SAY NO

to

Coffee

DATES

THE ULTIMATE GUIDE
FOR **WOMEN**
STRUGGLING TO
DATE ON THEIR
OWN TERMS

SHAW **DRAKE**

SAY N⃠ to *Coffee* DATES

SAY N⊘ to Coffee DATES

THE ULTIMATE GUIDE FOR **WOMEN** STRUGGLING TO DATE ON THEIR OWN TERMS

SHAW **DRAKE**

To the woman
who always reminded
me that I am worthy...
I love you, mom!

CONTENTS

PART 3:

A WOMAN'S MARKET

PART 4:

THE MAKING OF A WOMAN

PART 5:

THE MAN

PART 6:

MASTERING THE MARKET

PREFACE

THE DATE

THIS WAS MY MOMENT! I was searching for love for so long, and I was determined to find it. Another Valentine's Day had just passed, and instead of spending the night in the arms of my man, sipping rosé and indulging in decadent chocolate-dipped strawberries by the fireplace, I had just left yet another Galentine's Day event. You know, the dinner party that all the single ladies attend so they do not feel lonely, unloved, or forgotten.

With all the prayers that I sent up to the heavens, surely God had forgotten me. That, or my husband accidentally hopped into the wrong DM when God told him my name. I mean, perhaps Shaw Drake was not as uncommon as I thought.

Regardless, I was done waiting and decided I would take control of my love life, once and for all. I hit the ground running, joined a popular dating app, swiped right on every guy that I felt could be a potential partner, and accepted ten date offers that spanned over the next ten days. I did *not* come to play.

While each date was an opportunity to meet my future husband, I could not help but feel the most hopeful and excited about this one particular guy. Let's call him number seven.

He had a seemingly perfect profile: a smile that could brighten any room, the physique that showed he was a regular at the gym, and words so sweet, my ovaries exploded! I kid you not. My heart fluttered at his first message to me, and damn if his voice didn't send chills up my spine.

We spoke briefly over Facetime to arrange the details, but mostly to ensure the other was not catfishing. Let me tell you, he did not disappoint. He gave me the address for our date, showed great enthusiasm about meeting me, and I ended the conversation right there—just in time before my anxiety got the best of me.

With my hand over my chest, I took long, deep breaths to calm myself down. My heart pounded and my mind raced as I was at the precipice of planning our private beach wedding on Makena Cove Beach in Maui, Hawaii.

Okay, perhaps I was a little over the top, but this man was different. Over the next six days, I went on a date with a different man each night. Some were great, others … not so much, but all were forgotten by the time Wednesday rolled around.

I was meeting number seven. Finally! I couldn't have been more ready.

Stepping into my closet, I pulled out a red, mid-length dress, my staple—the perfect combination of sex appeal and class. I took the time to pamper myself, oiling my skin, spritzing on *Chanel Coco Mademoiselle Eau de Parfum,* and paying close attention to every detail of my appearance. From the light beat on my face and the bounce of my curls, to the shape of my nails and my favorite charms for my lucky bracelet—nothing went overlooked.

I listened to some nineties R&B to get into the mood until my Uber driver arrived. I grabbed my coat, checked my clutch to make sure I was not forgetting my essentials, and strutted toward his freshly detailed SUV. My driver jumped out to open my door, and I noticed him checking me out. My efforts had not been in vain.

"So, who's the lucky fella tonight?" he asked, as he skated through DC's evening traffic.

"It's my first date with this guy. I am very excited about him," I replied. We continued with our casual banter until we arrived at the address number seven had given me.

He pulled over, stopped the car, and said, "Well beautiful lady, he's going to be blown away when he sees you. I wish you all the best."

He opened my door, and I hit the ground in my stilettos. After checking my reflection in his window, I turned around, looked up, and read the large neon sign hanging above the door of the building.

I had been dropped off at a coffee shop.

Instantly, I felt shame within myself. I did not know what was happening. I was not even sure if this really was happening. Was I dreaming? No way would he consider a coffee shop "a nice place" for a first date, especially after he took the time to mention that he loves seeing a woman in heels during the three minutes we spoke over the phone. Who the hell purposely wears heels to have a cup of coffee?

"Okay, okay. Calm down, Shaw," I said to myself. "This is an innocent mistake. Just go inside to stay warm and call him. Everything will be fine girl!"

I entered the shop, stood by the front door, and called him. "I think I came to the wrong place."

"Is that you in the red dress?" he replied.

Now, I had two options at that moment: I could turn around and walk out the door, or I could proceed with the coffee date.

I considered the first option, but two things kept me from doing so. First, I had taken an Uber to meet him, and even if it only took five minutes for another one to arrive, I risked the chance of him following me outside and questioning me, ultimately making me more uncomfortable than I already was. Secondly, I simply could not muster up the courage to say no. I did not want to be the next viral video of a woman being berated for turning down a man.

So, I proceeded with the date, and I am almost certain I drank at least four cups of coffee over the course of two hours. I do not even remember what the conversation was about. It is all a blur now and it was all a blur then. Finally, I summoned the courage to excuse myself from the table, ordered an Uber, and came back and lied to him. I told him I had to leave soon because something came up. I know, I know. It was the most obvious lie to leave a date early, but I could not think of anything else at the time. I didn't feel like my truth was valid, which was that I simply didn't want to be on a coffee date with him or any other man pursuing me.

For weeks, I wrecked my brain trying to figure out what exactly I did to be offered a coffee date. Did I come across as cheap? Did I come across as money hungry and he wanted to ensure I wasn't only using him for his funds? Was my conversation not interesting enough that he was scared to be stuck on a two- to three-hour date with me so soon? Did I appear as if I had no other men vying for my interest? Did our brief conversation over the phone make it seem like coffee shops were my thing? Did he explicitly state or even suggest that our date would be at a coffee shop, and I just missed it because I was so enamored by his voice?

The questions in my mind persisted. Until one day, I decided none of those things mattered. Why? This man did not know me! He simply saw an attractive woman on a dating app, swiped right, and received an alert that we had matched. If I did not stop myself, I could have come up with endless possibilities as to why he made the offer that he did.

Though here is the thing, I didn't know him either. I wasted weeks of my life trying to figure things out instead of simply asking him why he felt it was appropriate to take me out for coffee to get to know me. So, I asked. I am sure you can imagine my face when he replied, "Well, how am I supposed to know what you are worth when I am just getting to know you? I take every woman on dates like this to gauge our interest in one another, as well as our chemistry. If it doesn't work out, I don't lose much. If it does, then we can start going on nicer dates in the future."

I hung up the phone and promised myself that I would never accept a coffee date again. I would never accept a low-effort, pre-date again. No matter how difficult or uncomfortable it might be, I would never give a man the satisfaction of enjoying two hours of my conversation when I did not enjoy a minute in his presence.

That moment was the inception of *Say No to Coffee Dates*, and I am not talking about the book. No, this became my real-life mantra for any man that would pursue me. At that time, my self-confidence was low. My hope that I would ever enter a healthy, long-lasting relationship was low. If I am being honest, my will to even keep dating at that point was especially low. No matter what, I decided that saying no to coffee dates would be my baseline for any possible relationship down the line, and let's be honest, that bar wasn't even that high.

I took to social media as I usually do, and I began publicly sharing many of my dating experiences with my audience. The good. The bad. The ugly. What became evident to me and those following along with my dating stories was, the more I dated, the better my experiences became.

I wrote this book because after sharing those dating experiences, so many women started to ask me, "How do you do it?" They weren't just asking how I had so many date offers, but they specifically wanted to know how I was able to consistently secure high-quality dates for myself. They were also struggling to date on their own terms, and they wanted answers, fast!

Now, it took me almost three years to write this book. So, I suppose my answer was not fast. I wanted to ensure there was no fluff, no nonsense, and no reason you, too, cannot change your dating life around.

One thing I know for sure is this: the only women who feel like the dating scene is a cesspool, either do not know how to date on their own terms or have not given themselves a real fighting chance to find their ideal guy. In a world of eight billion people, once you know how to date, and you actually begin to date, it is impossible to not find exactly what it is you are looking for.

A whole new world of dating opportunities awaits you, and I am here to guide you every step of the way. So, read the book. Digest the material. Do the work. You *will* discover for yourself that you've got what it takes to leave the single life behind, forever.

This is your moment!

◆

INTRODUCTION
THE QUANTUM
LEAP

NOTHING IN LIFE IS FAIR. Not everyone's starting point in life is the same. Karma in this lifetime may or may not be real, and cheaters do temporarily win. If you feel like you have done everything by the books and still find yourself in unfavorable, meaningless, and draining relationships that leave you with unanswered questions, just know you are now in a better position by reading this book. So, *woman*, applaud yourself. Take a deep breath and get ready to unlock the keys that will allow you to better navigate the dating world by dating on your own terms from this moment forth.

First, let me be clear about what this book is not. This book is not anti-men—sorry to my misandrists out there. It isn't based on a certain type of man, whether black, white, or purple; young and hot,

xix

or silver-haired and debonair. Nor is it about becoming the ideal woman, baking the perfect key lime pie, or figuring out how to show up looking your absolute best every single day. And for crying out loud, you do not have to stop holding men accountable, become a *YES* woman to every man you encounter, pretend to enjoy watching the NFL (if that is not your thing), or perpetuate misogynistic ideas that many men and women have bought into.

Instead, this book will teach you how to recognize and let go of dusties once and for all, choose from higher quality men, and discover which type of men and relationships are most ideal for *you*. Regardless of your age, education level, physique, motherhood status, number of past relationship failures, skin tone, hair texture, or anything else that the gurus like to use as identifying factors in your dating market value, you *will* walk away learning to date on your own terms.

I am going to let you know this now; it is highly unlikely that the first man you meet will be the guy of your dreams. You are constantly evolving. The more you learn to understand yourself, the easier it becomes to identify your ideal partner. In the meantime, that ideal man may change, because who you choose today is not who you *must* choose tomorrow. Let me say that again.

Who you choose today is NOT who you must choose tomorrow…
Unless that choice is
YOURSELF!

So, instead of focusing on frivolous things like how to wear your hair, which designer bag you should carry to allude you are already *that* girl, or what self-proclaimed high-value men think of you, you will concentrate on things that truly matter.

This book aims to help you develop yourself holistically so that you are perpetually attracting who and what you need now to become who and what you want to become in the future.

You see, that is exactly what this book is all about. You will learn how to make sure your next decision is your best decision over and over again, inevitably propelling you to the next step toward your happy ever after.

Think of it as a ladder. Step-by-step, you will elevate yourself closer to your ideal relationship without having to discard your non-negotiables, become a shell of an individual, fit into a size six jeans, or marry someone who was meant to be in your life for only a season.

Dating should be fun, not frustrating. Dating should feel easy, not exhausting. Experiencing healthy, romantic relationships should not be dependent on how well you can assimilate to anyone else's standards of beauty or faux femininity. When you learn how to harness the power within, you will stop accepting less than what you truly want, and you will no longer equate your value and self-worth to the level of service you can provide for others. You are much more than what you can bring to the table.

You are **valuable** beyond measure. You, my sister, deserve so much more than coffee dates.

Now, I will warn you. The ideas of this book may not be the easiest for you to digest. You are starting a process that will help you to see situations completely different. This new way of thinking may have already begun for you, and you may be feeling responsible for the decisions you have made in the past.

So let me tell you first, there is nothing wrong with holding yourself accountable. Likewise, there is nothing wrong with acknowledging how society has helped groom you into making some, perhaps many, of the poor decisions you have made. Be sure to show yourself grace as you embark upon this journey of becoming who you were created to be. Please understand that no matter what you have been through in the past, believing you are worth your heart's desire, practicing self-preservation, and positioning yourself to be cherished greatly is truly a radical act of self-love.

Let's face it, women have bought into the lie floating around the dating scene for years that men marry who they want while women marry who they can, *if* they can. We have accepted that men are the only ones in the position to do the choosing. Consequently, we have given our power away freely to these mediocre men to ultimately make one of the most important and impactful decisions of *our* lives, which for many, is deciding what relationships we will enter and who our husband will be.

That is not okay, sis! Being chosen should not be your only goal. Being the chooser is something you should also aspire to. No, I am not encouraging you to get down on one knee because you want to upgrade yourself from being an overworked girlfriend or a forever fiancée to a man clearly content with using you as a placeholder.

I am not suggesting you shoot your shot toward every man that looks good, smells good, can hold a decent conversation, and bears an enticing imprint on his summer gray sweats. I am not advising you to become the aggressor in your pursuit of finding love. And I most certainly am not suggesting you think like a man and act like a ... Well, you know the rest.

I am simply affirming you that you alone are worthy. I am reminding you that you have a voice and a choice. You do not have to fake relationship goals on social media, live unhappily, share community peen, or settle for mediocre and emotionally unavailable men. You do not need to serve as a mule or turn tricks for a man to try to find true, romantic love. You surely do not have to forsake men all together, only to then feel shamed by both men and women for your singleness.

While this book can help you shorten the time it takes for you to enter the relationship of your choice, there is no rush. There is no such thing as a perfect age at which a woman must enter her long-lasting relationship or marriage. It is purely power tactics men use as a result of our patriarchal society to make us feel otherwise, to make us feel like our time is running out.

Women are not inherently the problem if we do not marry young, or at all. There are too many factors to explore why a woman would decide to remain in her singleness. One of the main considerations is the pool of men in which many of us have been taught to choose from. They simply do not meet the standard.

Yet, women are expected to make sound judgments in their relationships, oftentimes without any real support from their culture, counsel from their spiritual leaders, or guidance from their more experienced female family members. Pop culture continuously champions toxic relationships. Many religious institutions focus on teaching women to keep themselves in order to be chosen without providing the same level of attention to build quality men worthy of doing the choosing; and it is sad to say, but sometimes mothers just do not know what is best. A woman undergoes so many societal pressures to quickly enter a relationship and start a family, but no grace is given if her choice leads her to an unfavorable situation.

This is why I am writing this book.

Despite these taboo truths, I learned firsthand that the room to err is very small before judgment comes knocking at your door. At a young age, I made romantic and life-altering familial decisions that society ridiculed me for, and I later came to regret, like entering a marriage that did not offer the amount of financial security necessary to sustain a quickly growing family and remaining in a marriage after being cheated on by more women than he could remember. I was even convinced by my spiritual leaders that it was my duty as a wife to be there for my husband through his sexual addictions, despite the fact that it was killing me inside, despite that it was a threat to my physical, mental, and emotional well-being. I learned whether I stayed or left, I would be judged by someone who felt they knew better about my life than I did.

So yes, I have been there—young, ignorant to life, and parenting multiple kids without the consistent financial or emotional support of their father. I felt society's kicks long before I even realized I was down. As a result, I spent years trying to compensate for my children now living in what I viewed as a *broken* home, which was draining to say the least. I spent even more years trying to wash away the shame that consumed me and worked tirelessly to prove my worth to worthless men. I even stooped so low as to fight multiple women (on social media), who were equally foolish to compete for the same low-hanging fruit.

At some point, I realized my self-worth was nonexistent. I began doing things to try to increase it. I went back to college and completed my bachelor's degree, started successful businesses, and accumulated multiple stamps in my and my children's passports. I prioritized physical fitness and found myself in the best shape of my life. However, while I felt worthy in many areas of my life to create and receive all that my heart desired, I *still* felt unworthy to date the kind of men I was interested in. It seemed like I was succeeding in every area of my life, except for the dating market.

Then, something clicked. I realized that while I could never undo my past, my past did not have to define me. I was not helpless, nor hopeless. Just like I took control of and leveled up in my education, body, and finances, I learned I could do the same in my relationships. I also learned that if I *never* entered what I felt would be my ideal relationship, I would still lead a great life with a promising future.

I would still fulfill my life's purpose because my relationship status most certainly did not define my happiness. With that mindset shift, I went from assigning blame to others to owning the power I had over my own life.

I stopped seeing myself as the victim and began rewriting my overcomer's narrative. The struggles I used to have in my love life no longer existed. The unworthy men that I could not keep were replaced with men of substance who valued me. The standards that were too high for the dusties to meet were raised even higher by the new men I began to date.

I am not saying things happened overnight, though I must admit, the change happened pretty damn fast—not just for me, but for many of the women I have taught over the last few years.

Now, it is your turn. You may not be a divorced mother of multiple kids like me. You may have never dated dusties in the past. You may have always listened to sound advice, unlike most of us. You may have no personal regrets and are simply interested in learning tried and true strategies to circumvent some of the relationship pitfalls you have witnessed loved ones go through.

Regardless, if you are reading this book, you surely have your own reasons that led you to wanting better for yourself and your love life. No matter the reason you have decided to date on your own terms, the fact is you have made the quantum leap. Therefore, my promise to you with this guide is to teach you how to:

- Let go of pick-me behaviors
- Develop yourself holistically
- Debunk dating myths
- Create the dating market of your dreams
- Decenter men
- Date more efficiently and effectively
- And ultimately, say no to coffee dates

Before we go any further, here is a declaration that I encourage you to make to yourself. Please reread and recite this as many times as you need and be prepared to create your own personal declaration in chapters to come.

Declaration

Today, I honor my present, release my past, and welcome the woman I am to become. I adopt new, more positive beliefs about myself with ease and give myself permission to discard all ideas that no longer serve me. I speak peace, love, and abundance over my love life. I hold the power to choose and am worthy of being chosen by my ideal partner. I have the mental fortitude to withstand the time it takes to create my greatest dating life transformation to date.

The Market Maker Method™

A Woman-focused Framework for Dating on Your Own Terms

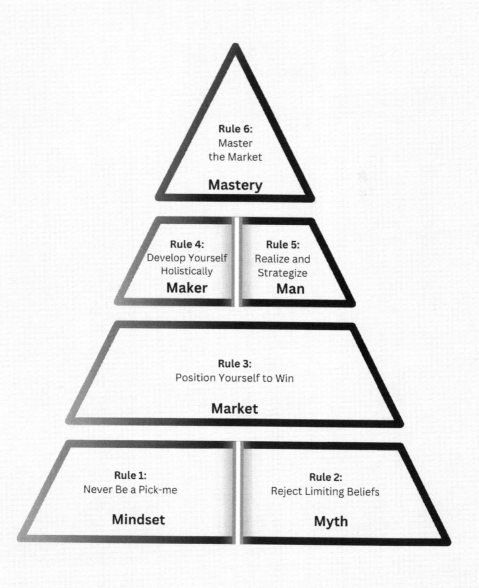

Overview

This book utilizes *The Market Maker Method™*, a woman-focused framework for dating on your own terms. This framework consists of six key components: mindset, myths, market, maker, man, and mastery. The book is broken down into six parts, each with a corresponding key component and rule.

Rule 1 - Never be a Pick-me.

Rule 2 - Reject limiting beliefs.

Rule 3 - Position yourself to win.

Rule 4 - Develop yourself holistically.

Rule 5 - Recognize and strategize.

Rule 6 - Master the market.

In part 1 of this book, you will study *The 3 Archetypes of a Pick-me Woman™* and the self-destructive mindsets pick-me women have that impede their ability to form healthy relationships. Even though they do not realize it, their negative sentiments regarding relationships are deeply ingrained, and over time, they become a part of their identity.

In part 2, using *The Dating Market Myth-Busting Model™*, you will learn to unpack several myths within the dating market, which are external factors commonly responsible for women settling for men they do not want. Together, parts 1 and 2 act as the foundation for part 3. Without them, part 3 will be unusable.

Part 3 is the core of *The Market Maker Method™*. Here, you will learn how to implement *The DECIDE Model™*, which serves as the blueprint to truly creating the market of your dreams. Many of the teachings derive from my experiences trading currencies within the foreign exchange market. You do not need to have any prior knowledge of trading terminology to comprehend the concept because everything will be conveyed in an easy-to-understand way. The Market Maker concept will help you realize how to create and position yourself among the correct market of men, one in which your ideal partner exist. This concept also serves as the backbone for many chapters to follow.

In part 4, *The SHAW Self-Development Model*™ will guide you through a four-step process to improve yourself holistically to become the market maker you need to be.

In part 5, you will learn to utilize *The DRAKE Diamond Model*™ to attract and retain better quality men into your life. Together, parts 4 and 5 are used to facilitate ease when applying *The Market Maker Method*™ to your dating life.

In Part 6, you will explore *The Market Mastery Model*™, which presents six unique concepts that empower you to assertively navigate the dating world. This crucial stage is not to be taken lightly, as it equips you with the tools you need to confidently pursue your desires and master your market.

All parts begin with a "Before You Begin" section, which should provide you with any necessary context and set the stage for the chapters to come and end with "A Moment to Reflect" section that summarizes the key takeaways and provides additional prompts for reflection.

You will soon come to realize that *Say No to Coffee Dates* is not just full of demands, theory, and fluff. It truly is the ultimate guide for women struggling to date on their own terms. Each new concept presented is accompanied with detailed explanations, actionable steps to take, and evaluating metrics to determine whether you are on the right track. The beauty of *The Market Maker Method*™ is that it can be applied in a way that is unique and most beneficial to you. No woman's process will be identical to another. So, while I encourage you to share this book with as many women you feel could benefit from it, there is no reason to compare your journey with the next.

The strategies taught here are timeless, effective, and in many ways, innovative. Get ready to change your dating approach forever. Let the dating begin!

PART 1

DEATH OF A PICK-ME

Definitions from Shawdrism Language

dust·y \ ˈdə-stē *noun*
> a man who is broke and delusional with nothing to offer but audacity

di·ve·stor \ ˈdə-ˌves-tər *noun*
> a person who consciously and exclusively seeks romantic or intimate relationships with individuals from a racial background different from their own, often driven by specific preferences, beliefs, or stereotypes.

low-hang·ing fruit \ ˈlō-ˈhaŋ-iŋ-ˈfrüt *noun*
> a man who is for everybody; easy to get, harder to return and usually has very little to lose

ma·ni·pu·la·tion \ mə-ˈni-pyə-ˌlāt-shən *noun*
> the art of lying to a man in order to enter a relationship you don't actually want; a short-sighted tactic for a long-term goal

pick-me \ ˈpik -ˈmē *noun*
> a woman who is willing to sacrifice herself to win the approval of or receive validation from a man

prag·ma·tist pick-me \ ˈprag-mə-ˌtist - ˈpik -ˈmē *noun*
> a woman who, driven by a belief in practicality, tolerates men's undesirable behaviors, including infidelity, as a trade-off for preserving family cohesion and financial stability

re·pre·sen·ta·tive pick-me \ ˌre-pri-ˈzen-tə-tiv -ˈpik -ˈmē *noun*
> a woman who manipulates her own identity, either consciously or unconsciously, to align with her partner's desires, often sacrificing her authenticity for the sake of securing a relationship

self-se·lect·ed wo·man \ ˌself-sə-ˈlek ˈwu̇-mən *noun*
> A woman who is a mastermind of her own life, opportunistic in her dating approach, and the heroin of her own story; the inverse of a pick-me woman

war·ri·or pick-me \ ˈwȯr-yər, ˈwȯr-ē-ə ˈpik -ˈmē *noun*
> a woman who, driven by a sense of competition or submission, tolerates and endures unhealthy relationship dynamics, often sacrificing her own needs and self-respect, to maintain her status as "chosen"

Part 1: Death of a Pick-me

The Market Maker Method™ Component 1: Mindset
1st Rule: Never be a Pick-me.
Framework: 3 Archetypes of a Pick-me Woman™

There are so many derogatory terms that are gender specific. These terms reserved for women by men are often, but not always, in direct relation to the sexual behaviors women exhibit. However, if you ask many modern-day women what one of the worst terms a fellow woman could call her, pick-me would surely be toward the top of that list, and with good reason.

So, what exactly is a pick-me? The term pick-me describes a woman who is willing to sacrifice herself to win the approval of or receive validation from a man. She is not to be confused with a woman who is in a healthy relationship and is simply treating her man well.

Thus, in this section, I will share my *Death of a Pick-me* story so that you understand you are not in this alone. We will then analyze The *3 Archetypes of a Pick-me Woman*™ to understand the mindset of pick-me women, explore their behaviors, examine their intentions, and categorize them into three different archetypes: the warrior, the pragmatist, and the representative. Although the behaviors of each type materialize in different ways, all three archetypes have one thing in common—centering men. As a woman looking to take control of her dating life, this is the last thing you want to do.

And finally, we will explore the inverse of a pick-me, which is a self-selected woman. We will learn how she thinks, behaves, and views the world in a way that is beneficial for her.

Before You Begin

Welcome to this journey of self-reflection and transformation. This is not a one-time event where you read the book, make a few changes, and then everything is magically fixed. Just like in *Alcoholics Anonymous* (AA), where members are reminded of their commitment to sobriety every day, this journey requires daily effort and dedication. In a world full of pick-mes, it is not always easy gaining or maintaining your self-selected status, but the good news is you are not alone. You have a community of women who are on the same path, and together, we can support each other and grow.

To get the most out of this section, I suggest following these steps:

1. Read each chapter slowly and thoroughly.
2. Pause and reflect on the information being presented.
3. Take note of any personal experiences or insights that come to mind.
4. Trust the process and be open to the transformation that is possible through this journey.

Part 1 is designed to be reflective and serve as a mirror to see yourself more fully. For this reason, it is important to set the tone and let you know that my intention is to speak from a place of love and not judgment. I, too, was once a pick-me woman, specifically, every type of pick-me that you will learn about in the upcoming chapters. As such, I understand what it is like to have that knee-jerking reaction to deny pick-me behaviors. Most importantly, I understand the struggle and the journey it takes to transform into a self-selected woman.

My goal for you is to use Part 1 as a tool for personal growth and transformation, so be gentle with yourself and lean into the process.

Questions That Might Arise

What does it mean if I see myself in one of the pick-me archetypes?

If you see yourself in one of the pick-me archetypes, it is important to be empathetic and understanding toward your feelings of self-discovery and reflection. I assure you that recognizing and understanding the traits of a pick-me is a step toward growth and transformation. I want to further emphasize that being a pick-me is not a permanent state. You have the power to change and evolve. Be kind to yourself and avoid self-blame or shame. Focus on the journey ahead and the positive steps you can take toward becoming self-selected.

What does it mean if I cannot identify with a self-selected woman?

If you do not see parts of yourself reflected in the self-selected woman chapter, rest assured that everyone's journey to self-selection is unique. "The Self-Selected Woman" chapter is not meant to be prescriptive or a one-size-fits-all approach. The traits of a self-selected woman are ideals to aspire to, but not necessarily a fixed destination. I encourage you to focus on your own personal growth and evolution, rather than comparing yourself to others or feeling like you have failed.

What if I have trouble with self-reflection and introspection?

It is natural to feel overwhelmed or uncomfortable when starting to reflect on one's own behaviors and beliefs. However, remember that growth and transformation require effort and discomfort. Try to approach each reflection exercise with an open mind and a willingness to learn. Additionally, consider talking to a trusted friend or therapist for support as you navigate this journey.

What if I feel like I am not making progress?

Personal growth can be a slow process, and it is not always easy to see the changes in ourselves. Focus on the small steps and victories along the way, rather than looking for a big, overnight transformation. Additionally, regularly review your notes and reflections to see how far you have come. Do not give up.

The 3 Archetypes of a Pick-me Woman™

A Mindset Deconstruction of Women who Hold Male-Centric Views

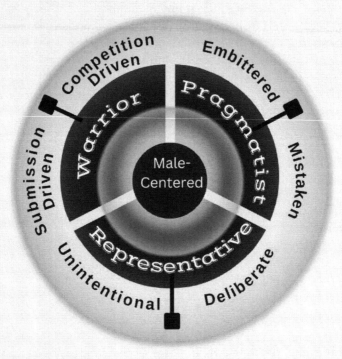

DEATH OF A PICK-ME

CHAPTER 1

I THOUGHT I STOPPED BEING a pick-me when I started handling men the way they handled me; when I was able to fully match their energy, wit, finesse, dominance, and show up as my most authentic self. The truth is, I was still operating within the confines of a patriarchal system, still seeking validation from men, still allowing their perceptions to shape my identity. I was still a pick-me, but in a more sophisticated guise.

The real transformation, the real death of my pick-me self, only began when I made a conscious decision to dismantle the structures that held me captive. This meant challenging societal norms, questioning the beliefs that were handed down to me, and forging a new path that was uniquely my own. It was a journey of self-discovery and self-affirmation, a journey that led me to redefine my values, my relationships, and ultimately, my identity.

My personal *Death of a Pick-me Story* began when:

◊ I started to decenter men from my narrative and recenter myself.

◊ I learned to show more grace to women than I showed loyalty to men.

◊ I stopped bashing women who had not reached the level of awareness I felt I had.

◊ I learned that sisterhood meant respecting women's decisions even when they did not align with *my* belief system.

◊ I no longer condemned women for being different, desiring less, and accepting more BS than me.

◊ I made it a point to remember that my purpose was tied to my ability to connect with women from a place of love.

◊ I stopped judging women for being *my* definition of mediocre.

◊ I learned that hypergamy was not for every woman. Some women were suited for isogamy; others would still choose hypogamy, no matter what, and that was okay.

◊ I understood that women had a right to choose who they had sex with, dated, or married, because the consequences of those decisions would be theirs to bear, not mine.

◊ I learned to understand women who are now divestors, as well as those who will forever be race loyal.

◊ I chose to acknowledge that women who are intentionally side chicks have the right to be, regardless of how it makes me feel. The same way they could purposely deal with a dishonorable man is the same way I could choose to walk away from one.

◊ I learned to respect women who were content with little in life while still championing women who want it all.

◊ I learned that we all have our *own* life to live, and while our differences could affect our desire to befriend one another, we all are just trying our best.

Not being a pick-me is more than just creating standards for the men we allow to pursue us, it is also challenging social norms under patriarchy that has made many of our sisters feel and become less protected, less accepted, and more marginalized than others. So, while I am no longer a pick-me, my recovery had less to do with how my views of men have changed, and more to do with how my views of women have shifted. I respect women in their absence and hold no space for any man to use another woman as a stool to prop me up or use her as a comparison to communicate why I am such a good woman.

I stopped being
a pick-me when
I PICKED ME!

Once I became woman-identified, a woman's woman, and my sister's keeper, my full transformation happened. This, sis, is what I desire for you. My goal is that you unlearn all that does not serve you, embrace your womanhood, and see the value of true sisterhood and community. Why? Well, men are not coming to save us. We must save ourselves!

In the next three chapters, we will be looking at the different pick-me archetypes. While doing so, I want you to look for similarities and differences. For instance, while the warrior pick-me views men as superior, the pragmatic pick-me views men as inferior. However, they both lack boundaries within their relationships. Whereas the representative pick-me values her intelligence over all else, the pragmatic pick-me values her practicality the most. Yet, they both lack true authenticity in their pursuit of and existence within relationships.

You will began to notice that how women perceive men is not the only factor that defines their pick-me behaviors, nor is it how they self-identify. It is a combination of their many attributes, what they are willing to sacrifice in order to secure and maintain a relationship with men, as well as how they view other women.

If you go on any social media platform, you will witness women proudly proclaiming that they do not owe any loyalty to other women. While this sentiment may stem from the importance of practicing self-preservation, it is truly a problematic statement. The reasoning behind these proclamations is often that men do not concern themselves with what other men do, so women should likewise not worry about the actions or affairs of other women.

The issue here is that these women are basing their moral compass on the moral compass of men, which is asinine. Men should never be the standard by which women hold themselves. Any progress that women have ever made has happened because women decided to go against the status quo and not adhere to the normality created under patriarchy and enforced by society.

This leads us to a crucial realization: true empowerment and growth come from within, not from conforming to external standards or comparisons. It's about recognizing our unique value and taking care of ourselves, not measuring ourselves against others.

It is important to note that one of the key aspects of awakening from pick-me behavior is the practice of self-care and self-love. This includes taking time for yourself, practicing self-reflection, and learning to prioritize your own needs and desires. One way to practice self-care is through journaling, which allows you to process your thoughts and emotions and gain a deeper understanding of yourself and your motivations.

Additionally, therapy can be a valuable tool in learning how to let go of the pick-me mindset and focus on your own well-being. Mindfulness exercises such as meditation or yoga can also be helpful in promoting self-awareness and reducing stress and anxiety. By prioritizing self-care and self-love, you can begin to shift your focus away from the pick-me mindset and toward centering yourself and your own needs.

If you do not discover anything else, you must recognize that getting a man or landing a relationship is not worth losing yourself. It is not worth your dignity, nor is it worth your authenticity. It is not worth harboring ill feelings toward women who do not even know you exist and it is not what determines your value. As you embark upon this Market Maker journey, I want you to always remember that you alone are worthy of all that your heart desires.

You do not need to lie, pretend, or lower your standards for what you believe you deserve.

You will never be **right** for the **wrong** man.

But you will always be more than enough for your ideal partner.

> "WHEN WE CENTER MEN, WE FORGET THAT THE WORLD IS BIGGER THAN THEM. WE FORGET THAT WE ARE BIGGER THAN THEM."
>
> *— Chimamanda Ngozi Adichie*

THE WARRIOR

CHAPTER 2

A WARRIOR PICK-ME (WP) is the type of pick-me most women think about when they hear the term. She is not remotely discreet in her male-centered ways. She boasts and brags about how well she treats her man when it is obvious the treatment is never truly reciprocated. Although she may not be able to easily recognize this, she has extremely low standards, if any at all, for the men she chooses.

She does, however, recognize that her level of commitment to their relationship is far greater than her partners, but she simply does not care. She happily basks in her "taken" status despite the price she must pay. And, oh, the price is great. For her to maintain her status, she must sacrifice herself at every turn.

She embodies **struggle love** and is the epitome of self-destruction.

A warrior pick-me hardly sets or enforces boundaries, which are necessary for any healthy relationship. Because of this, she is rarely single. Low-value men love to be with women like her. They receive so many benefits with little to no investment or any real expectation to reciprocate. As long as those benefits remain, a man will stay with her until he can no longer manage the parts of her that he is not attracted to, find someone new to harm or house him, or land someone he feels is more aesthetically pleasing or closer to his desired phenotype.

In addition to her lack of boundaries, the warrior pick-me often struggles with codependency, becoming excessively emotional and psychologically dependent on her partner. She may find herself in relationships where she is constantly sacrificing her own needs and wants for her partner. This can lead to her feeling trapped and unable to leave the relationship, even if it is unhealthy or abusive. She can spend ten years with a low-hanging fruit or one year with ten dusties. Regardless, she proudly proclaims, *I've got a man*. Despite this pick-me experiencing constant heartaches, let-downs, and betrayal, her self-perception is anything but a victim.

Another aspect of the warrior pick-me is her tendency to be overly jealous and possessive in relationships due to her incessant fear of losing her man. She may become obsessed with her partner's every move and become enraged if she perceives any threat to the relationship, even if it is unfounded. This can lead to toxic dynamics and a lack of trust in the relationship.

Still, she delights herself in how well she can endure because one of her main core values is strength. So as ironic as it may seem, considering her behaviors, the last thing she wants to be seen as is weak. Because of this, she will prove her strength a million times over. The most prominent reason she is called a warrior is because whenever she perceives a threat to her relationship, she is prepared to go to war. To make matters worse, her perceived opponents could be anyone or anything—her friends; family (children are not exempt), strangers; her man's job, hobbies, and other love interests; and even her very own man if she believes he is sabotaging their relationship in any kind of way. For her, it is truly not about the man himself. It is about parading herself as a chosen woman. She experiences his flaws and inadequacies on a regular basis and knows he is not good to her, but she understands everything has a price and will sacrifice her finances, friendships, future, and self to preserve her status.

Now, to further understand her, I will break it down another step. There are two types of warrior pick-mes, ones driven by submission and others driven by competition. Despite the differences, the outcome remains the same. Let's take a look.

Warrior Pick-Me Archetype

	SUBMISSION DRIVEN	COMPETITION DRIVEN
IDENTITY (HOW SHE VIEWS HERSELF)	Helpmate	Contender
PARTNER PERCEPTION (HOW SHE VIEWS HER MAN)	The Leader	The Prize
BELIEF (HER IDEAS SHE HOLD TO BE TRUE)	Mistakes are inevitable for growth	Mistakes will lessen if she does her part
DUTY (HER OBLIGATION TO THE RELATIONSHIP)	To uplift her man	To support her man
RESPONSIBILITIES (LIABILITIES ASSUMED IN THE RELATIONSHIP)	Provide peace Maintain his good reputation Love without conditions	Provide pleasure Defend his poor reputation Teach him how to love
WEAPONRY (TOOLS USED TO ENDURE)	Forgetfulness Persuasion Humility Grace	Forgiveness Demands Wit Mercy
FEAR (HER IDEA OF DEFEAT)	Losing him because she is unworthy.	Losing him to another woman who reaps the benefits of her labor
MOTTO (HER RELATIONSHIP IDEOLOGY)	All is fair in love and war.	What one woman won't do, another woman will.

A submission driven warrior pick-me (SDWP) is a woman who enters a relationship with a man to be his helpmate. She enjoys being able to uplift her man whom she views as her leader and understands that no one is perfect. She strives daily to be his peace and love him unconditionally while ensuring his image is always good in the eyes of other people. When he abuses her in any way, she humbles herself before him to try and understand what she has done wrong to provoke him to make the decisions he did.

She then tries to persuade him to do differently the next time. Regardless of whether he has proven himself to have changed, she grants him grace and chooses to forget all that was done. She uses forgetfulness as a tool of self-preservation as well as an incentive for him to stay. She strives to prove herself but inwardly believes at any moment he could leave her for someone better. Despite her hardships, she believes the end justifies the means.

On the other hand, a competition driven warrior pick-me (CDWP) is a woman who is competitive by nature. She knows that there are many women who would love to be with a man like him. Therefore, she views her man as the prize. From the beginning until the end, she truly believes she is winning. She, in no way, feels the need to fake like her relationship is perfect. She feels the harm he causes her, and instead of processing it as reasons to leave the relationship, she looks within herself to see where she is wrong so that she can become better for him.

This man does not know how to properly love her, but she is always ready and willing to teach him how to love. She will defend him publicly and scold him privately. Her weaponry is completely different from the SDWP. Instead of forgetting his wrongdoings, she chooses to forgive him repeatedly. Instead of trying to persuade her man to be better, she verbally demands that he gets his shit together. She regularly tries to outwit him, but sadly, it is never enough.

Ultimately, she grants him mercy. She could be a vengeful woman if she desired, but she is smart enough to realize her doing so would be the death of her relationship. After all the struggles she has endured with him, she simply cannot lose him to the next woman, and she knows there is *always* the next woman.

Now, if you take a good look at those descriptions, you will notice that many, if not all, of the aspects outlined in the chart are positive. This speaks more about the good within these women than the not-so-good within the men they are dealing with. However, make no mistake: These women are dangerous—to themselves and other women. When you look beneath the surface, you will surely see they hold much power. However, they wield their power just to mismanage their vaginas and yield their wombs for the fodder of mediocre men. They fight their sisters, betray their friends, and punish themselves behind low-hanging fruit. They will cast spells to keep his attention, pretend they are bisexual to please him, and still end up brokenhearted. They have yet to learn.

If you choose to not engage in such self-destructive behaviors with them, they will make statements like: *This is why you cannot keep a man, all is fair in love and war, or what you will not do, the next woman will.* They can influence you in subtle ways and have you questioning yourself if you truly are making the best decisions or if you are a bit delusional with your standards.

While pursuing a healthy relationship, it is unwise to have a woman of this ilk in your circle. They will project their insecurities and shame you for your standards. These women are facing serious challenges, and while there is always hope for growth and healing, being mindful of what you share with warriors and keeping some aspects of your life private may be the wisest approach.

THE PRAGMATIST

CHAPTER 3

THE PRAGMATIC PICK-ME (PP) woman is not as easily recognizable as the WP. Her perspective remains consistent whether she is single, a widow, a newlywed, or in a forty-five-year marriage. The existence of her relationship or the length thereof does not dictate nor change her actual views on men. Her core values are family, security, and duty, all of which she believes are practical things a relationship should consist of. She does not fancy herself by imagining a perfect man or a perfect relationship. She does not have high hopes or regard for men.

Before she ever places men on a pedestal, she would **die**.

She believes men are just that—men, humans with flaws whom she feels she must learn to tolerate at a very basic level to receive the benefits of having an adult male presence within her home. So why then is this seemingly grounded woman classified as a pick-me? The answer lies in her willingness to prioritize the relationship and her sense of duty over her own well-being and self-respect.

If you have yet to realize, the PP's focus on duty can lead her to lower her standards in a relationship to such an extent that she practically sets the bar in hell. By accepting flaws and behaviors that might be deeply troubling, she risks creating a dynamic where her own needs and values are secondary, setting a bar that not only compromises her own fulfillment and happiness but may also undermine the very foundation of the relationship itself.

Yes, she can proudly claim that her man financially provides or contributes, but outside of finances, almost anything goes within their relationship. She refuses to hold men accountable and excuses their undesirable traits to preserve the cohesion of her family and her financial security. She is both male-identified and male-centered. This means that she places men and their needs at the center of her life (male-centered), often prioritizing them over her own needs and desires. Furthermore, she identifies strongly with male perspectives and values (male-identified), often to the point of excusing or rationalizing behaviors that are detrimental to her own well-being.

Her belief that "all men cheat" is deeply ingrained in her pragmatic worldview. Not in a condemning way, but in a way that removes the onus from the man to remain faithful and places the onus onto the woman to overlook his unfaithfulness or any other undesirable traits he may demonstrate. She also regularly centers him by hyper-focusing on and justifying his struggles without giving a reasonable amount of concern for her own needs or the consequences she endures as a result of his shortcoming.

This woman will never preach being in love and receiving

great sex are enough to sustain a relationship like some other pick-mes. Most times, she has never experienced real, romantic love and regularly questions herself on whether her orgasms are real. She will, however, tell you that relationships take work, compromise, and long-suffering and encourage you to not jump at the first sign of trouble. This is not because she wants you or herself to remain in an insufferable relationship. No, she honestly would like to see women thrive. In turn, she sets the bar so low for men that she never truly experiences what it feels like to be in a healthy, loving, mutually beneficial relationship.

A common trait of the pragmatic pick-me is her tendency to downplay her own needs and wants in relationships. She may believe that it is her responsibility to make the relationship work and will often put the needs of her partner before her own. This can lead to her feeling unfulfilled and resentful in the relationship. Another aspect of the pragmatic pick-me is her tendency to be passive-aggressive in relationships. Instead of directly confronting her partner about issues in the relationship, she will hint at them or use passive-aggressive tactics to communicate her dissatisfaction. This can lead to misunderstandings and a lack of effective communication in the relationship.

Pragmatic pick-me women tend to play some leadership role in your life. Sometimes, they are your mother, friend, mentor, or perhaps the matriarch of your extended family. Although they refuse to be your *yes woman* when it comes to your relationship woes, they are generally positive women, always looking on the bright side and searching for ways to help save someone's relationship. Because of this, they are even more dangerous than warrior pick-mes because women tend to welcome and seek out the advice that these pick-mes offer, making the advice more readily accepted.

Now, to understand the pragmatic pick-me more, we can categorize her into two types: the Embittered and the Mistaken. Let's explore this further.

Pragmatist Pick-Me Archetype

	EMBITTERED	MISTAKEN
IDENTITY *(HOW SHE VIEWS HERSELF)*	Experienced	Calculated
PERCEIVES PARTNER *(HOW SHE VIEWS HER MAN)*	Privileged	Incompetent
BELIEF *(HER IDEAS SHE HOLD TO BE TRUE)*	Men won't be faithful	Men can't be faithful
POSTULATES *(ASSUMES TRUE FOR BASIS OF REASONING)*	Men control access to relationships and marriage	Men are not wired for monogamy
EXPECTATIONS	Expect the unexpected	Prepare for the worst, hope for the best
ROLE *(REGARDING PATRIARCHY)*	Participant within patriarchal societies	Victim of patriarchal societies
FINANCIAL STANDARDS	The price he pays for her to deal with his wrongdoings	Reward for accepting his wrongdoings
MOTTO *(HER RELATIONSHIP IDEOLOGY)*	You gotta pay the cost to be the boss.	The grass isn't greener on the other side.

The embittered pragmatic pick-me (EPP) is a woman who has been through the trenches with men. She has a lot of unpleasant personal experiences in relationships and carries unhealed trauma from her past. As a result, she has concluded men just will not be faithful. She does not believe they are incapable of being loyal, but she accepts they are privileged in the fact that the collective society almost expects men to cheat and women to forgive.

Despite many women suggesting that infidelity is a deal-breaker, she observes that it often isn't for most women. So if she threatens to leave her man because of infidelity, chances are slim that she would gain the satisfaction of her man feeling the consequences. After all, she knows that he could easily find another woman to accept his behavior. This leaves her with two possibilities in her mind. She could end the relationship and replace it with another one that also and almost inevitably results in infidelity, or she could remain in the relationship and require him to pay a higher price, not just financially, but in ways that cater to her specific needs and desires.

This could encompass him being frequently refused intimacy, carrying out extraordinary acts of service, showering her with extravagant presents, expressing his affection for her publicly whenever she demands, or simply tolerating her trust issues and heightened emotional responses without significant resistance. In essence, she leverages his indiscretions to dictate the terms of their relationship, creating a dynamic where he must continually 'pay' for his past mistakes.

Honestly, the EPP barely even likes men anymore. She has experienced so much pain and heartache over the years and has never fully recovered from it. Despite all of this, she still does not see herself as a victim. Instead, she is simply a participant in a patriarchal society and leverages her hand by requiring the man to pay the cost to be the boss. The saddest part about the EPP is that she is never truly okay with being cheated on, no matter how much she pretends it does not hurt.

Now I must acknowledge there are some relationships where a woman may willingly accept her partner's extramarital affairs, often without a mutual agreement that she can do the same. This understanding, though not necessarily formalized, comes with its own set of rules and boundaries, and it's distinct from a situation where both partners agree to see other people. The Embittered Pragmatic Pick-Me (EPP) does not fit into either of these categories. Unlike those who have an understanding with their partner about extramarital affairs, the EPP tolerates her partner's infidelity, even though it goes against her personal morals and the agreements she and her partner made during the onset of their relationship. This distinction is crucial, as it highlights the difference between a consensual arrangement, even if one-sided, and a situation where one partner's behavior is excused or overlooked, despite being a breach of trust.

The mistaken pragmatic pick-me (MPP) is a woman who has drawn conclusions about marriageable men from assessing not only the men she has personally dated but all the men in her orbit, including her male relatives, friends, and colleagues. She has done her calculations and has deduced that all men cheat, even if no man has ever cheated on her. In fact, in scenarios where she believes that a man has not cheated yet, in her mind, it is only a matter of time before he does. Although it is wise of her to not judge every man based on the men she has personally dated, she has still made a costly miscalculation.

While the notion that all men cheat is problematic in and of itself because men are not a monolith, the bigger issue at hand is the MPP's reason for acceptance. She believes that men are incapable of committing themselves to one woman. Though if that were true, her logic falls short just like the EPP in that she never considers that her views of men have been shaped by those she has encountered personally or within her orbit. She also does not consider there are ways for a man to enter ethically non-monogamous relationships that do not require the cheating, lying, and other abusive characteristics that come alongside infidelity. In this scenario, it would require the man to have good character, a healthy ego, and open communication. Instead, she commits herself to relationships where the man banks on her moral compass to remain faithful to him despite his dishonorable ways, despite her knowingly and painfully sharing community peen.

The mistaken pragmatic pick-me is so dedicated to centering the man and justifying his behaviors that she disregards her own emotional needs and sexual safety to amicably give the man what he requires. She does all of this because she sees herself as a victim of patriarchy that at least rewards her with financial compensation due to her partner's infidelity. She is not requiring that he financially compensates her; she simply believes it is all a part of how things work in real-world heteronormative relationships.

But what exactly does this look like for a woman who has not already been cheated on? A mistaken pragmatic pick-me who has not yet experienced infidelity in her relationship operates under the assumption that it is only a matter of time before it happens. This belief, which stems from her perception of men and relationships, is inherently flawed, and she sees infidelity as an almost inevitable part of the relationship landscape.

She is so committed to centering her man and his needs that she often neglects her own emotional wellbeing. She might suppress her feelings, desires, and needs in order to maintain harmony in the relationship. She might also downplay her own achievements and aspirations, instead focusing on supporting her partner's goals and ambitions.

In terms of sexual safety, she might ignore her own comfort and boundaries, prioritizing her partner's sexual desires over her own. She might consent to sexual activities she is not entirely comfortable with, or she might not voice her needs and preferences out of fear of upsetting her partner or causing conflict.

Even though she has not been cheated on, she might already be mentally preparing for the eventuality. She might be setting aside money, building up her own career or skills, or creating a support network outside of her relationship. She sees these actions not as an assertion of her independence, but as a necessary precaution against the anticipated infidelity that could leave her destitute and alone.

In essence, she is a woman who, despite not having been wronged yet, is already living in the shadow of betrayal. She is constantly on guard, always ready to forgive and rationalize her partner's potential missteps, all while neglecting her own needs and desires. This is the reality of a mistaken pragmatic pick-me who has not yet been cheated on.

As you can see with both pragmatic pick-mes, they did not start off centering men. It was a result of their mindset and belief system surrounding the possibilities and probabilities of securing nontoxic relationships. It was a result of their lived experiences and the environments around them that caused them to make a last-ditch effort to not remain single forever. Do not be fooled; they still paid a hefty price, and they will encourage other women to do the same.

You can hear a EPP tell her daughter, "*If you live long enough, you will see that all men are the same.*" You will hear a MPP tell her best friend, "*At least he's paying the bills, girl. What more could you ask for?*"

They genuinely believe that they are giving good, practical advice and that the receiver just has not accepted the truth. These women are dangerous. They will have you lowering your standards until you find yourself enduring emotional abuse, all in the pursuit of perceived family stability and financial security. While they may benefit financially, the emotional and psychological toll is immense, as they sacrifice their own needs and well-being in a misguided demonstration of duty.

◆

THE
REPRESENTATIVE

CHAPTER 4

BEFORE EVER MEETING A MAN, an *evolved* woman has her own ideas, personality, interests, values, belief systems, passions, goals, and hobbies. She has spent years strengthening her self-awareness and developing herself into the woman she is now. She has experienced some difficulties in life, but she has used intelligence, strategy, wit, and resilience to continue herself on her path of success, navigating her life as if it is a chess game, always looking several steps ahead, and anticipating her opponent's next move. In full control of her life, she knows how to go after what she wants and is gifted in managing new spaces with ease.

She knows what to say, when and how to say it, and who she should say it to. Her social skills are impeccable and her ability to read the room is evident. She is indeed a force to be reckoned with. Nevertheless, this is exactly where things for her, the representative pick-me (RP), can all go wrong.

She is too **smart**
for her own good.

I am certain you have heard this idiom before. But if you haven't, it simply means that a person's intelligence begins to hamper their ability to do less difficult things; their knowledge somehow works against them or causes them harm. Unfortunately, this idiom perfectly describes the representative pick-me. She has become so accustomed to occupying spaces others have not fully welcomed her, that she has not yet discovered how to create spaces for herself, free from struggle, ridicule, or the need to assimilate to be accepted. So, she methodically takes all that she knows and applies it to her relationships. While there is sound logic in her approach, it is the misemployment of that knowledge that becomes her downfall.

Her efforts to find the perfect partner are clearly secondary to many of her other life's achievements, which is well within her rights and oftentimes a great decision. By the time a RP pursues serious relationships, she feels like her time is running out. This timeline that says a woman needs to marry or be in a serious, committed relationship by a certain age (usually regarding her ability to birth a child) causes some women to become desperate. When a woman becomes desperate to find a man, she often whitewashes herself to attract the man. Or even worse, she becomes a chameleon and completely misrepresents who she is for the fear of not entering the relationship she thinks she wants in the timeframe she has allotted herself. She will say everything she believes the man wants to hear even though most of it does not align with who she is at her core.

For instance, consider a woman who is naturally independent and enjoys her personal space. She meets a man who expresses his preference for a woman who is always available and deeply involved in his daily life. In her desire to secure a relationship with him, she might start to downplay her need for independence and personal space, and instead portray herself as someone who is always available and eager to be involved in every aspect of his life.

While it is completely normal and healthy to show interest in your partner's life and to make compromises in a relationship, the problem arises when this behavior is driven by fear and desperation, rather than genuine interest and love. If she starts cancelling her personal plans frequently to accommodate his schedule, constantly checking up on him to the point of neglecting her own needs or showing excessive interest in his daily activities to the point of losing her own interests, she is not being true to herself.

Similarly, it is wonderful to share hobbies and interests with your partner. However, if she starts to mirror his interests and hobbies, even if they are not genuinely appealing to her, just to make herself more appealing to him, she is misrepresenting her true self. For example, if he is an avid sports fan and she has no real interest in sports, it is one thing to watch a game with him occasionally out of love and compromise, but it is another thing to pretend to be an avid sports fan herself.

In essence, she is molding herself to fit into his ideal image of a partner, even if it means suppressing her true self and personal preferences. This is a clear example of a woman saying everything she believes a man wants to hear and behaving in a way she thinks he wants, even though it does not align with who she is at her core.

The most obvious problem with this tactic of getting a man is the inability to maintain this charade. At some point, the authentic woman shows up, only for her and her new partner to realize that the two are completely incompatible with each other. The man begins to feel bamboozled into a relationship because it was pure, yet subtle, manipulation that led him to entering the relationship with her in the first place.

Oftentimes, you will hear women complain about being with lying ass men. But the truth is many women are liars too, constantly lying to themselves and deceiving their partners. When you decenter men, which we will discuss thoroughly in later chapters, you stop looking for ways to manipulate them into a relationship. Instead, you will begin prioritizing your wants and desires and make yourself available to a man who will be compatible with you. Now, to better understand the RP, let's break her down into two types: the Unintentional and the Deliberate.

Representative Pick-Me Archetype

	UNINTENTIONAL	DELIBERATE
IDENTITY *(HOW SHE VIEWS HERSELF)*	A Pawn	A Grandmaster
PERCEIVES PARTNER *(HOW SHE VIEWS HER MAN)*	A King	An Opponent
STYLE	Positional	Aggressive
STRATEGEM	End game sacrifice	The Queen's Gambit
GOALS	To become the queen	To checkmate her opponents King
INSTINCT	To become what he wants	To pretend she's who he wants
FEAR	Another pawn becoming the queen	Losing to a weaker opponent
MOTTO *(HER RELATIONSHIP IDEOLOGY)*	It's not how you start, but how you finish.	Win before you start!

The URP is a woman who sees herself as a pawn, but not in a negative sense. She understands that in the game of chess, there is a term called queening, which means a pawn (the least powerful piece) can become a queen (the most powerful piece). She applies this principle to her life, knowing that her starting point does not dictate her finish. She prides herself on being self-made and credits her ability to advance professionally to her work-ethic and commitment to win at all costs. She values consistency and growth and believes slow and steady wins the race.

In her pursuit of a relationship, the URP is not consciously studying the man to become what he wants. Instead, she is subconsciously adapting to his preferences, often misinterpreting them due to her own insecurities or misconceptions. She may hear him express his desires or needs, but she may not fully understand them or may project her own assumptions onto them. This is not a deliberate act of manipulation, but rather an unintentional result of her desire to fit in and be accepted.

The URP is often a habitual shape-shifter, adjusting her behavior and personality to match the environment she finds herself in. This is not a conscious strategy, but rather a subconscious coping mechanism she has developed over time. She may come off as shy or reserved to men, when in reality, she is just uncertain of who she needs to be in his particular environment. She is unknowingly highlighting different aspects of her personality to gain a foothold in his life, with the hope that he will eventually embrace her true self in its entirety.

The URP's aim is never to manipulate, although she is doing so unintentionally. She sees the potential within herself to become a queen and is simply looking to partner with a man who she feels would be her equal: her king. However, in her quest to become the queen, she unintentionally sacrifices pieces of her authenticity, molding herself to fit into the image she believes the man desires. This is not a deliberate act of deception, but rather an unconscious result of her desire to be accepted and loved.

In essence, the URP is a woman who is intelligent and strategic, yet unaware of the extent to which her subconscious fears and desires are driving her actions. She is not intentionally manipulating the man, but rather unintentionally adapting herself to fit into his world. This makes her a complex and intriguing character, one who is both smart and unaware, strategic and unintentional.

On the other hand, a deliberate representative pick-me (DRP) is used to winning, despite any odds against her. Unlike the URP, she has every intention of using manipulation to get the man she desires and the relationship she deserves. She views life through the lens of chess. However, instead of seeing herself as a piece to be played, she sees herself as the grandmaster, the highest title that a chess player can achieve. She has experienced much professional success and believes all the years spent developing herself is now about to pay enormous dividends romantically, which will allow her to dominate the dating scene once and for all. Her time is currently spent orchestrating the most ideal scenarios that would prevent her potential partner from ever escaping her world. Her truth—no woman is better than her and no man can keep up.

The stratagem a DRP employs is called the Queen's Gambit, one of the oldest and greatest known chess openings. With this strategy, the player sacrifices her pawn temporarily to gain control of the center of the board. From the beginning, she deliberately sacrifices her authenticity, something she holds little regard for, and pretends to be exactly who her potential partner wants. She does not have time to waste, so she is as aggressive as possible in her approach, and she asks him all the pertinent questions, hoping to quickly secure a place in his future.

Did you have to work through childhood traumas and what were the indications of your healing?

Where do you see yourself in five years?

What are your top two love languages?

What are you looking for in a wife?
Gender-role beliefs? Ideal partner?
Spirituality? Finances?
Children? Sex Frequency?

She knows what she wants, and she has a very extensive, yet quick, vetting process that allows her to filter out all the men who do not meet the basic qualifications she uses to determine whether they will advance to the next phase with her.

As you can see from both types of representative pick-mes, the RP is a highly intelligent woman. She has the innate ability to identify and transfer skills from one aspect of her life to another. But sadly, her methodical ways just are not enough. Despite having all these accomplishments, a RP does not believe in herself. She does not believe she is exactly who someone would want. She does not see herself as a pick-me, even though that is precisely what she is. Instead, she sees herself as a high-value woman with options, deserving of the best man out there. However, she does not understand that good men are not all the same; they are not a monolith. Yes, there are high-value traits worthy men possess, which we will discuss more in later chapters, but they are not all packaged in the same exterior.

She does not understand that her goal should be to partner with a man who is aligned with the truest version of herself rather than trying to become or pretend to be who a man wants or who society tells her she should be. While she is convinced that she is growing into the woman she intends to be, her evolution is dangerous because though growth means change, change does not always mean growth.

And when **securing a man** becomes her impetus for change, she ambles toward the precipice of despair.

Her intrinsic nature is overtaken by her extrinsic goals, and after years of developing herself into the woman she was created to be, she looks into the mirror and is unable to recognize the woman looking back.

This woman is dangerous, not only to herself, but to many other women who aspire to be successful professionally. She seemingly has it all—the house, car, time-freedom to vacation on a whim, and the outward appearance that says she *knows* her shit. Still, financial success simply is not the key to landing your most ideal partner, and when you have not done the work, the right work, you launch a pursuit of male subjugation and begin to view romantic relationships with men as a feat to be conquered, instead of seeing it as a partnership in alignment with the core of who you are.

The Paragon of a Self-Selected Woman

A Mindset Deconstruction of Women who Center Themselves

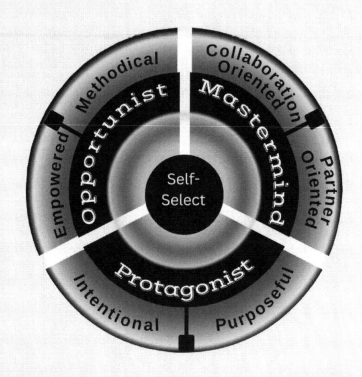

*Inverse of a Pick-me Woman

> " A POWERFUL WOMAN IS ONE WHO FEELS SECURE IN HERSELF, WHO KNOWS HER WORTH AND HER STRENGTHS, AND WHO IS ABLE TO EMPOWER OTHERS. "
>
> *- America Ferrera*

THE SELF-SELECTED WOMAN
CHAPTER 5

THE SELF-SELECTED WOMAN IS THE antithesis of a pick-me. She heralds authenticity yet conceals upcoming movements. She welcomes her failures and mitigates her pain. She is resolute in her pursuits yet pivots when necessary. She is intolerant of stagnation yet a proponent of rest. She is not well rounded yet a maven of her interests. She is hard to find yet easy to recognize. Above all else, she is committed to her purpose and acceptant of her journey, regardless of her relationship status with men.

A self-selected woman seeks out the support of a community. This can include female-only spaces, sisterhoods, or mentorship programs. She understands the importance of patronizing safe spaces and empowering environments for women to share their experiences and learn from one another. One of her core values is service. She deeply enjoys supporting other women in their journey toward becoming self-selected women, whether it is through online forums, in person events, or simply in her day-to-day interactions with other women.

This, sis, is what separates her from pick-me women. Although she may be difficult to access when you have not done the work, she exists within you already. She is the quintessence of womanness, the matriarch of her progeny, the healed version of the broken girl, and the prototype of femininity.

Embracing the self-selected woman within is not merely a theoretical concept; it's a tangible and achievable transformation. It's about recognizing your inherent worth, embracing your unique journey, and taking intentional steps towards self-empowerment and fulfillment. It's a path that requires reflection, courage, and commitment, but the rewards are profound and life-changing. As we embark on this exploration of the self-selected woman's characteristics and strategies, know that this is not just about understanding an archetype; it's about unlocking a new way of being, a new way of relating to yourself and the world around you. It's about becoming the woman you were always meant to be.

Thus, in the following sections, we will delve into practical examples and strategies that will help you embody the characteristics of a self-selected woman. We will explore how she navigates relationships, handles challenges, and cultivates her personal growth. By the end of this chapter, you will have a clear roadmap to guide your transformation from a pick-me to a self-selected woman. Let's get into it.

The Self-Selected vs The Pick-Me

	PICK-ME	SELF-SELECT
	WARRIOR	**MASTERMIND**
IN RELATION TO MEN	Submissive Driven	Partner Oriented
IN RELATION TO WOMEN	Competition Driven	Collaboration Oriented
	PRAGMATIST	**OPPORTUNIST**
HER DISPOSITION	Embittered	Empowered
HER JUDGMENT	Mistaken	Methodical
	REPRESENTATIVE	**PROTAGONIST**
METHOD OF CONTROL	Unintentional	Intentional
METHOD OF PROCUREMENT	Deliberate	Purposeful
WHO SHE CENTERS	**MEN**	**SELF**
HER FEARS	Utilized in Decision Making	Acknowledged in Decision Making
HER RESPONSIBILITY	Self-Sacrifice	Self-Preserve

The Mastermind Vs The Warrior

A self-selected woman is a mastermind of her life. Her skills allow her to execute at the highest degree of planning for the future she is creating. No longer does she operate through trial and error, but through conscientious design, and therefore has no time to aimlessly date men whose potential is not bolstered to a proven past. Besides, most men believe she is not easy to partner with. Her truths are not easily digestible, and her convictions remain impenetrable. Her virtue is bound by the covenant she has made with God, and she gives no man the power to alter the trajectory of her life's path.

She does not view freedom as the ability to do whatever the hell she wants. Rather, she sees it as granted permission to take whatever is rightfully hers. She understands that abundance is her birthright and is never afraid to lose anything that belongs to her. She knows that if something is meant for her, it will find its way back, and if not, she trusts in her ability to create new opportunities.

She practices **self-control** and is the personification of **self-awareness**.

Men learn quickly that she only reserves space in her life for those who are useful to her. It is not about creating a relationship rooted in transactions; it is about partnering with a man who edifies her by utilizing his resources of his own volition. She knows what she needs. She knows what she wants. And she knows she will never settle.

She has no desire to imprison a man. If he does not want to be in a relationship with her, she is quick to release him. Unlike the warrior pick-me, who is always ready for battle and willing to fight anyone she feels would threaten her relationship, a self-selected woman is always ready to retreat and prepared to orchestrate the smoothest transition to bigger and better things.

She is not focused on finding a man worthy of her submission. Instead, she aims to partner with a man who has submitted to his purpose. She does not view other women as competition. Instead, she looks for ways to collaborate with, mentor, or be mentored by them. There is no reason for her to compete. Other women could never be her; and she knows very well that the man is not the prize.

The Opportunist Vs The Pragmatic

The self-selected woman is opportunistic in her dating approach—not in a way that is harmful to others, but in a manner that allows her to leverage who she is and what she has in order to create what she needs and the type of relationship she requires. She does not assume the worst or hope for the best regarding men; she cultivates relationships that allow her to capitalize on her position no matter the outcome, and with very little regard to patriarchal conditioning because it no longer dictates her decisions.

Unlike the pragmatic pick-me, who is embittered by her past and/or mistaken in her calculations, the self-selected woman is empowered by her experiences and methodical in her analyses. She does not believe that all men cheat because she understands that accepting that belief would never render a favorable outcome for her. Instead, she makes herself inaccessible to men who are operating with an unhealthy state of mind because she understands that whoever she aligns herself with begets the power to influence her in subtle yet impactful ways. Therefore, she sets the bar optimally high, and allows nature to take its course.

Like the pragmatic pick-me, the self-selected woman operates the way she does as a result of her mindset and belief system. But instead of concentrating on the probabilities of her securing a healthy relationship, she focuses on the ratio between the opportunities and disadvantages that each relationship brings.

There is not a price a man could pay for her
to dishonor herself.

This is because she does not have a love for money, security, comfort, stability, etc that is rooted in the need for someone else to provide that to her. What she does have is a contract with the universe rooted in abundance, and she understands that the genesis of prosperity follows the exodus of excuses. She makes none for herself and accepts none from her partners or pursuers.

For a self-selected woman, any relationship she enters is an opportunity for growth. You will hear her tell her daughter, "If you keep your eyes open, you will see that who you attract is never your problem, but the men you select should always be a part of your solution."

The Heroine Vs The Representative

Unlike the representative pick-me, whose main focus is getting casted in someone else's story, a self-selected woman is the heroine of her own. No matter how many times she is passed over, she always centers herself, believes she is worthy, and views herself as the protagonist of a story worth telling. She is too smart to be somebody's fool and too in love with her mind, body, and soul to even think about misrepresenting any part of herself that she has purposefully cultivated.

A self-selected woman does view life through the lens of a game. However, her preferred choice is poker, not chess. While chess arguably requires more skill and analytical abilities among all great players, poker is more reflective of how she navigates her life. This is because of two primary reasons. First, she understands that while intelligence is positively correlated to success, it does not guarantee it. Second, in life, she understands that you must be able to anticipate the moves of several people at a time—not just one—while still making the best decisions with the hand you have been dealt.

She practices self-preservation. After all of the hard work that has gone into developing herself into the woman she has become, she refuses to exhaust herself trying or pretending to be someone she is not. She strives to meet a man who likes her for who she is—a woman of integrity who values free will and would never use manipulation as a tool to secure a relationship or capture a man. So to avoid sacrificing her authenticity, she takes her time getting to know a man step-by-step to ensure he is a viable suitor.

Although she may not have a husband or child yet, she does not live with regret.

She knows that **working toward a goal** is always better than wishing upon a star.

She accepts that her journey is unique and does not view herself as less than for not being what society expects her to already be: a wife and a mother. She has intentionally created the life she deserves and is willing and ready to share it with others when the opportunity arises.

The Awakening

The transition from a pick-me to a self-selected woman is a journey of self-discovery, growth, and empowerment. It is about reclaiming your power, asserting your worth, and choosing a life that aligns with your values and desires. It is a journey that requires courage, resilience, and a commitment to self-love and self-respect; and for the self-selected woman, it is a journey that is absolutely worth it.

The transformation from a warrior pick-me to a self-selected woman is not a battle against men or other women, but a battle within yourself. It is about confronting your fears, insecurities, and self-doubt. It is about challenging the beliefs and narratives that have held you back and kept you stuck in patterns of behavior that do not serve you. It is about letting go of the need for external validation and learning to validate yourself.

The journey from a pragmatic pick-me to a self-selected woman is a process of redefining your relationship with yourself and others. It is about letting go of bitterness and resentment from past experiences and embracing the potential for growth and healing. It is about shifting from a scarcity mindset, where you may feel you must compete for resources and attention, to an abundance mindset, where you believe there is enough for everyone. It is about learning to trust your intuition and make decisions that align with your values and goals, rather than being driven by fear or the desire for security.

The transformation from a representative pick-me to a self-selected woman is a journey of authenticity and self-expression. It is about shedding the masks you wear to please others and embracing your true self. It is about letting go of the need to fit into a certain mold or meet certain expectations, and instead, defining success on your own terms. It is about recognizing your worth and refusing to settle for less than you deserve. It is about learning to express your thoughts, feelings, and desires openly and honestly, without fear of judgment or rejection. It is about stepping into your power and taking control of your narrative, rather than letting others dictate your story.

Ladies, this journey is not linear. There are ups and downs, successes and setbacks. There are times when you may feel like you are taking two steps forward and one step back. But with each step, you becomes more self-aware, more confident, and more aligned with your true self.

As a self-selected woman, you must understand that this journey is not about becoming perfect or achieving some idealized version of womanhood. Instead, it is about becoming the best version of yourself, and that version is constantly evolving. You must know that you will make mistakes along the way, and be able to see these mistakes not as failures, but as opportunities for growth and learning. And although it may be surprising to hear, the real, defining, and measurable distinction between you being a self-selected and a pick-me woman lies in the day-to-day choices you make to choose (or not to choose) yourself.

That is it. It all begins with you.

A Moment to Reflect

As we conclude Part 1, let's take a moment to reflect on the key takeaways and engage in some introspective journaling. This will help consolidate your understanding and facilitate a deeper personal connection with the material.

Key Takeaways:

1. Understanding the Pick-Me Woman: The Pick-Me woman is characterized by her willingness to compromise her own needs, desires, and identity to secure a relationship. She often operates from a place of fear and desperation, rather than self-love and self-respect.

2. The Three Types of Pick-Me Women: The Warrior, the Pragmatic, and the Representative each have unique characteristics and behaviors. Understanding these types can help identify patterns in your own behavior or the behavior of others.

3. The Self-Selected Woman: The Self-Selected woman is the antithesis of a Pick-Me woman. She is authentic, self-aware, and does not compromise her identity for the sake of a relationship. She operates from a place of self-love, self-respect, and abundance.

4. The Journey to Becoming a Self-Selected Woman: This journey is about self-discovery, growth, and empowerment. It requires courage, resilience, and a commitment to self-love and self-respect.

Journaling/Reflection Prompts:

Remember, this journey is not about achieving perfection, but about growth, self-discovery, and becoming the best version of yourself. Take your time with these reflections and be honest with yourself. This is a safe space for you to explore your thoughts and feelings, and to chart your path towards becoming a Self-Selected woman.

Identify Your Patterns: Reflect on your past and current relationships. Can you identify any behaviors that align with the Warrior, Pragmatic, or Representative Pick-Me woman? How have these behaviors impacted your relationships and your sense of self?

Envision Your Ideal Self-Selected Woman: What does the Self-Selected woman look like to you? How does she behave in relationships? How does she handle challenges? What are her values and beliefs?

Your Journey to Becoming a Self-Selected Woman: What steps can you take to start your journey towards becoming a Self-Selected woman? What beliefs or narratives do you need to challenge? What fears or insecurities do you need to confront?

Your Relationship with Abundance: How can you shift from a scarcity mindset to an abundance mindset? How would this shift impact your relationships and your sense of self?

PART 2

DEBUNKING MYTHS

Definitions from Shawdrism Language

au·then·tic·i·ty \ ə-‚then-'ti-sə-tē *noun*

The ability to be who the hell you are while evolving into who the hell you want to be.

fem·i·nine en·er·gy \ 'fe-mə-‚nin 'e-nər-jē *noun*

The nurturing force that births creation, honors intuition, and gracefully navigates life's winding paths.

in·tu·i·tion \ ‚in-‚tü-'i-shən *noun*

That gut feeling that whispers the truth even when logic is still fumbling for the light switch.

log·ic \ 'lä-jik *noun*

The mental compass guiding decisions, built on the foundation of past knowledge and experience.

mas·cu·line en·er·gy \ 'mas-kyə-lən 'e-nər-jē *noun*

The driving force that constructs, employs logic, and moves unswervingly along life's linear path.

pret·ty priv·i·lege \ 'pri-tē 'priv-ə-lij *noun*

The golden ticket in the lottery of patriarchy, granting unearned perks to those who fit society's beauty standards.

Part 2: Debunking Myths

Market Makers Method™ Component 2: Myths
2nd Rule: Reject limiting beliefs.
Framework: The Dating Market Myth-Busting Model™

In Part 2 of this book, we will delve into the myths and misconceptions pervasive within the dating community that prevent women from achieving the relationships they desire. Debunking myths is an essential part of the journey toward mastering the market and dating on your own terms.

Using *The Dating Market Myth-Busting Model™*, the four chapters in this section will examine and challenge long-held beliefs about women. This section will provide a fresh perspective on topics, such as femininity, the dangers of dating wealthy men, the misconceptions surrounding single-mothers, and the value of virginity.

These are controversial topics that have been widely debated, but often without a clear understanding of the facts. By exploring these myths and understanding their origins, we can empower ourselves to make informed choices and navigate the dating world with greater confidence and self-assurance. It is important to approach these chapters with an open mind and a willingness to question our preconceptions.

If at any point you feel overwhelmed, take a break and come back to it when you are ready. Remember, this is a journey, and progress takes time. With the knowledge and tools provided in this section, you will be well on your way to mastering your market and finding the relationships you desire.

Before You Begin

Welcome to the part of your journey where we debunk myths. This section is not intended to be comprehensive. Rather, it should serve as a guide to help you understand exactly how to debunk any dating myths designed to tear you down.

To get the most out of this section:

1. Approach each chapter with an open mind and a willingness to question your preconceptions.
2. Use Evidence-Based, Critical Thinking, and Personal Experience approaches to evaluate the validity of each myth.
3. Consider cultural, historical, and societal factors that may influence your dating behaviors and beliefs.
4. Align the information with your values, beliefs, and goals for your dating life.
5. Engage with the writing prompts and questions at the end of this section to deepen your reflection and understanding.

Part 2 is designed to be illuminating, shedding light and bringing clarity to areas where you may be unaware or misinformed. For this reason, it is important that you understand the societal implications of these myths, even if they do not personally apply to you. These topics often come with shame and guilt, so learning how to approach them with confidence and self-assurance can help you navigate other negative sentiments that may arise in your personal dating journey.

My goal for you is to leave this section feeling empowered and equipped with the tools to make informed decisions about your dating life, regardless of outside commentary.

Questions that Might Arise

What if I find it hard to let go of some of these myths? They've been ingrained in me for so long.

It is completely normal to find it challenging to let go of long-held beliefs, especially when they've been a part of your worldview for a significant period. Remember, change is a process, not an event. It is okay to take your time to digest the new information and gradually adjust your perspective. You might find it helpful to revisit these chapters, engage in further reading, or even discuss these topics with trusted friends or a counselor.

How can I reconcile my personal beliefs with the debunked myths presented in this section?

Your personal beliefs are shaped by your experiences, values, and the information available to you. When you encounter new information that challenges these beliefs, it is an opportunity for growth and learning. Start by examining your beliefs and the myths debunked in this section. Ask yourself why you hold these beliefs and whether they serve you in your current life and goals. It is okay if your beliefs evolve over time - this is a natural part of personal growth.

How can I apply the Evidence-Based, Critical Thinking, and Personal Experience approaches to other myths?

These approaches are versatile tools that you can apply to any belief or assumption. When you encounter a new myth, start by looking for evidence. Is there reliable, scientific data that supports or refutes this belief? Next, apply critical thinking. Finally, reflect on your personal experiences. Do they align with the myth or not? By using these three approaches, you can form a well-rounded understanding of any myth you encounter.

What if my cultural or religious beliefs align with some of these myths? How can I navigate this conflict?

This is a valid concern. Cultural and religious beliefs are deeply personal and can significantly influence our perspectives. If you find that some of these myths align with your beliefs, it is okay. The goal is not to change your beliefs, but to provide a broader perspective. You can acknowledge the information presented while still holding onto your beliefs.

THE
DATING MARKET MYTH-BUSTING
MODEL™

Evidence-Based Approach	Critical Thinking Approach	Personal Experience Approach

3 APPROACHES TO DEBUNK DATING MYTHS

Evaluates the statement based on scientific evidence and research. This method involves using credible sources, such as academic journals and studies, to determine the validity of a statement.

Applies critical thinking skills to evaluate the statement. This method involves analyzing the statement from different perspectives and considering alternative viewpoints to determine its validity.

Evaluates the statement based on personal experience. This method involves considering the experiences of individuals who have interacted with the statement and determining if it holds true in their personal experiences.

Questions TO ASK YOURSELF

Evidence-based — What is the evidence that supports or refutes this statement?

Critical Thinking — Are there any assumptions, biases, or prejudices underlying this statement?

Personal experience — Does this statement align with my values, beliefs, and goals for my dating life?

Cultural context — Does this statement consider cultural, historical, or societal factors that may influence dating behaviors and beliefs?

Self-reflection — Does this statement align with my personal experiences or observations in my dating life?

> "FEMININITY IS DEPICTED AS WEAKNESS, THE SAPPING OF STRENGTH, YET MASCULINITY IS SO FRAGILE THAT APPARENTLY EVEN THE SLIGHTEST BRUSH WITH THE FEMININE DESTROYS IT."
>
> —Dr. Gwen Sharp

BUSTING THE MYTH OF FEMININITY
CHAPTER 6

"YOU MUST LEARN TO BE FEMININE" is one of the greatest dating myths ever. It is a problematic statement as it implies that there is a certain way that women should act or behave to be considered feminine. This belief is often perpetuated by societal and cultural norms, as well as by what is portrayed in the media. However, the true essence of feminine energy is much more than just being soft-spoken or submitting to men. It encompasses a variety of traits and characteristics unique to each individual woman.

In this chapter, we will explore the concept of authenticity in relation to femininity, and how trying to conform to a certain archetype of femininity can be detrimental to a woman's sense of self. We will also delve into the idea of creating versus building, and how feminine energy is geared toward bringing new things into existence, while masculine energy is focused on building and constructing.

Next, we will discuss the difference between circularity and linear thinking as it pertains to femininity. Additionally, we will discuss the importance of embracing your intuition, and how to use it as a guide in your relationships and decision-making. Lastly, we will explore the importance of rest and self-care and what that specifically looks like as a self-selected woman.

It is important to note that femininity is not a one-size-fits-all concept, and what may be considered feminine for one woman may not be the same for another. The goal of this chapter is to help women understand that they do not have to conform to societal expectations of femininity to be considered a "real" woman, and to instead embrace their unique qualities and traits.

Authenticity Vs Facade

The concept of femininity has often been distorted and repackaged in a way that can make many women feel as though they do not fit the 'feminine' mold. This distorted image often portrays femininity as being soft-spoken, submissive, cooperative, and less opinionated. This is what I refer to as the 'facade' of femininity - a superficial, one-dimensional portrayal that does not capture the full depth and diversity of feminine expression.

On the other hand, authentic femininity is about embracing who you truly are as a woman. It is about expressing your unique qualities, traits, and perspectives, even if they do not fit the traditional mold. Authentic femininity is not about being soft-spoken or submissive, but about being true to yourself and your values.

Just as there is a "pretty privilege" that women receive for being more conventionally attractive in their society, there is also a privilege for women who conform to this facade of femininity by being more cooperative and less opinionated than others. However, this does not mean that being cooperative or less opinionated is inherently feminine. Rather, these are traits that have been associated with femininity due to societal and cultural norms. The point I am trying to make here is that femininity is not about conforming to these norms, but about expressing your authentic self.

One of the scariest truths is that women can exist in a space for a lifetime that they were never meant to exist in. It is not uncommon for a woman to remain married to a man for forty years, find relief when he passes, and never desire to remarry or even have close relations with men anymore despite still being full of life and energy. It is not because their late husbands were awful to them, it is because they were finally free from having to pretend to be a woman they never truly were. They finally got the opportunity to live for themselves again, and they never want to go back.

You do not have to become that old and sometimes bitter woman before finding your freedom to be yourself and live out your purpose. You can choose to be you today and let go of the facade that you have been hiding behind. While it might be a bit scary, it will be one of the most rewarding gifts you can ever bestow upon yourself.

Building vs Creating

In the dating scene, it is not uncommon to hear a man say, "I am looking for a woman I can build with." This statement often reflects a desire for partnership and shared goals. However, it is important to understand the difference between 'building' and 'creating.' To build is to form or construct something by combining materials or parts, often associated with masculine energy. On the other hand, to create, associated with feminine energy, is to bring something into existence without the prior existence of the materials or elements used.

When a man says he is looking for a woman to build with, he is often expressing a desire for a partner who can complement his strengths and compensate for his weaknesses. He may have a vision for the future and is looking for someone who can help him realize that vision. This does not necessarily mean he is looking for a submissive partner or a 'yes woman.' Rather, he may be seeking a partner who can bring her own unique skills, perspectives, and ideas to the table.

However, it is important to note that women, particularly those who embrace their femininity, often play a different but equally important role in a relationship. They are creators, bringing into existence things that did not exist before, often in ways that go beyond their experience and available resources. For example, a woman can transform a house into a home, infusing it with love and warmth that goes beyond the physical structure. Similarly, a woman can contribute to a business in ways that go beyond the tangible, such as by fostering a positive culture or implementing innovative strategies.

It is important to understand and embrace these distinct roles. A woman's role is not to compete with a man or to be his equal in the sense of doing the same things he does. Rather, her role is to complement him, to bring something unique and valuable to the relationship that enhances both their lives. This is not about being less than or subservient to a man, but about recognizing and honoring the unique strengths and contributions of both genders.

Circular Vs Linear

Have you ever noticed that when communicating with men, it is sometimes difficult to get them to make certain connections? It's not because they all are playing ignorant or willfully dismissing us. It's not because they do not believe the conversation is worth having. The simple reason is this. Men and women have different ways of processing information and reaching conclusions due to the unique ways in which our brains are wired. Men tend to be more direct and solution-focused, while women have a greater ability to connect seemingly unrelated information and experiences. Men are direct and to the point. They have an opinion and state their solution. They do not need to openly analyze how and why they reached their conclusion, only that they did. Women, however, have the ability and propensity to connect almost anything together, openly analyzing all possibilities in their mind.

This is because masculine energy is linear and feminine energy is circular. Women can exist in the present and connect something that is currently happening within a situation to an experience that happened ten years ago. Thus, the ability to make connections and understand patterns is not a sign of being stuck in the past or jaded, but rather a result of their divine feminine energy. Men who are operating in their masculine can easily recognize *patterns*, which happens within their conscious mind. Women who are operating in their femininity can more easily recognize *habits*, which are typically done subconsciously. We will learn more about this in Chapter 18.

It is important to recognize and appreciate the differences in communication styles and to understand that they can be beneficial to the family unit. When a woman recalls past events or makes connections between different experiences, it's not because she has not moved past certain things. Instead, it is a manifestation of her divine feminine energy, which allows her to see patterns, anticipate potential issues, and bring a holistic perspective to the relationship. This ability is not about dwelling on the past, but about using all available information to make the best decisions for the family's future.

Therefore, when you find yourself in conflict, instead of being defensive, you can explain to your partner that what they are witnessing is not a sign of unresolved issues, but rather, an expression of your feminine energy at work. You can explain to them that while you appreciate their single-minded focus and ability to keep your family's progression oriented forward, you also need them to recognize that your responsibility to the family is different–that being able to make certain connections is necessary because it creates an added layer of protection to the family unit.

By embracing and understanding the unique power of your femininity, you can alleviate confusion and improve your relationships with your partner and family.

Intuition Vs Logic

A woman who is operating in her femininity uses intuition instead of logic. Intuition is the feeling that something could happen, whereas logic is recognizing something has already happened. Being intuitive is trusting your gut instinct rather than waiting for logic to validate your feelings. This is why you can often hear men tell women that they are constantly jumping to conclusions. And the truth is women are. It is in our nature. But it's important to distinguish between intuition and another feeling that can sometimes be confused with it: insecurity. While intuition serves as a guiding force, insecurity can lead to confusion and self-doubt.

Intuition is the impetus of change and is useless without action. You are not intuitive without reason because intuition serves as a warning and signals you to do something different than you otherwise would. Insecurity, on the other hand, is a deep-seated feeling of uncertainty or anxiety about oneself, often stemming from a lack of confidence in one's worth or abilities. Unlike intuition, which is a protective force, insecurities often lead to self-doubt and can undermine the health and harmony of a relationship. Now if you have not done the work, you will not be able to tell the difference between your intuition and your insecurities, causing many unnecessary problems.

Remember this, your intuition will always be validated with logic in the near or far future, but your insecurities will remain unjustified, no matter how much you try to reason with yourself and your partner.

Intuition is used to protect, whereas insecurities can destroy.

Logic, however, is the ability to draw conclusions based upon having knowledge or experience with a situation prior. While logic is both useful and necessary for both partners to demonstrate, it should not be weaponized against intuition.

You are dishonoring your divine feminine when you attempt to move without emotion and intuition, and you are disrespecting the masculine parts of yourself when you refuse to ever use logic and reason. The goal is to honor both the feminine and masculine and allow them to work hand in hand, in both you and your partner. The divine feminine is the highest expression of your feminine energy. It is not possible to operate in your divine feminine unless you embrace the masculine because the divine feminine encompasses both feminine and masculine energy just as the divine masculine encompasses both masculine and feminine energy.

Resting in Your Femininity

When I first started learning more about being a feminine woman, everything I saw and heard was leading me to this idea of a soft life, especially as a black woman. I wanted to get away from the strong black woman trope so badly that I began to reject anything that could be interpreted as work and feel repulsed by any man that wanted a woman to work. I desired to have a man to rescue me from the hard life that I had been accustomed to.

However, I realized at some point that I did not need a man to rest in my femininity and it made a hell of a difference in my life. Instead, I began to operate in my divine feminine always. That means sometimes I create, sometimes I shake shit up, sometimes I must shut shit down abruptly, and if any person is in my way, they just might feel my wrath. Sometimes I tap into the masculine parts of myself. And of course, sometimes, I rest!

But **with or without** a man, I am feminine.

I accepted that my life is not majorly soft, but it is purposeful. It is evolving. It is more primitive to womanhood than it has ever been before. With that acceptance, I have allowed myself to expand far beyond where I was energetically and consciously. I am now able to experience all my power instead of limiting myself to only being seen as feminine through the eyes of men who do not even know there are different archetypes of femininity and who refuse to stop conflating masculinity with power and authority.

Anyone trying to teach you that femininity is not powerful is setting you up for an extremely difficult life. It is doing you a disservice to only rest when someone grants you that opportunity. You must value and believe in yourself more. Control your life more. Be accountable to yourself more! You must become the captain of your own ship and secure with the woman you are at your core.

Stop arguing with men about whether you are a feminine woman. If his masculine energy cannot connect with your feminine energy to the point where he has to ask you about it, you two are not compatible or there is still more healing, growing, and evolving necessary on one or both parts. He is not at fault, nor should you be concerned about his limited vision. Femininity is not just love and light, it is also dark and sometimes lethal. It is not about submission. It is about cohesion. It is not about being led to a good life. It is about being driven to creatively employ your soft and hard skills for the betterment of yourself and the people you care about.

So, do not sell yourself short by being this performative pick-me version of a feminine woman. You do not need to silence your voice. You do not need to wear pink, flowy dresses with kitten heels if that is not your style. It is impossible to suppress all negative emotions and you do not need to even try.

Be authentically you. You cannot fake femininity. It is your essence. You simply need to learn to tap into your full feminine power to properly navigate the spaces and relationships you want to exist in.

There is room for you to authentically show up, and you are worthy of showing up. Let go of this idea of how you should act as a woman and accept that you simply are a woman. Remember, women are not a monolith.

True Femininity cannot be ~~WORN~~, although it can be **SEEN.** It cannot be ~~TAUGHT~~, but it can be **FOUND.** It cannot be ~~TAMED~~, but it can be **HARNESSED!**

A self-selected woman is one who encompasses both feminine and masculine energy and knows when to operate within one versus the other at any given time. Limiting yourself to being all feminine is impeding the possibility of partnering with a man operating in his divine masculine. You cannot operate in your divine feminine without acknowledging and learning to use your masculine traits and energy.

There are some women who try to suppress any trait or energy they feel is masculine and they wonder why they are not seeing growth in their lives at the rate in which they are expecting. Striving to be all feminine is not a brag. It is not possible, and it is surely not the key to dating on your own terms.

> ## THERE IS SOMETHING ABOUT POVERTY THAT SMELLS LIKE DEATH.
>
> "
>
> "
>
> — *Zora Neale Hurston*

BUSTING THE MYTH
OF RICH MEN
CHAPTER 7

THE STATEMENT "RICH MEN ARE DANGEROUS" alludes to the idea that the more money a man has, the more likely he is to be abusive. The biggest reason this myth does not make sense is because the data simply does not support it. Statistics show a much stronger correlation between poverty and intimate partner violence (IPV) than it shows wealth and intimate partner violence.[1] While correlation does not equal causation, the facts remain. The likelihood for a woman to experience IPV increases the less money there is in the household.

It is easy to understand when you consider all the stressors that come with living in poverty or paycheck to paycheck. The Covid-19 pandemic in 2020 is recent proof of that. Reports of domestic violence from lower income families increased drastically during the pandemic.[2] Men who are poor are not inherently bad people, and men who have attained decent wealth are not inherently good people.

However, living in poverty for an extended time can have negative effects on almost anyone.

This is in no way meant to excuse the horrible behavior that some poor men display toward others, but it should serve as a cautionary tale to remove yourself from those men and environments as best as you can to avoid unnecessary conflict within your home. When a woman makes it clear that she has high financial expectations for the men she dates, one of the first things people will say to her is "rich men are dangerous." They do this as a scare tactic to keep her from pursuing the type of relationship and man she wants.

Now, I will be very honest with you, the truth is rich men could cheat, but so could poor men. Rich men could be abusive, but so could poor men. Rich men could leave a woman for the next baddest woman within his reach, but so could poor men. Rich men could abandon their families, but so could poor men. Rich men could be dangerous, but you have guessed it, poor men could be as well.

This entire notion that it is okay to categorize an individual's character by their socioeconomic class is absurd. No class is all encompassing of good qualities, neither is any class all-encompassing of poor qualities. A man's financial status does not dictate how poor or well he will treat you, but it could indicate how much he could financially benefit you if he so chooses. So why is it that so many people want to warn women about the dangers of entering a relationship with a rich man? There are a few reasons why this is the case. Let's look at it from a mindset perspective: the scarcity mindset, the victim mindset, and the fear-based mindset.

Scarcity Mindset

A man operating from a scarcity mindset will be the first to tell women that rich men are dangerous. These men do this because they believe that if too many women adopt higher financial standards for their partners, it will reduce the size of their dating pool. They know they are poor. Yet, they lack the ambition, knowledge, skills, and self-motivation necessary to level up their lives financially. Because they are complacent with who and where they are in life, they want all the women they believe they currently have access to, to remain accessible to them. Instead of these men investing into their self-development, they take the easy way out by gaslighting women into believing dating a poor man is safer.

The truth is a portion of the poor men who preach rich men are dangerous do not believe that being a rich man is synonymous with being a dangerous man. They know it is illogical because if their theory were correct, that would automatically mean they too would become a danger to be with if they ever became rich. They would immediately and consequently become a danger to any woman they would like to pursue despite having no intentions of harming women just because their income has increased.

However, the other portion of men who hold this belief are oftentimes some of the most abusive men that have ever existed. They are the ones who are currently abusing their partners and abandoning their children. They are the ones asking women, "What do you bring to the table?" knowing they do not own a home to even put a table in. They are the ones who are unable and unwilling to commit themselves to a woman despite having the expectation that she remains faithful and loyal to them. They are the ones who use all their spare time arguing on Beyoncé's Internet that women are gold diggers and low vibrational if they have a modicum of a financial standard for their prospective partners.

These men have a scarcity mindset. Instead of believing that there is enough knowledge and wealth to go around, they limit themselves and others with half-witted tactics they feel will keep them in the game.

Victim Mindset

Men operating from a victim mindset feel life is not fair and, despite what they may tell you, does not actually believe that rich men are dangerous. They believe that people at the top of anything, those with power, must have made it there due to corruption. They make a subconscious decision to never be at the top with them.

They blame all their shortcomings on something or someone else. Usually, it is the economy, their supervisor, all of their exes, their mother, or "the system." They believe that the cards they were dealt with would never allow them to become rich. Because of this, they do not believe women should have any financial standards. They see themself as a great partner who is loving and supportive, albeit, unable to financially support their family or future family.

Instead of these men focusing on improving their future, they are stuck in the past, always pulling old stories out to prove to others why they are in their current situation in hopes of gaining sympathy. They are not interested in leveling up, not because they do not necessarily want to do the work, but they honestly believe it is simply impossible. They are always defeated in their minds and can never see any wrong in the decisions they made that perpetuated this life of gloom. So, their vision of what could be is constantly hampered by their ideas of what was and who caused it. And, of course, they were never the culprit.

Men who hold this belief can be very dangerous, not just physically, but mentally. They will use passive-aggressive, backhanded compliments, like "You're cute on the outside, but no man wants a woman who is materialistic," or "You need to lower your standards or you are going to die alone." These men have a victim mindset, and they will project their insecurities on women they have access to. Instead of accepting responsibility for their failures, mistakes, and inability to achieve their most basic goals, they lash out at women and accuse them of being shallow for having no interest in an unambitious, victim-minded man like them.

Fear-Based Mindset

Women are not immune to perpetuating the myth that rich men are dangerous. In fact, some women, whether they are friends or strangers, can be the most vocal proponents of this idea. These women are often operating from a fear-based mindset, a direct consequence of their own insecurities and low self-esteem.

A woman with a fear-based mindset might have never experienced a relationship with a financially stable man. She might be used to struggle and hardship, and she might have come to view these challenges as indicators of true love. For her, the idea of a good man is tied to how well she is treated, with little regard for his financial stability. Anything outside of her normal experience can evoke fear and insecurity.

This fear is often rooted in ignorance. Despite her own accomplishments, beauty, or intelligence, she might not believe that she is worthy of a relationship with a man who is financially secure. She might have accepted mediocrity for so long that the idea of wanting more for herself seems foreign, even dangerous.

In addition to fear, low self-esteem plays a significant role in this mindset. A woman with low self-esteem might not believe that she can fall in love with a financially stable man who treats her well. She might not believe that she can leave an abusive relationship and never return. She might not believe that she is worthy of more. As a result, she might project her insecurities onto other women, warning them against seeking relationships with rich men.

However, it is important to remember that these fears and insecurities are not reflections of reality. They are distortions created by a mindset rooted in fear and low self-esteem. As a woman, you have the right to seek a relationship with a man who is financially stable, respectful, and loving. Do not let the fear-based mindset of others deter you from pursuing the relationship you deserve.

BUSTING THE MYTH OF SINGLE MOTHERS
CHAPTER 8

MOTHERS WHO FIND THEMSELVES BACK IN the dating market are constantly being told that their motherhood status devalues their worth to marriage-minded men. I can easily explain why many mothers are actually great candidates to become wives; however, it is necessary to discuss the opposing views made by men who are on the market. Men and women see things differently and considering the woman's perspective only in this situation could leave you uninformed on the reasons men prefer to not date mothers.

The first thing you must realize is that men who hold these views are not viable options for mothers. If you are a mother, do not try to coerce a man into dating you if he states he will never marry a woman who is already a mother. It puts both your and your children's safety at risk. Now, let's look at some of the most common reasons mothers are told they hold less value in the dating market and understand why these reasons are invalid and not a true reflection of society, especially considering mothers are marrying everyday.

Bitter Baby-Mamas

The most popular explanation I have seen men give in regard to why they do not want to date single mothers is that single mothers are bitter baby-mamas. The term "bitter baby-mama" is often used to describe single mothers in a negative light, implying that they are constantly embittered and resentful toward their co-parent, relationship status, and even their own children. While it is true that parenting can be challenging, especially for single parents who bear most of the responsibility, it is important to remember that bitterness can emerge during the natural grieving process.

Bitterness is not a recognized stage of grief, but it is a common emotional response that many people experience as they navigate their way towards healing. Many single mothers have gone through a period of bitterness but have since moved on and are even grateful for their newfound independence. As such, it does not make sense to suggest that all single mothers are bitter, as this implies that their feelings are constant and never-ending. Most single mothers have successfully navigated through all stages of grief and are ready to move forward in their lives. To say that single mothers are bitter baby-mamas is not only inaccurate, but it also perpetuates harmful stereotypes.

It is important to note that even if a single mother has experienced bitterness in the past, it does not define her as a person or make her any less worthy of love and companionship.

Furthermore, bitterness is a natural feeling that can arise from any type of loss or disappointment, not just from being a single mother. Everyone has their own unique experiences and emotions, and it is important to acknowledge and validate those feelings. Remember, bitterness is a temporary feeling that can be overcome with time and healing.

It is also important to not let negative stereotypes and myths hold you back from pursuing the life and relationships that you want. Single mothers can be loved and respected just like anyone else. Most importantly, if you are a single mother, you should not allow anyone to make you feel like you are not good enough for love and companionship, because you are. Trust me!

Women with children are receiving marriage proposals every day. They are being pursued by men of substance every day. They are leading amazing lives every day. While being a single mother is not easy, and requires immense strength, resilience, and dedication, a season of bitterness will never outshine a lifetime of love and fulfillment. Men who are emotionally intelligent understand this.

Indicative of Poor Judgment or Horrible Character

Some men claim that outside of becoming a widow or sexual assault, it is 100 percent the woman's fault for becoming a single mother. They claim that there are only one of two reasons that could have resulted in that outcome. Either she was a poor picker of men, realized her partner was trash, and then she left. Or she was so insufferable that a man decided to leave both her and his child behind. Essentially, men who feel this way believe that the woman should have chosen or conducted herself better.

The problem in the first scenario is that it unjustly takes all responsibility away from the man. While I do believe that women decide who we have a child with, women can only make decisions based upon the information that we have at the time. Now, there are times when women disregard certain traits of a man, indicating that he might not be a good father or a good partner. However, there are also plenty of times where men simply change up.

I can agree that the woman is responsible 100 percent for who she chooses to have a child with, but I will never agree that the woman is then responsible for every decision the father of that child makes from that point forward. Women have autonomy over our bodies, but we can never dictate what any person outside of us does. There have been far too many times a man woo, provide for, remain faithful to, and dote on a woman, only for him to become a subpar father or an abusive husband four years down the line.

This does not mean that the woman made a poor decision to marry or have a child with that man. It does not mean that their values at the time were not seemingly aligned. It does not mean that she trapped that man, and he did not want to be in a relationship or have a child with her. Absolutely no one can foresee everything. Blaming a woman for motherhood is reasonable to a degree. However, blaming a woman for being a single mother without identifying circumstantial factors such as the evolution of her child's father is absurd.

The second scenario, which suggests a woman's character was the reason a man would leave if he was actually a good man, is more common to hear among self-proclaimed good men who have fathered children they do not take care of. Are there some women who are insufferable? Of course. Does this represent the majority of single mothers? Perhaps, if you ask the fathers in these scenarios. But if you ever sit longer than five minutes with many of these men, you will notice very common grievances they make about these women, which are rarely about the woman's character.

On the following page, take a look at a few translations of the things they would say, along with an empathetic interpretation that acknowledges the potential unhealed trauma in men:

Guy: *She tried to change me.*

Interpretation: *She was encouraging growth and change in areas I was not ready to address. This could reflect my own resistance to personal development or fear of change.*

Guy: *She nagged about every little thing.*

Interpretation: *She repeatedly expressed her needs and concerns, which I may have overlooked or dismissed. This could indicate a need for better communication and understanding in our relationship.*

Guy: *She changed.*

Interpretation: *She evolved and grew as a person, which is a natural part of life. This could reflect my own discomfort with change or a struggle to adapt to new dynamics in our relationship.*

Guy: *She is too emotional.*

Interpretation: *She expresses a wide range of emotions, which may be uncomfortable for me due to societal expectations that men should limit their emotional expression. This could point to a need for me to expand my emotional literacy and understanding.*

Guy: *She let herself go after having the baby.*

Interpretation: *Her body and priorities changed after childbirth, which is a natural and common experience. This could reflect my own unrealistic expectations and a need to better understand and support the physical and emotional changes that come with motherhood.*

Guy: *She never wants to have sex and she used to want to have sex all the time.*

Interpretation: *Her sexual desire has changed, which could be due to a variety of factors including increased responsibilities, hormonal changes, or emotional stress. This could indicate a need for me to be more understanding, supportive, and proactive in addressing these issues together.*

These interpretations are not meant to excuse or dismiss the feelings of the men expressing these concerns. Instead, they aim to provide a more empathetic perspective that acknowledges the potential unhealed trauma and societal pressures that men face. It is important to remember that these situations are complex and involve the feelings, experiences, and perspectives of both parties.

Lastly, you will also notice that many men are unable to explain the reasons they have left their children and their children's mothers. It's primarily because they know deep down inside that it has far more to do with their own character and needs than it does the character of the woman or the needs of the child.

No benefits to being a stepparent.

I remember being in a room full of single people. A man made a provocative statement: "There is no benefit for a man raising another man's child. There is only sacrifice and suffering. If I am wrong, tell me how the child of a woman I would have been interested in could benefit me in any way, because it is obvious how having a stepfather could benefit a child."

The room fell silent. Shortly thereafter, women began to respond by saying things, like "Worrying about how a child can benefit you is the problem. Your focus should be on the woman and how you two can come together to create the life you want," or "That does not even make sense, how does any child benefit a parent, whether they are biological, step, or adopted?" or "Men who are looking for a child to benefit them are the kinds of men who are looking to use a person, and he already knows how he can use the woman to his benefit but is looking for ways to benefit even more through her offspring."

I will admit, I understood where all these ladies were coming from. However, while several women responded to the statement at hand, none of them actually addressed it. I believe this was for a few reasons. First, these women had probably never been asked this before and were unprepared. They probably had no clue how a stepchild could possibly benefit the man. Lastly, they probably felt attacked if they were single mothers and immediately shifted their focus to defending themselves, although the question was not personally directed toward any one woman.

I did not respond because I know how to read a room. There was no answer a woman could have given that would have sufficed because the men in that space were not asking to learn new information. Instead, they were seeking ways to support the ideas already cemented in their minds, just as they did with each question prior.

The truth is if you are committed to not seeing something, you never will, even if it is staring you dead in the eyes. But for the men and women who truly want to know how it is that a child could possibly benefit the stepfather, here are a few reasons.

First, there are few men who are excited about engaging in all the responsibilities and sacrifices that come with having a newborn in the home. Sleepless nights, diaper changes, and deciphering between cries to understand what a child is trying to communicate is not something that men instinctively think about when they decide to have children. However, you hear a lot of them talk about how they look forward to being able to play sports with their sons, pamper their daughters, and have family game nights with their wife and children. The excitement of parenting children daily does not generally start for men until the child is old enough to verbally communicate in a way that does not require them to decode every cry, sentence, or tantrum.

This is not to say that men do not enjoy having young children around, because many do. Many of them, however, expect for the woman to do most of the parental labor during the youngest years of that child's life, despite breastfeeding being the only true task that is exclusive to motherhood after the child is born. Often, resentment is built between the parents when the woman feels like she is not being supported enough in the day-to-day affairs of parenting the child.

77

Though, if a man enters a woman's life who has a child above the age of six or so, the man essentially gets to avoid all of the responsibility that he never really cared for, the resentment from the mother he could have potentially received and can move straight into the more desirable parts of fatherhood. Most people do not have many memories before that age, so the child will feel like the stepfather was in their life from the very beginning and will honor him for it.

Also, two of the most primitive things that men do are provide and protect. Becoming a stepdad enables a man to expand his scope of protection and provision almost instantaneously. While those things would then require more effort and sacrifice on his part, it is not a deterrent because men genuinely find great pleasure in doing these things for their families. Subsequently, the more opportunities a man gives himself to protect and provide, the more opportunities he gives himself to receive the rewards and satisfaction he desires.

It is not about men being charitable to women and children, but rather connected to all of humanity. It is not about their level of nobility so much as it is their source of identity. A man who can only identify family as someone with whom he shares a biological connection, is a man with an encumbered consciousness of self. This is because humans are not designed to use biology as the sole metric to identify who we are to ourselves or who we are to and among other people.

Thus, a man choosing to parent a child who is not biologically related to him further catalyzes his ability to define and reaffirm who he is through a broader and deeper level of awareness, accounting for sociocultural influences, personality traits, cognitive abilities, behavioral patterns, biological responses, spiritual beliefs, and more, which aggregately describes who he truly is. Additionally, choosing to be a stepparent helps to cultivate an identity among others that is based upon intrinsic merit and acquired value demonstrated over an extended period.

When we explore the hierarchical rewards and satisfactions of men, we will find that two of the top components are respect and appreciation. Without these two present, men will not amount to their fullest potential, nor will they be compelled to remain near those who are not demonstrating it. The more a man has the propensity to not solely define fatherhood by his biological connection to a child, the more deliberate he becomes in his parental efforts, the greater accountability he takes for how he influences the child in his care, and the less likely he is to expect respect and appreciation that he has not earned.

People value more in life the things that they work most for. Being respected and appreciated by someone with whom you may share no obvious similarities can be truly rewarding in the end. This is not to suggest that men do not feel highly respected and appreciated by their biological children because many of them do. Nonetheless, consider the profound satisfaction that comes from nurturing a child into adulthood. This child may not share your inherent gifts or traits, as they are not biologically yours. Yet, they grow up to attribute much of their success to your influence and presence in their life. Isn't it deeply rewarding when a child, who may not share your physical characteristics, embodies your principles, values, and love, and shows you respect and appreciation for your fatherly influence?

While men may have different and valid reasons to prefer a childless woman over a mother, the only men who see no benefits in dating a woman with a child are the ones who only assess the value of their fatherhood by the existence and distribution of their seeds, rather than their influence on and development of their children.

BUSTING THE MYTH OF VIRGINITY

CHAPTER 9

IF I AM BEING HONEST, LATELY, no man that I have been romantically interested in has ever asked me how many sexual partners I have had in the past. This could be due to various factors, such as my age, the types of men I date, or even a broader societal shift towards accepting sexually liberated women. Who really knows? However, I know that this is not the case for everyone. Some of the younger women I have coached have had to contend with questions and judgments about their sexual history, a reflection of the persistent myth that virginity somehow determines a woman's value.

This myth is not only outdated but harmful, and in this chapter, we will explore why. We will discuss several reasons people use to support their stance that virgins are more valuable in the dating market, including misconceptions about women's inherent value, men's desire for purity, and what desirability looks like from a male perspective.

Before we delve deeper, let's acknowledge that a woman's virginity, like her body, belongs solely to her. Choosing to remain a virgin until marriage can be a unique and personal decision, one that may set a woman apart from societal norms and pressures. However, this choice should be made freely, without fear or coercion, and in alignment with one's personal beliefs and values.

Inherent Value

Myth: *Women are born with value and lose it over time, whereas men are born without value and must earn it over time.*

This pervasive myth pivots around two central points: physical beauty and virginity. Let's explore each aspect and debunk the flawed assumptions behind them.

The idea that women are born with value based on physical beauty suggests that men primarily seek physical attractiveness, while women are interested in financial security. Some even argue that a woman's mere existence is enough for her to be marriage material. However, this perspective oversimplifies the complex dynamics of attraction and compatibility. In reality, men consistently demand more than just physical attractiveness, considering other qualities such as personality, intelligence, and shared values when determining a woman's suitability for marriage. Therefore, the notion that women are born with value that diminishes over time is fundamentally flawed.

Some men argue that a woman's virginity, like her physical beauty, is an inherent value. They contend that because a woman's first sexual experience is irreversible, it holds a unique, priceless status. This perspective is akin to the notion of buying a brand-new car: once it is driven off the lot, it is considered 'used', and its value immediately depreciates. Regardless of how well the car is maintained or how few drivers it has had, its status shifts from 'new' to 'used', and that is all that matters.

This analogy, although widely used, fails to recognize the complexity and individuality of human relationships. Unlike a car, a woman's worth cannot be reduced to a single aspect of her life or experience. The idea that virginity is a one-time commodity that loses value once "used" is a reductive and harmful narrative that overlooks the multifaceted nature of human beings.

It is important to note, however, that men's virginity is not subjected to the same scrutiny. Men often view their sexual experiences as conquests, with each new partner serving to bolster their masculinity. The idea that a woman's value decreases with each sexual encounter is a manipulative narrative that serves to keep men ahead in the game. By convincing women that their societal contributions and acquired skills are less valuable than a one-time sexual experience, men can maintain their perceived superiority.

The notion that virginity equates to a higher inherent value is fundamentally flawed. Consider this: every woman who has experienced abuse, be it physical, emotional, or otherwise, was once a virgin. Her virginity did not shield her from harm. It did not prevent her from being cheated on, abandoned, or treated as a second-class citizen. It did not protect her from any form of abuse or from becoming a baby-mama. This stark reality underscores the fact that a woman's virginity does not inherently increase her value or guarantee her safety and respect.

Men who hold these views are reducing a woman's worth to a single aspect of her life, ignoring her complexity, individuality, and the many qualities that make her valuable. It's essential to recognize that these perspectives are not universal truths but rather societal constructs that can be challenged and changed. If you ever encounter someone who holds this view, remember that your value is not determined by your sexual history or anyone else's opinion. You have the right to define your worth, and you can articulate your beliefs with confidence and grace. By understanding and embracing your own value, you can contribute to changing the narrative and fostering a more respectful and compassionate view of women's sexuality.

Purity and Paternity

Myth: *Men have a predisposition to prefer the purest women to prove paternity.*

When I first encountered this myth, I was unsure of its origins. It was challenging for me to comprehend because the argument supporting this statement was a non-sequitur, a type of logical fallacy. The reasoning behind it did not follow a logical progression. With that said, let's explore this statement to see why this is the case.

First, it is important to acknowledge that because men do not bear children, they never truly know whether a child is their biological offspring. Well, that is up until recent times where DNA tests have become available and accessible to many men. But regardless, women never have to worry about whether they have propagated their own genes. Because of that, women often find it difficult to understand the insecurities of men when it comes to male paternity because their maternity is proven through birth alone. Just like most women naturally desire to become mothers, men naturally desire to father children. It is an internal wiring that has helped humanity to exist for as long as it has. It is the most primitive (not only) explanation for the sexual desires between men and women.

Now, the reality is this: a man's desire to ensure paternity is not directly correlated to his desire to sleep with a virgin. It is linked to his desire to receive loyalty from his partner, which explains why men generally respond more angrily to physical cheating than women do. If virginity is what ensures male paternity, men would only mate with women they perceive to be virgins. However, this has never been the case. At no point in history have men refused to mate again with the mother of their first child simply because she is no longer a virgin. On the contrary, they want more and more children with her. Her virginity then is not what ensures anything. Instead, it is her fidelity and commitment to their relationship that a man values above all else. Also, in modern times, it has become more common for a man to knowingly have a child with a woman who was already a mother before having met him. Again, virginity was not a factor.

From an evolutionary psychology perspective, prevalent human behaviors have emerged as 'psychological adaptations', developed to address recurring challenges in the environments of our ancestors. During the medieval times, men realized that they were not able to know the true paternity of a child. They created many ways to try to rid their jealousy and reduce their paternal insecurities. They created laws that favored them, which forbade women to marry without being a virgin as well as consequences for women who did not uphold the law. But even with these adaptive responses, men still seldomly took care of children who were not biologically theirs because virginity was never what they truly cared about. If a woman made a man feel or believe that she was loyal to him, he believed that the children born into their union were indeed his biological offspring.

There is a misquoted statistic that men who propagate this myth often refer to. It says that almost 30 percent of men are raising children that are not actually their biological children, insinuating women are regularly committing infidelity that result in pregnancy and delivery. This is simply not the case. In situations where the father attests paternity, with the overwhelming majority of these cases involving fathers who are not in committed relationships with the mother, there is approximately a 30 percent chance that the presumed father is not the actual biological father.[3] However, when the child is being born to a committed couple and paternity is not questioned, the probability of a man unknowingly raising a child who is not biologically related to him drops to less than 1 percent.

This conversation is significant because there is no scientific data or historically supported claim that a woman's premarital sexual experiences suggest a higher likelihood that children born within the marriage will have a biological father different from the husband.

Desirability

Myth: *If a nonvirgin, never-married woman requires a man to marry her before having sex, that man is less desirable to her than the man she did not require marriage from.*

I remember speaking to a group of men who explained why it made no sense for a nonvirgin, never-married woman to make them wait until marriage for sex. They rationalized that women sleep with who they want and men sleep with who they can. I agree with this statement. However, they went on to explain different tiers of desirability among men. They did not say tiers per se, but this is how I will categorize them to make things clear.

Tier 1 - a man who offers the least amount of benefits and receives sex within the shortest amount of time.

Tier 2 - a man who offers the least amount of benefits and receives sex after an extended time.

Tier 3 - a man who offers a lot of benefits and receives sex within the shortest amount of time.

Tier 4 - a man who offers a lot of benefits and receives sex after an extended time.

These men claim that offering the ultimate proposal (marriage) to a nonvirgin, never-married woman, means that he is not as desirable to her as other men. However, studies have shown that since 2010, around 95 percent of women who become married have engaged in premarital sex. It also shows that 72 percent of women have had at least two sexual partners.[4] This means that only a small amount of women had premarital sex with only the man that eventually became their husband. The vast majority of married women had sex before marriage and at least one of their partners was not the man they married. Some argue that this is because men have now lowered their standards for what they are looking for in a wife. But the truth is most men simply do not care if a woman has been sexual with another man before having met them.

Men with healthy self-esteem do not assume they are less desirable just because a woman chose to have sex with other men before they met her. On the contrary, many of them pride themselves on being that woman's best partner in many ways. Men are not regularly proposing to women who do not make them feel like they are the most desirable, even in the instances in which they are not. It is preposterous.

Desiring a woman with little to no sexual experience is not a problem in and of itself. The problem arises when the only reason a man can see himself as most desirable is if there was no other man to compare himself to. This sentiment exposes more about how the man feels about himself than it does how he feels about a woman. It makes no sense because it goes against the very nature of men. Men are naturally competitive. Men who feel this way are clearly in the minority of men and perhaps are the ones who also have the worst self-esteem comparatively.

A Moment to Reflect

As we conclude Part 1, let's take a moment to reflect on the key takeaways and engage in some introspective journaling. This will help consolidate your understanding and facilitate a deeper personal connection with the material.

Key Takeaways:

1. **Femininity is not a weakness:** Femininity is a strength and a source of power. It is not about being submissive or passive, but about embracing your unique qualities and using them to your advantage in the dating market.

2. **Wealthy men are not inherently dangerous:** While there are risks associated with dating wealthy men, these risks are not exclusive to this demographic. It is important to approach any relationship with caution and to prioritize your safety and well-being.

3. **Single mothers are valuable:** Single mothers are not devalued in the dating market. They are strong, resilient, and capable of providing a loving and nurturing environment for their children. Their status as mothers does not diminish their worth or desirability.

4. **Virginity does not determine value:** A woman's value is not determined by her virginity. It is determined by her character, her actions, and her contributions to society. Virginity is a personal choice and should not be used as a measure of a woman's worth.

Journaling/Reflection Prompts:

Remember, this journey is about empowering you to navigate the dating market with confidence. Use these reflections to examine your beliefs and guide your path forward. The goal is to align your choices with your personal values and desires, not societal expectations. This is your safe space to explore and chart your path towards becoming a woman in control of her dating life.

Reflect on the myths debunked in this section: How have these myths influenced your dating behaviors and beliefs? How do you feel now that these myths have been debunked?

Consider your personal beliefs and values: How do they align or conflict with the information presented in this section? How can you reconcile these differences?

Think about your dating goals: How can you apply the Evidence-Based, Critical Thinking, and Personal Experience approaches to achieve these goals? How can the debunking of these myths help you navigate the dating market more effectively?

Acknowledge any feelings of guilt or shame: How can you address these feelings and move forward? How can understanding the societal implications of these myths help you navigate these feelings?

PART 3

A WOMAN'S MARKET

Definitions from Shawdrism Language

a wo·man's mar·ket \ ə ˈwu̇-mənz ˈmär-kət *noun*

A dating market where women set the rules and the closing bell never rings.

bar·ri·ers of en·try \ ˈber-ē-ərs əv ˈen-trē *noun*

The velvet ropes and bouncers of your dating sphere, keeping the undesirables at bay.

con·flu·ence \ ˈkän-ˌflü-ən(t)s *noun*

A harmonic convergence of internal and external metrics signaling when to enter or exit a relationship.

en·try sig·nal \ ˈen-trē ˈsi-gnəl *noun*

The green light in your dating traffic system, indicating when it's safe to proceed into a romantic relationship.

ex·it stra·te·gy \ ˈek-sət ˈstra-tə-jē *noun*

Your pre-planned escape route from a relationship, designed to minimize collateral damage.

glass cei·ling \ ˈglas ˈsē-liŋ *noun*

Invisible barriers in your relationship that only become apparent once you've bumped your head a few times.

in·va·li·da·tion point \ in-ˌva-lə-ˈdā-shən ˈpoint *noun*

The final straw that breaks the camel's back, prompting you to hit the eject button; your relationship's stop loss.

mar·ket ma·ker \ ˈmär-kət ˈmā-kər *noun*

A woman who sets her own dating rules, creating an exclusive market tailored to her needs.

rules of en·gage·ment \ ˈrülz əv in-ˈgāj-mənt *noun*

The relationship Geneva Conventions, outlining how conflicts will be handled in your romantic interactions.

TROMP \ ˈträmp *noun*

An acronym for Top-tier Rotation of Marriageable Prospects; the crème de la crème of your dating options.

A Woman's Market

The Market Maker Method™ Component 3: Market
3rd Rule: Position yourself to win.
Framework: The DECIDE Model™

Intentionality is key. You do not accidentally get the person you desire. Instead, you must decide to create and implement a system that will allow you to positively change the manner in which you date once and for all. In this section, we will discuss the inception of *The Market Makers Method™*, followed by the exact steps to create the dating market of your dreams, which is called, A Woman's Market—the only market that never ends.

First, I need you to understand something. The focus will be on your goals for your future, not the men of your past. We will discuss a few important topics that focus on men, but sis, that is it! The reason is this—placing most of our focus on men and trying to combat their million ways of keeping us in a state of despair will forever keep us in the passenger's seat. We will always find ourselves on the defense, trying to maneuver around their mental gymnastics, and we will likely look like a clown while doing so. That's not the goal.

The goal is to systematically place ourselves in a position to win, think offensively no matter what, and create the relationship we want on our own terms. We will never truly learn the heart of a noncommittal man, but we can learn how to filter out any man who is not aligned with who we are and where we are going. In order to do this, we will utilize *The DECIDE Model™,* a six-step blueprint that allows a woman to create her ideal dating market. The steps are as follows: design the relationship, establish barriers of entry, create rules of engagement, identify entry signals, develop an exit strategy, and employ a TROMP.

Before You Begin

Welcome to Part 3 of your journey, where we delve into the concept of creating your own dating market. This section is designed to empower you, providing you with the tools to take control of your dating life and establish your own rules.

To get the most out of this section, I suggest:

1. Read each chapter slowly and thoroughly.
2. Reflect on the strategies and concepts presented.
3. Consider how these strategies can be applied to your own dating life.
4. Engage with the exercises and questions at the end of this section to deepen your understanding.
5. Trust the process and be open to the transformation that is possible through this journey.

Part 3 is about more than just understanding the dating market; it is about actively participating in it and shaping your experiences. Even if you feel confident in your dating skills, this section offers new perspectives and strategies that can enhance your approach.

The goal of this section is not to dictate your dating life, but to equip you with the knowledge and tools to make informed decisions that align with your personal values and goals. These chapters may challenge some of your existing beliefs and practices, but remember that growth often comes from discomfort.

My hope for you is that by the end of this section, you will feel more confident in navigating the dating market, setting boundaries, and advocating for your needs and desires. Remember, this is your journey, and you have the power to shape it

Questions That Might Arise

What if I am not comfortable with some of the strategies presented?

It is okay to feel uncomfortable with new concepts and strategies. Remember, this is your journey, and you have the power to shape it in a way that aligns with your values and aspirations. Take what resonates with you and leave what does not.

What if I am not sure how to apply these strategies to my own dating life?

That's okay. The strategies presented in this section are meant to be a guide, not a strict rulebook. Take your time to understand each concept and think about how it might apply to your own experiences.

What if I feel like I am not making progress?

Remember, personal growth is a journey, not a destination. It is okay to take your time and move at your own pace. Celebrate small victories and be patient with yourself.

What if I have questions or need further clarification?

Feel free to revisit previous chapters or seek additional resources if you need further clarification. Remember, this is a learning process, and it is okay to ask questions and seek help.

The DECIDE Model™

A 6 Step Blueprint to Creating Your Ideal Dating Market

Step	Focus	Key Actions	Outcomes
DESIGN the Relationship	What is your goals and desires for a relationship?	Define what you want in a partner and what your relationship should look like	A clear vision for your ideal relationship
ESTABLISH Barriers of Entry	What criteria must a potential partner meet before considering them?	Establish a list of deal-breakers and standards for your relationship	Increased confidence in attracting the right partner and avoiding the wrong ones
CREATE Rules of Engagement	How will you and your partner communicate and interact?	Create boundaries, expectations, and agreements for your relationship	Increased communication and understanding in the relationship
IDENTIFY Entry Signals	What are the signs that a potential partner is the right fit?	Look for signals that a potential partner is aligned with your values and relationship goals	Increased ability to identify compatible partners and make informed dating decisions
DEVELOP an Exit Strategy	How will you handle a breakup or end the relationship if needed?	Identify what actions you will take and how you will handle the end of the relationship	Increased peace of mind and a plan for handling difficult situations
EMPLOY a TROMP	How will you manage, create, and employ a true rotation of marriageable men?	Prioritize relationships with the most potential and make changes as needed	Increased options of connecting with your ideal partner

FOUNDATIONAL GUIDANCE

CHAPTER 10

A part of my life's purpose is to help women learn to better navigate their romantic relationships and date on their own terms; however, I am a forex day trader by profession. That means, I trade currencies in the foreign exchange market and exit each position that I take the same day as I enter it, usually within a few hours.

By far, it is been one of the most challenging things I have ever learned to do. It has required a level of discipline I thought I had, but realized I did not, as well as a will to succeed even when the odds were stacked against me. Because of that, I have taken a lot of what I have learned as a trader and implemented that knowledge into other areas of my life. So, I want you to follow along with me for a bit as I explain an important forex concept before circling back to romantic relationships.

In forex, there is a term called market makers. Market makers are the large institutions who actually control the direction of the markets. When I say *large*, I want you to think of major banks like Citibank, JP Morgan, UBS, Barclays Bank, Deutsche Bank, BAML, Goldman Sachs, HSBC, Morgan Stanley, etc., as well as governments and hedge fund managers. Everyone else trading in the forex market is called retail traders. No matter the strategies, tactics, or styles of trading the retail traders use, they are always operating within the parameters set by the market makers.

It is possible to have a successful trading career as a retail trader, but you must know that you are indeed playing in someone else's territory. You are participating in a market where 90 percent of all retail traders lose 100 percent of their invested money and stop trading altogether, leaving only 10 percent of retail traders who end up becoming consistently profitable within the market. Although it is not true, this explains the reason so many people believe that trading forex is a scam.

No matter their intelligence, desire, or commitment to win, most retail traders fail and never receive back what they put into the market. They never learn how to align themselves with the market makers to consistently stay on the winning team. Most traders never realize that they could have found massive success had they simply learned to create their unique edge within the forex market and never given up. While it is true that 90 percent of retail traders lose 100 percent of their initial deposited funds, it is also true that 100 percent of retail traders who are successful are the ones that simply never gave up.

When trading currencies in the forex market, one of the most common mistakes retail traders make is making emotionally based decisions when trading. They have no real plan in place to inform their decisions and end up allowing their emotions to dictate their trading. The moment they lose a trade or two, their emotions run high, and they begin to make irrational decisions, trying to force the market to give them back the money they lost and causing them to lose even more in the process.

Once a trader learns the importance of creating a plan and following a system, their trading improves significantly and their view of the forex market shifts into a more positive light. They learn to fully trust their system, despite their emotions, even when an individual trade does not produce the results they were hoping for. They begin to understand that while every trade is not a winning trade, their system is 100 percent working in their favor, doing what it is designed to do, and ultimately leading them to the success they are looking for.

This market maker concept explains why many women also feel like they are being scammed in their relationships. They believe the dating market was designed for women to lose themselves while only receiving a fraction of the return on their investment from the man they entered the relationship with.

As bad as it sounds, they are correct. They are playing a losing game. They are entering a man's market and trying to outwit him in a relationship that was inherently designed to benefit him more, and many times, at the expense of the woman. It is not because the woman is unintelligent. It is not because she is inexperienced. It is not because her eyes are glued shut and she is unable to see what is going on around her. Still, this is the reality for many women.

The society in which we live has given men so many privileges over their women counterparts that cause women to experience such difficult times on the dating scene. If we are being honest with ourselves, we know that this will not stop anytime soon. So, where does that leave us?

If we are participating in a man's market, supported by society, how can we ever get on the right side of the market? How can we ever create enough power to move the market in the direction we want it to go? It almost seems impossible.

But, what if I told you that just like the market makers, you could create a market for yourself where you will always win in the end. No, you alone cannot change the dating market for every woman out there, but you are the only person needed to create the dating market most ideal for you. You just need to know the formula. So how exactly can we do this?

There is an idea floating around that says, "It takes two to tango." It suggests that both parties must be willing to put in the work for the relationship to succeed. While there is some truth to that statement, it leaves out an imperative qualifier—the power held by the creator of that relationship. I understand the importance of having both people take responsibility for the quality of the relationship they are in, but a successful relationship starts well before either person enters it.

When people are intentional about what they want in a relationship, they must first envision themselves in that relationship and create it in a way that is both welcoming and undeniably attractive to the type of person they want to partner with.

Dating casually can become complicated because it requires little to no planning or boundaries. It requires no consistency, and it leaves no real ability to measure the effectiveness of your dating habits. However, intentional dating, also known as courtship, is all about structure. It is all about committing yourself to one strategy that allows you to consistently show up in your most authentic self.

This is what this section is all about, learning to create a winning dating system that will move your relationships from the edge of complexity to the edge of simplicity and ultimately allow you to date on your own terms.

Here is the best part. Just like the retail traders in the forex market can align themselves with the market makers to win in the end, so can the men who participate in a woman's market. The goal is not for you to win and the man to lose. What man wants to be in a relationship where he is not winning while he is with you? The goal is to design the market in a way that guarantees you will win in the end and ensures that your ideal partner does the same.

The following chapters will help us to do just that. In the context of this book, a "market maker" refers to a woman who is in control of her dating options, creates her own opportunities, and sets her own terms in relationships, rather than being at the mercy of the "market" or the men who are available to date. It is a woman who makes the rules and chooses the relationships that are right for her, as opposed to being passive and accepting whatever comes her way.

◆

> " THE BEST WAY TO DESIGN A HAPPY RELATIONSHIP IS TO CREATE A SHARED VISION OF WHAT LOVE MEANS TO BOTH OF YOU. "
>
> — *Gloria Steinem*

DESIGN THE RELATIONSHIP

CHAPTER 11

THE BEST WAY TO PREDICT YOUR relationship is to create it. Instead of leaving everything to chance or hoping that the relationship will miraculously look exactly like you want, you can methodically create the relationship you know would be beneficial to you. A way to do this is by focusing on the two key phases of relationship design: framework and functionality. The framework is all about creating the structure for your relationship, which consists of the foundation, pillars, and covering. Functionality is all about how well your relationship makes room for you to thrive and grow.

Framework

Foundation

The foundation is the bedrock upon which your relationship will be built. It is the first element you need to establish because everything else will rest upon it. This is the stage where you identify your most profound values. Are they respect, friendship, and trust? Perhaps they are legacy building, commitment, and intimacy? Or maybe love, loyalty, and spiritual alignment? You need to pinpoint the essential elements that, if upheld, will anchor your relationship, and if violated, will signal its dissolution.

The number of core values you establish for your relationship does not have to be fixed. However, remember that these values are meant to guide you in your quest for companionship. If you have an extensive list of thirty-seven core values that a man must independently share, finding the perfect match might be an uphill battle. Conversely, if you focus solely on one aspect, your net might be cast too wide. The ideal number may vary for each woman, but I suggest starting with three deep-seated values and expanding if necessary.

Your foundation represents your **non-negotiable** boundaries.

These boundaries must always be respected. If any part of your foundation is breached, the entire relationship will suffer. It is crucial to distinguish between boundaries and expectations here. Boundaries are standards that must be upheld in your relationship, while expectations may not always be met and can often be unrealistic or unnecessary.

Identifying damage to your foundation is not always straightforward. You will not immediately realize that your commitment is weak after the first disagreement. You will not label your partner as an unsuitable friend after the first instance of disrespect. Instead, issues with your relationship's foundation will gradually impact everything else built upon it.

Much like a house, signs of foundational problems in a relationship can be subtle. You might notice uneven floors, cracks in the walls, or signs of water damage before realizing there are deeper foundational issues. Without constant vigilance in maintaining your foundational values, you might end up paying a steep price for repairs that could have been avoided with regular upkeep.

Pillars

While the foundation of your relationship is paramount, the pillars that provide support between the foundation and the covering are equally crucial. These pillars represent the daily mechanisms that validate and indicate the health of the relationship. They can include elements like compromise, emotional intelligence, reciprocity, conflict resolution, communication style, sexual compatibility, and more. It is relatively straightforward to recognize when one or more of these relationship health indicators are weakening.

However, the faltering of a single pillar does not necessarily mean the entire relationship will crumble. These are your relationship's red flags. There is a common belief that you should exit a relationship at the first sight of a red flag, but if that were the case, long-lasting relationships would be nearly impossible. Instead, red flags should serve as warnings that something is not right. They should prompt you to take note and initiate a conversation at an appropriate time to address the concerns.

The concept of red flags did not originate with the NFL, but football provides a useful analogy for understanding how red flags function within relationships. In American football, according to NFL Football Operations, coaches have red flags that they can throw onto the field before the next snap. This signals to a referee to initiate an instant replay review of the previous play.[5] Essentially, when a red flag is thrown, a coach is challenging a call they disagree with. This does not guarantee a favorable outcome for the coach, but it does allow them to address the issue immediately before the game proceeds.

The most successful coaches rarely throw red flags, but when they do, they win the majority of their challenges. They understand that not everything needs to be addressed. Other coaches have a 50/50 or lower success rate when they throw their red flags. This is significant because the success rate of red flags thrown can affect perceptions of a coach's value within the game. The best coaches understand that they cannot challenge every referee's call. They respect the game, the rules, and decisions made outside of their control. In American football, not every play can be challenged. Some plays, like scoring plays and turnovers, are automatically reviewed, so a coach does not need to challenge them.

Considering these NFL red flag rules, let's look at five key takeaways and relate them back to red flags within relationships:

1. Raising concerns in a relationship is about exploring a situation further, not about assigning blame or asserting correctness.

2. Use red flags judiciously. Excessive false alarms can erode trust and reduce your partner's willingness to engage.

3. Not every situation requires a lengthy conversation. It is important to acknowledge that both partners have flaws.

4. Avoid challenging your partner's feelings. It can be hurtful and unhelpful to the relationship. Instead, listen and understand their perspective.

5. Some issues demand immediate attention and should be addressed promptly, such as instances of physical or emotional abuse.

When designing the pillars of your relationship, consider when, where, and how often you will address the red flags that will inevitably arise.

Covering

The third component of your relationship design is the covering. This element is crucial as it provides an external support system for the couple. The covering is intended to add an extra layer of protection to your relationship. When conflicts emerge within the relationship, the covering offers guidance and neutral perspectives to help resolve the issues. It can be seen as a safety net, protecting the relationship from harm and preserving its integrity. This could include professionals such as therapists, relationship counselors, mediators, spiritual leaders, mentors, or other impartial individuals who can provide advice and support.

The covering serves both individuals within the relationship by outlining where they can seek counsel when they cannot resolve a conflict between themselves. The covering can also play a role in regular relationship maintenance and upkeep, ensuring that both partners receive the support they need to maintain a healthy and fulfilling relationship.

Once you have identified the foundation, pillars, and covering, it is time to move on to the second phase of relationship design: functionality.

Functionality

Functionality is a critical aspect to consider in your relationships. Reflect on the potential cost of remaining in a relationship that does not serve you. Recognize the difference between a low-functioning relationship and one that fosters growth and helps you reach your full potential. The right relationship can be the catalyst for becoming the best version of yourself, rather than keeping you stagnant. Let's delve into the significance of functionality in crafting your ideal relationship using the concept of a "glass ceiling."

The term "glass ceiling" is often used to describe an invisible barrier that hinders a person or group from rising beyond a certain level. Marilyn Loden first coined this metaphor in 1978 to describe the limitations high-achieving women faced in the workforce.[6] However, this concept can also apply to the constraints many women experience within their personal relationships.

Every relationship you enter will have boundaries—some set by you, others set for you. Therefore, before entering any relationship, particularly a romantic one, it is crucial to consider the limitations, boundaries, and expectations you will encounter. Understand your current position as an individual and how your freedoms and constraints might change as you transition from single to committed. Honesty about these aspects, both with yourself and any potential partner, is essential. Avoiding these discussions or being dishonest could significantly hinder your growth and suppress your aspirations throughout the relationship and beyond.

A significant factor that can hinder your growth is residing in an unsuitable environment for an extended period. This phenomenon is evident in various examples around us. Consider a pet fish, for instance. It is common knowledge that a fish tank should be appropriately sized for the species it houses. We often hear, "Fish only grow to the size of their tank." However, the tank's size is not the sole or actual cause of the fish's stunted growth.

So, what is the real reason? Fish release hormones in their waste, which can accumulate over time and inhibit the growth of less dominant fish. If the tank's water is not regularly refreshed, the fish could suffer from the waste's adverse effects. If the fish cannot swim as much as their species requires in their natural habitat, their skeleton could deform, affecting their internal organs. Malnourishment can occur if the fish is not fed adequately. If the tank's temperature is too cold or too warm, the fish could die from freezing or suffocation due to insufficient oxygen.

While housing a fish in a tank may have benefits, such as protection from predators, an environment that is too small, unhealthy, unclean, or at an inappropriate temperature can prevent the fish from reaching its full potential. It is crucial to note that only one of these issues can shorten the fish's lifespan, although it is often a combination of several. Ultimately, the fish dies, not merely because the tank was too small, but because the tank's collective conditions did not allow it to live to its fullest potential.

Another example is a tree. During a house-hunting experience in Mexico, I came across a beautiful home with a palm tree in the foyer, just a foot or two shorter than the vaulted ceiling. I asked the realtor how the tree had not reached the ceiling after being planted there for so many years. He explained the same concept—the tree would only grow as tall as its environment allowed.

What does all of this have to do with a woman dating on her own terms? Let me tell you. When evaluating a potential partner, one of the critical aspects to consider is how the relationship can foster your personal growth and development. It is not uncommon for a woman to enter a relationship in a healthy state in all the crucial aspects, only to leave in the same or worse condition. The issue is not always about how a woman enters a relationship, but often, it is about who she enters it with.

Just as a healthy fish can be placed in a tank that ultimately stunts its growth, or a tree can be planted in a home that prevents it from reaching its maximum height, a woman can enter a relationship that lacks the space, support, and resources necessary for her to flourish.

You need the room to evolve into the best version of yourself. This evolution cannot occur if you choose a partner who does not comprehend the importance of utilizing your gifts at the highest level possible. It cannot happen if your partner lacks the resources to support you in the ways you need most. It will not happen if he does not possess the tools needed to nourish your spirit with things that uplift you in times of need. The day will never come if you stay with a partner who is comfortable with you being harmed by the things and people he allows within your relationship. Simply put, it will be impossible for you to use your gifts at a higher level if your relationship is restrictive.

Entering a relationship free of a glass ceiling implies that you will not be expected to remain the same woman you were when you first joined. Your partner will not always perceive you as the younger, less developed woman he initially fell in love with. Not only will your partner have the foresight to envision you in your elevated state, but he will also take pride in aiding you to reach there, having prepared himself to serve you even before he met you.

If you consider the original concept of the term 'glass ceiling' and apply it to your romantic life, you will start posing significant questions to your potential suitors, such as "What benefits are you offering?" or "Once I achieve these milestones, will there be any expectations you would have of me that could impede my upward mobility?" Based on his responses, you will be able to discern whether a glass ceiling exists or not, and you can then proceed to your next criterion for evaluating your suitor.

> " BOUNDARIES ARE A MEASURE OF SELF-RESPECT. THEY SET THE LIMITS FOR APPROPRIATE BEHAVIOR FROM OTHERS. "
>
> — *Beverly Engel*

ESTABLISH BARRIERS OF ENTRY

CHAPTER 12

WHEN TRADING IN THE FOREIGN EXCHANGE MARKET, most traders use leverage, which is essentially borrowed money, to gain more buying power. This means a trader can use a small amount of their money, leverage a much larger amount of their broker's money and enter a larger position. The benefit of increasing your position size in forex is to potentially increase your return. A trader does not have to leverage their money. They can always choose to only trade what they deposited into their trading account. But despite a person's wealth, individual traders never make this choice. Why is this?

Successful forex traders understand that whether you invest $100 or $10,000 in a single position, the probability of winning or losing that trade is the same. Investing more does not make a trade riskier and investing less does not make your position safer. It is the trading system that you employ that will determine the probability and outcome of your investment. Let me explain how this same concept applies to the dating market.

When you create your unique dating market, you give yourself the ability to determine your starting point. You can decide to give access to men who are unable to provide you with any leverage or you can give access to men who can comfortably provide you with leverage that can 10X your returns. And let's be clear, I do not mean this in a financial sense.

So, why would any woman in her right mind choose to put in the same level of work, time, and effort to receive a fraction of the return she could have received had she simply partnered with a man who could provide her with leverage?

They say, *If a man gives a woman a house, she will turn it into a home.* If you give a woman sperm, she will then produce life. If you give a woman groceries, she will turn it into a meal. If you can multiply what is given to you, why choose to start out small? We should not despise small beginnings, but we should be looking for the greatest investments, especially when the effort is the same.

Any man I have ever been in a relationship with has benefited greatly by having me as their woman. Many have been able to retire young, start successful businesses, and even broaden their aspirations in life. Some of their lives have changed forever in a positive way, and you better believe that in turn, I benefited from their elevation.

This is exactly why you must choose the right man to invest in. If he comes to you with little benefits, you have the ability to multiply whatever those benefits are. However, if he comes to you already developed in many ways, you can put in the same effort to multiply those benefits for both you and your partner. The entire purpose of becoming the market maker is to learn to date smarter, not harder. It is to position yourself in the most ideal relationship that will allow you to take what your partner has to offer and increase it for your benefit.

Years ago, I had entered a new circle of friends. We were all single and went out to a local lounge to have a girl's night. While we were there, one of the women received a call from her brother who was in prison and scheduled for release within a year. She was so excited to tell her brother about the new friend she had met and how amazing she was. She was referencing me. This part of the conversation lasted all of five minutes, and she insisted I get on the phone with him to get to know him because she just knew that we would make a beautiful couple.

Ladies, I kid you not. There was not one woman in our entire party that could understand why I refused the call, and I could not understand how they thought so much of me but still believed in their hearts that a current, convicted felon would make a great partner to me. Wait! Before I go any further, let me say this. If you are a woman who has a husband with a questionable history and an amazing reformation story, let me be clear.

I do not care about your unicorn.
Life's not about chance.

It is about positioning yourself to increase the probability of receiving your heart's desire in the path of the least resistance. I knew then I needed to separate myself from that group of women, and I did just that.

When you learn to date on your own terms, you must accept that not everyone will understand why you are so exclusive. If you want to see the maximum growth in your life, you must exclude those who can only add little to no value.

You should not consider every man you meet as a potential partner. So, as a market maker, it is important that your dating pool is not all-encompassing. This is not an inclusive market. Your goal is to become as exclusive as possible, weeding out all the men who are incompatible with you. How do you do this?

113

Well, just like the United States has different parameters in place that makes it almost impossible for most people to become day traders in the foreign exchange market, the same should happen with your unique dating market. For instance, the US has a pattern day trading rule, implemented by the Securities and Exchange Commission (SEC) and the Financial Industry Regulatory Authority (FINRA) that prevents retail traders from taking more than three trades per trading week if they do not have $25,000 or more to deposit into their trading account.[7] I will not get into all of the arguments made for or against this rule, but at the very least, it prevents people without a certain amount of money from playing what is considered a rich man's game.

Your barriers of entry will be **unique** to you.

You can have as many or as little qualifiers that you feel are necessary, to include, but not limited to, financial, character, educational, belief systems, alignment of goals, parental status preferences, etc. Everyone will have their own barriers of entry based upon what is ideal for them.

Some women may decide to never date a man with children. Some women can decide to only date men who have shown a clear history of leadership outside of romantic relationships. Some women may require the man to make a minimum amount of annual income or have an overall net worth. There is no right or wrong stipulation you can choose; however, do know that you must use methods of exclusion.

One of the best ways to do this is by having proper vetting techniques. Proper vetting techniques are ones that will allow you to receive critical information without appearing intrusive or making him feel uncomfortable. When you are becoming a market maker, you must be sure to examine key aspects about your potential partner to make sure that he would be a good fit for you on a surface level before you can even think to evaluate him on a deeper level.

I do not just mean the amount of money he has, his aesthetics, or his level of education. These may be preferences for you, but those things do not actually give you the information you are looking for. We will cover how to curate critical conversation to obtain important information, but first, let's discuss criminal history.

Criminal History

Before ever going on a first date with a man, you need to receive his first and last name, date of birth, and a city that he has lived in for more than two years. This will allow you to do a quick background check on him. This is for people who live in America, specifically. Getting this information from him is not difficult to do, especially if you met him organically through your offline social network (friends, colleagues, school, etc.).

If a man is not willing to give you this basic information, he is not a good candidate for even a first date. Let me also state that unlimited basic background checks can be purchased at a monthly subscription for less than $30 a month. It is definitely worth the investment when you are dating intentionally. This will not tell you everything there is to know about an individual, but it will show things, like past or pending criminal charges, sex offender registry, liens, and other legal things from his past that could affect his or your life in the future.

Their background check may reveal some things that are inconclusive. You can bring those things up in non-attacking ways on later dates. The goal here is not to make a full character assessment with the information you find. However, it gives you the minimum framework you need to build a character assessment on each person, and it takes no more than five minutes.

Financial Stability

Over the phone, through a dating site, or on your first date, you can ask more questions. You do not want to ask, "How much money do you make?" Instead, you can ask a series of questions, like "What do you do for a living? How long have you been in this field? Are there any certifications that could give greater opportunities for upward mobility? Is this your dream job?" You can even ask questions about how he feels about the job and what ways he is using that job to benefit his future.

If he is entrepreneurial, you can ask questions, like "What are some of the difficulties you have faced building your company? Do you currently have all the skills, resources, finances to accomplish this goal?" You can also ask questions that have nothing to do with the nature of his business, such as "What type of lifestyle does this provide you and are you happy with it right now? Do you have the freedom to travel once or twice a year? If you want or have children, will your income right now be sustainable for an increasing family size?"

Most people will tell you that asking questions about money on the first date will turn a man off. But the truth is that it is simply the way you phrase your questions that makes all the difference.

Marriage-mindedness

I have met too many women who desire marriage and have never spoken about marriage to their boyfriend of three years. They are silently waiting for their man to randomly ask the question. After a while, the woman becomes anxious because it is taking him longer than she was comfortable waiting for, and she then blames the man for being commitment resistant. The problem with this is the woman never had a clear discussion in the beginning with that man that she was interested in marriage within a certain time frame. So, to avoid this, you must feel comfortable having this conversation early on. Yes, even on date one.

How exactly do you do this? You ask as many clarifying questions surrounding marriage. Do you plan on marrying in the future? Are you dating with the intent of marriage right now? Are you ready for marriage? Do you have a minimum timeframe that you believe you must court a woman before becoming exclusive? Do you have a minimum timeframe of exclusivity before proposing? Do you have a minimum timeframe for being engaged and setting a date to marry?

Your goal is to ask questions and allow the man to speak more than you speak on the first date. Do not make him feel like anything he is saying is wrong. Allow him to speak his truth without judgment and he will speak as freely as you need him in order to gain the insight that you are looking for. There is an art to this, so even if you find that your date is becoming agitated with certain questions, it is okay. Either the amount or order of your questions made it seem like an interrogation, or he was simply uncomfortable talking about marriage.

You can get better at this over time to notice the difference for yourself. If he is not comfortable even after you have mastered the art of interrogation, he simply is not a good candidate for you.

Children

This is also an important first date topic. You want to ask directly if he has children, and if so, was he married to the child's mother. Again, allow him to explain. This will give insight on how he views bringing children in the world. You do not want to have trauma-based conversations on the first date, but you do want to understand his history if he is a parent.

If he has four children by three women whom he has never married, you can ask him about that in a non-confrontational way.

You should also ask him about his relationships with his children, and the frequency in which he is a part of their daily lives. Some women prefer dating men without children. Some women prefer dating men only if their children are adults or are not being raised in his home 100 percent of the time. Some women prefer to date men who share 50/50 physical custody. Some women prefer dating a man who has sole custody. No matter what your personal preference is, allow him to answer without judgment.

If he does not have children, you can ask him about his intent to have them or not. This is not the time to get into the nitty-gritty details of his parenting philosophy. You do not have all the time in the world for the first date. A conversation surrounding kids should really take no more than two or three minutes to discuss and receive all the information you need. Be prepared to answer his questions as well, but be sure to keep your answers succinct.

Spirituality and Religious Beliefs

For many individuals, spirituality and religious beliefs form the core of their identity and worldview. They influence our values, our understanding of the world, and how we interact with others. If you are a woman for whom faith plays a significant role, it is essential to consider this when entering the dating market.

If sharing the same faith is a non-negotiable for you, it is crucial to address this topic early on. Do not hesitate to bring up this topic on the first date. It may seem daunting or too personal, but remember that you are seeking a partner who aligns with your core values. Discussing this early on can help you understand whether your date shares your beliefs or is open to understanding and respecting them.

This approach may lead to more first dates, but it will also save you from investing time and emotional energy into relationships that may not fulfill your spiritual needs. It is about quality, not quantity.

You are looking for a partner who complements your faith and supports your spiritual journey, not someone who merely tolerates it.

On the other hand, if you are more flexible about your partner's faith or lack thereof, you may choose to leave this topic for later discussions; however, it is still important to be open and honest about your own beliefs if the topic arises. Remember, a successful relationship is built on mutual respect and understanding, and this includes respecting each other's spiritual or religious beliefs.

In the end, your spiritual and religious beliefs are a significant part of who you are. Do not shy away from expressing them in your dating life. By being upfront about your faith, you are more likely to attract a partner who values and respects your beliefs, leading to a more fulfilling and harmonious relationship.

Interests and Hobbies

These are the more common and easier conversations for people to have on a first date. However, they are equally important to have during the vetting process. It is not because you are in search of a partner who naturally shares your favorite interests so that you two can now do everything together.

This is the time you can ask about the most impactful books they have read, or most enlightening films they have seen. If they are well rested already and have the freedom to do anything for a week, what would that week consist of? Would it be playing video games, going to chess tournaments, watching movies, trying new restaurants, traveling to a new city, hanging out with friends, finishing a business plan, or brainstorming on their next big move?

What a person does in their spare time is just as important as what a person does in their profession. If you are a woman who is looking to spend a decent amount of quality time with your partner, you want to know a few things. The first thing would be that he has the time freedom to give you without sacrificing his ability to earn or create income. Secondly, you want to make sure that you two have at least a few common interests, especially if you know that you are not that open to trying new things. Third, you want to have a small glimpse of what life would look like if you two enter a committed relationship with each other.

There is nothing more unsettling than to enter a relationship where either the man or woman is shamed for their interests. A man will begin to resent you for not allowing him to be himself. So, to avoid that, it is important to get to know what he enjoys early on.

If you know that you are triggered by men who play video games because a man from your past relationship prioritized his playing time over spending quality time with you, you must consider that. You must first learn that video games are not inherently bad. While it can be addictive, so can binging every new show that is released on Netflix.

You do not want to be that woman that takes all her past trauma into a new relationship and expects a man to be okay with being punished for what another man did. This does not mean there will not still be things you need to work through, but being aware of the real reasons you were hurt and not simply blaming them on hobbies is a great starting point.

> IF YOU'RE NOT ASKING YOURSELF HOW YOU'VE CONTRIBUTED TO THE CONFLICTS BETWEEN YOU AND YOUR PARTNER, THEN YOU'RE NOT BEING BRAVE IN CONVERSATIONS OR WITH YOURSELF.
>
> —Dr. Gina Senarighi

CREATE RULES OF ENGAGEMENT

CHAPTER 13

In the process of creating a relationship that serves you, it is essential to establish clear boundaries. These boundaries, once set, guide the interaction within the relationship, teaching your partner how to engage with you. This process of mutual learning and adaptation means that even if two people enter a relationship with different styles of communication or engagement, they can still build and sustain a healthy and enduring relationship.

As a woman who is taking charge of her dating life, it is your responsibility to define your rules of engagement and communicate them to any potential partner. This gives them a clear understanding of your expectations and allows them to contribute their own important points. However, once these rules are set, they should remain firm, even after meeting a potential partner.

So, what exactly are these rules of engagement? They are the commitments you make to your partner that dictate how you will interact during times of conflict. To help you define these rules, consider the following questions:

1. How have your engagement styles varied in past relationships?
2. Did you communicate in the same way with all your past partners?
3. Did you express your emotions consistently?
4. Did you find it easier to maintain your character in some relationships than in others?
5. Did you adapt to mirror your partner's behavior, or did they adapt to mirror yours?
6. Did you notice different versions of yourself in different relationships, or were you consistent in your behavior?

Reflecting on these questions will help you understand your patterns of engagement and guide you in establishing your rules.

Many women may assert that they have always remained true to themselves, that they have never altered their behavior to suit a partner. However, the reality is that it is impossible to be the same woman with different men. What you can do is become intentional about how you engage with people in various relationship dynamics. Reflect on the inception of your past relationships. Analyze the day-to-day operations and interactions. Be honest with yourself: did you intentionally shape the relationship, or did you allow the relationship or your partner to dictate your engagement style?

After asking yourself these questions and identifying your starting point, you can adopt a new approach by establishing rules of engagement for all your relationships, not just romantic ones. These rules apply to friendships, familial relationships, and even business relationships. For the purposes of this book, we will focus on romantic relationships. Ideally, you should establish these guidelines before entering a relationship, but it is still possible and necessary to do so even if you are already in one. So, how do we go about this?

To create your rules of engagement, start by writing down how you would want to feel during a conflict with your partner. You might want to feel safe, assured, heard, valued, loved, etc. Then, list all the behaviors that would make you want to disengage during a conflict, such as screaming, name-calling, talking over you, minimizing your emotions, storming away, or not giving you the space or time you need to process. Once you have made this list, create as many promises to yourself and your future partner as necessary to ensure these boundaries are set and upheld.

Here are some examples of rules of engagement:

1. I will always assume you have the best intentions.
2. I will not raise my voice or talk over you during conflict.
3. I will ensure you feel heard.
4. I will apologize when I have hurt you, whether intentionally or unintentionally.
5. I will ensure you feel safe talking to me.
6. I will not terminate or threaten to terminate the relationship in the midst of an argument.
7. If asked, I will honor your request to pause the conversation and restart when things have cooled down.
8. I will not minimize your concerns.
9. I will not call you out of your name or label you as emotional, dramatic, ridiculous, a nagger, etc.
10. I will not blame my reactions or temper on you.
11. I will not use absolute statements like always or never.
12. I will not use your traumas against you.

This list is a starting point. You can add more rules as necessary, but once you complete this list for yourself, you should not remove anything. This list is meant for both you and your partner to honor. Adhering to these rules is paramount for the success of your relationship. Disregarding these rules should not become a norm within your relationship, and the moment they do, a call needs to be made to one of the coverings you both agreed to.

Having agreed upon rules of engagement eliminates much of the ambiguity that couples often grapple with. Neither party can claim they did not understand the importance of certain things because it was established and agreed upon in writing. Too many people wait until marriage to establish certain rules and make certain promises, but often, it is too late. Once a person feels comfortable regularly talking down to you, calling you out of your name, or blaming you for their lack of emotional discipline, it is going to take an intervention to avoid that in the future, if you even want a future with that person anymore.

Lastly, there need to be clearly communicated consequences if the rules are not upheld. And no, market makers, I am not suggesting you weaponize sex whenever something goes wrong. What I am suggesting is that there are predefined responses to not honoring the agreement made to one another.

Another important aspect of rules of engagement is having sufficient communication skills. This allows you to create a safe space for both you and your partner to grow and thrive. It encourages conversation during the most difficult topics, de-escalates conflict, and removes tension within the relationship. It also helps you and your partner to have empathy for one another. Men and women communicate differently. Often, both styles are ineffective and can be the sole cause of a breakdown in a relationship when things were otherwise going well.

I have never met a person with a poor communication style who admitted to being a poor communicator. This is especially true for people who are naturally articulate. While being able to clearly express your feelings is important, it takes much more than that. The most important thing is that your partner understands you, you understand your partner, and the language used throughout the conversations has created a safe space for both people to share their truths.

Learning to communicate better within your relationship would require much more than reading this chapter of the book. However, I want to make sure you have a solid understanding of what poor communication looks like as opposed to good communication.

Instead of saying	Try this
You said …	This is what I heard you say … Is that correct?
That's just ridiculous.	Will you clarify that for me?
You're doing too much right now. You're emotional and I do not have to subject myself to this.	I want to understand what you are saying fully, but emotions are high. Let's slow the conversation down a bit.
I cannot tell you anything because you are always yelling.	I do not feel safe to share my truths when you yell but I would love to hear your honest feedback. How can we fix this?

Be mindful that it takes active listening in order to do this. If your mind is racing and constantly focusing on what your rebuttals will be during times of conflict, you will find it difficult to truly understand what your partner meant. Sometimes, what they say is completely different from what they mean. The same is true for you. Both people have different life experiences that shape the lens in which they see and interpret things. So, asking as many clarifying questions as possible is paramount until you both feel like there is an understanding between the two of you, regardless of whether you agree on the outcome.

Verbal communication is not the only style of communication. We must also consider nonverbal cues. What we do with our body is important. Our facial expressions, arms, hands, necks, and overall posture have a lot to do with how we are received and perceived during times of conflict. To ensure that both people feel safe, try gentle touches, uncrossing your arms, learning to have a poker face (to an extent), and reaffirming that it is safe for your partner to share with you.

Whether you are right or wrong, no one wants to feel unheard. By learning to communicate more effectively, your relationship can thrive. These changes may seem impossible and unnecessary. But I promise you; it will help you a lot. Not only will you be able to understand your partner better, but your partner will learn to communicate with you just the same, even if he had no prior experience communicating in such a healthy way. This is a form of emotional contagion, which essentially describes the way a person reflexively copies the emotions and behaviors of another person that they observe.

These things can help you when you are just getting to know a person, exclusively dating, or in a full long-lasting relationship or marriage. Avoiding conflict is a sure way to damage your relationship. There will always be conflict, but your communication skills can help you navigate it in a healthy way and bring you and your partner closer.

THE MOST IMPORTANT THING IN TRADING IS TO KNOW WHEN TO ENTER AND WHEN TO EXIT.

"

- Linda Raschke

IDENTIFY ENTRY SIGNALS

CHAPTER 14

SUCCESSFUL FOREX TRADERS HAVE identified signals that inform them of the exact time they should enter a position. Depending on their trading strategy, they might use fundamental indicators, a method that relies on macroeconomic analysis. They might employ technical analysis, which can range from interpreting candlestick patterns on charts to utilizing pre-established technical indicators or discerning market trends from the chart itself. They may also apply sentiment analysis, gauging how significant news events might sway most retail traders and adjusting their strategy accordingly. Alternatively, they might blend different styles to suit their trading approach. Regardless of the method, successful traders consistently adhere to the same signals, maintaining their strategy steadfastly.

They are not experiencing FOMO, *the fear of missing out*. They do not believe they need to rush their decision to enter a position. They have clearly defined indicators according to their personal trading plan that tells them the exact moment they should trade. Be mindful that it is never only one reason that a trader will enter a position. It is a combination of things, which are called *confluences*.

Confluences help traders avoid entering a lot of trades that will ultimately go against them. If a trader uses only one metric to determine their entry, they will ultimately enter too many trades and potentially lose most of them. However, the more confluences that a trader has, the less opportunities they have to pull the trigger. They are okay with this because it allows them to take only the most highly probable trades they see, increasing their odds of winning the trade in the end. This concept I am explaining can easily be applied to women who are pursuing relationships.

Some women solely rely on one reason to enter or want to enter a relationship with a man. For example, many women see that a man is aesthetically pleasing to their eyes and that is enough for them to want to enter a relationship with them. They may meet a man and believe the level of wealth he has amassed is enough to forgo any other indicators they would usually apply in their vetting process. They may learn that he has no baby-mamas and believe that he is the perfect person to create children with. They may simply be tired of always being the bridesmaid but never the bride. They may have never met a man who strongly talks about marriage and building a family and believe he must be the one. But it is never only one thing that indicates entering a relationship with a person is a good decision.

In these situations, they take one visible appealing thing about a person and make presumptions about everything else. *Because a man is rich, he must be great with money, generous, and looking for a wife to give him children to pass the wealth down too. Because a man has a gift with words, he must be an effective communicator, a good listener, and emotionally intelligent as well. Because a man has not fathered any children outside of marriage before, he must be a man who values family, practices safe sex, and is simply looking for that one worthy woman to procreate with.* They become hasty in their decision to enter a relationship and many times become upset that the relationship is not what they thought it would be.

These women have not given themselves the opportunities to see red flags. They have not given themselves the space and time it takes to see if that man would be compatible with them. Much of the heartache that these women experience is due to the fact they decided to enter a relationship prematurely, simply hoping for the best.

Then, there are other women who do not base their decision to enter a relationship on the first appealing trait they witness in a man. Instead, they allow their circumstances to dictate when they should enter. They find themselves trying to demand exclusivity after they have discovered they are pregnant, once they learn the man has still been entertaining other women and they want to lock him down, or because they simply feel good when they are around him. They may also meet men, become love bombed, and believe they've found their perfect match, leading them to quickly jump into exclusive relationships. It becomes a vicious cycle, and they never learn why their exclusive relationships are not working in their favor.

The biggest downside to entering relationships this way is they never really gain control of their lives once they enter. They become defensive in all their decisions afterwards because they had no real reason to enter the relationship. They do not know what type of father this man would be. They do not know if he is generous by nature or if he simply uses gifts and affection to win their hearts. They do not know why he was still in the market and might assume it was because the other women simply did not demand exclusivity with them. They are truly ignorant. And with that ignorance, they make a big decision to enter a relationship with a man because of circumstances they had not planned for.

If you establish a clear set of rules for yourself and give yourself time to see those confluences play out, you will enter fewer exclusive relationships and there would be no FOMO when you do. There should be no feeling of unease or fear attached to your decision to enter an exclusive relationship with a man. You can make sure your transition into partnership is smooth by developing entry signals beforehand. Now, what are some examples of entry signals?

You can employ a mix of external and internal metrics. External metrics might include having sufficient free time to cultivate a new relationship, even if you are still learning how to do so, managing your personal finances in a way that prevents you from rushing into a relationship for financial gain, ensuring you have no unhealthy attachments to past partners, and preparing your children for the potential introduction of a new man in your life.

Additional external metrics could encompass the vetting process you have implemented with him, your observation of his actions aligning with his words, his clear verbal confirmation of his readiness to commit exclusively to you, and his ability to maintain consistency in the areas that are most important to you over a prolonged period.

Internal metrics are considerations such as your feelings. Are you more happy than unhappy when you speak to him? Do you feel safe to have honest conversations with him? Have you already started therapy to get to know yourself better? Do you feel like there is no rush in becoming his woman, but instead, you feel like it makes sense for you overall? Do you have the mental fortitude to pour into him as you expect him to pour into you?

Knowing what to look for makes your decision to become exclusive with a man easier. There is not necessarily this immutable list that he or you must check off for it to make sense. However, there is a holistic approach you can take to determine if it makes sense for you to enter that relationship with him which should include both external and internal metrics.

To gain more clarity while dating, here are some entry signals (confluences) that can be used:

1. Compatibility indicators such as shared values, goals, and interests.
2. Communication indicators such as effective listening, mutual respect, and understanding.
3. Emotional intelligence indicators such as empathy, self-awareness, and self-regulation.
4. Relationship history indicators such as past experiences and patterns in past relationships.

To create metrics of evaluation, you can create a list of criteria that you believe are important in a relationship, then assign a weight to each criterion. For example, compatibility might be worth 40 percent of the total evaluation, while communication might be worth 30 percent and emotional intelligence, 20 percent. You can then evaluate potential partners based on these criteria and use the weighted scores to determine overall compatibility. These are just examples; you should have your own criteria that you find important and weight it accordingly.

DEVELOP AN EXIT STRATEGY

CHAPTER 15

KNOWING WHEN TO ENTER A TRADE in the forex market is imperative, as we learned in the last chapter. However, even more crucial is knowing when to exit a trade. While developing as many confluences as possible to enter a trade, it does not benefit you at all if you do not know when you should exit. When retail traders lose all their funds, or the majority of them, it is not because they entered a bad setup. It is always because they did not exit in a timely manner or when the market told them that their directional bias was wrong.

They sold when they should have bought, or they bought when they should have sold. Instead of exiting the trade when it was completely going against them, they held on for different reasons. Some of them were sure that the trade would turn around in their favor to give them the profits they were looking for. Others hoped that it would reverse just enough to return the money they had invested in that trade.

However, in the end, it does not matter the reason. When trading in the forex market, it is wise for you to always have a *stop loss* in place for every position you enter. A *stop loss* is the exact price in the market where your *invalidation point* occurs. An *invalidation point* is the price that tells you your analysis is not correct. These terms are used interchangeably. Therefore, your stop loss represents a predetermined amount of money you are willing to risk before you even enter the trade.

This allows you to not lose every dime in your account. If you enter a position and set a stop loss for $100, you will protect yourself from losing $200 if the trade goes against you. If you set your stop loss for $100 and it never goes against you, that stop loss is still important. Believing that any trade is a sure win is foolish. It is merely a gamble at that point. You know when to exit your position once your invalidation points have been triggered. It protects you from having to make difficult and quick decisions when your emotions may be running high. It protects you from yourself and it protects you from the market. It allows you to walk away from that trade with the least amount of loss possible without walking away prematurely due to a small setback. Any successful day trader knows just how important this is and they do not enter trades without it.

This same concept can be applied to your relationships. While it is necessary to develop entry signals for your relationship, it is even more essential to create an exit strategy. We all know that leaving a two-month relationship is much easier than leaving a relationship of five years. Oftentimes, there are points of invalidation that showed up during the early stages of that relationship that you did not recognize or chose not to respect. But as a market maker, it is important to know what to look out for and to respect yourself enough to walk away.

Having an exit strategy does not mean that you are planning for your relationship to fail. It simply means that you are planning for you to succeed overall, even if that relationship does not work out in your favor. You do not deplete yourself so much that it takes you months or years to truly recover from that loss. You do not put all your eggs in that one basket in hopes that you will gain the ultimate reward in the end. You protect yourself from giving more than what you truly have to offer. You learn to let go when it is no longer serving you and trust yourself in the process of courtship.

I know a lot of women believe that the only way they can prove to a man their loyalty, devotion, and love, is to remain in a relationship with them even when it is hurting them. They trust the man's word that things will get better more than they trust their own intuition. But the truth is this. When a man believes that there are not any circumstances in which you would walk away, you give him no reason to not keep putting you in hurtful situations. You must learn to protect yourself. Since we all know that women get blinded by sex, love, money, and a host of other things, developing an exit strategy before you enter the relationship will always be quite useful. What exactly does this look like?

Just as you used both internal and external metrics to enter a relationship, you will use them as confluences to exit the relationship as well. External metrics that show a point of invalidation in your relationship can be obvious things like your partner being verbally, emotionally, financially, or physically abusive toward you. It could also be less obvious things like intentionally isolating you from friends and family so that you must rely on them for every need you have outside of yourself, preventing you from pursuing your goals regardless of everything else being aligned for you to do so, or even addictions that are negatively affecting your partner, such as drugs, alcoholism, porn, etc.

In the early stages of a relationship, you may not have any of those worries. There are other signs you can look out for, like being with an overly pessimistic person which can truly stagnate your growth as an individual, being with a person who labels their meanness as, *keeping it real,* or being with a controlling person who tries to parent you or manipulate you into doing what they always want.

Internal metrics to show a point of invalidation in your relationship can be things like never feeling seen, heard, or valued. Have you shared intimate information with men and it was used against you in a later argument? Do you feel like your mental health was better before entering a relationship with them? Have you stopped finding enjoyment in the things that mattered to you most? Do you feel anxiety around speaking to them for the fear of how they will respond? These are questions you can keep in your journal to remind you of tell-tale signs to leave a relationship.

It is unlikely that a physically abusive man will hit a woman the day they agree to be exclusive, so waiting for the most extreme examples of abuse is never the right decision. Evaluate your relationship at every stage to ensure that it is edifying to you.

Making the decision to leave a relationship is personal and when there are not clear signs of abuse, those reasons may vary from person to person. So, you need to get clear on what your points of invalidation are before you even enter the relationship so that if they ever happen, you will not have to think twice about it.

Contrary to popular belief, you do not have to remain friends with your ex in order to show that you are not damaged or bitter, and seeking closure from a man after a relationship has ended is never a good idea. You do not have to have that one last talk after your point of invalidation has come. Oftentimes, it is not even because you want to feel at peace with your decision to leave that relationship, it is because you are subconsciously seeking a reason to reenter what you have already discovered is a toxic relationship. Seeking closure outside of yourself is the easiest way to extend your recovery period.

Relationships go through cycles. You will not always feel in love. You will not always feel like he is perfect. You will not always believe that you are living out this fairy tale the way you possibly felt in the beginning stages of your relationship. But the natural relationship cycles are not a reason to believe it is time to jump ship. Do not let anyone tell you that you need to leave your relationship because you are not presently feeling butterflies over your man. It does not mean it is time to exit simply because you had three fallouts in a row, and you do not have to call it quits because you are feeling bored. Make sure that your exit makes sense, and your point of invalidation was indeed hit.

To clarify this further, invalidation points in a relationship can be different for everyone, but some examples may include:

- Infidelity
- Physical or emotional abuse
- Persistent lying or dishonesty
- Lack of mutual respect
- Failure to meet basic needs or boundaries
- Persistent disregard for your feelings or opinions
- Lack of effort or investment in the relationship
- Persistent toxic or unhealthy behaviors

To set a stop loss in a relationship, you can start by identifying your non-negotiables or deal breakers and creating a plan of action for when those boundaries are crossed. For example, if infidelity is a deal breaker for you, your stop loss could be a plan to immediately end the relationship if it occurs. Similarly, if you have identified a pattern of toxic behavior in your partner, your stop loss could be to seek counseling or therapy together before deciding to continue the relationship. It is also necessary to have open and honest communication with your partner about your boundaries and exit strategy, so that they are aware of what is expected of them.

Here are some tips on how to create a clear and effective exit strategy in a relationship:

- **Identify potential red flags:** Identify potential red flags that may indicate that the relationship is not healthy or may not be what you are looking for. This can include things such as dishonesty, lack of communication, lack of respect, and physical or emotional abuse.

- **Set clear boundaries:** It is vital to set clear boundaries for what is acceptable behavior in the relationship and what is not. This can include things such as how often you expect to communicate, what types of physical or emotional interactions are okay, and how you expect to be treated.

- **Communicate your exit strategy:** This can include things such as what you will do if the boundaries are not respected, what the consequences will be for breaking the rules, and what you will do if the relationship becomes unhealthy.

- **Have a plan for leaving:** Having a plan for leaving a relationship is important in case things do not work out. This can include things such as having a place to stay, having a support system in place, and having a plan for how to handle any shared assets or responsibilities.

- **Trust your intuition:** It is vital to trust your intuition and to listen to your gut when it comes to relationships. If something feels off, take the time to assess the situation and to act if necessary.

- **Practice self-care:** It is crucial to practice self-care and to take care of yourself both during and after a relationship. This can include things such as exercise, therapy, and spending time with friends and family.

- **Be prepared for emotional and mental distress:** Leaving a relationship can be an emotionally and mentally distressing time. It is important to be prepared for this and to seek support if needed.

EMPLOY A 'TROMP'

CHAPTER 16

COURTSHIP IS ALL ABOUT DETERMINING WHO the most ideal partner is for you. Oftentimes, women who are marriage minded only date one man at a time to show the man that they are fully committed to them. Women also make this decision because it takes effort and discipline to date multiple people at once. It could seem intimidating and overwhelming. However, unless you intend to enter an arranged marriage, you are going to need to be very intentional in how you choose to date and who you choose to give your time to.

The issue is not inherently with men being the ones to choose. The problem arises when a woman decides to commit to a man solely because she does not perceive any other promising prospects. At the point in which a woman is ready to enter a committed relationship with a man, she should have engaged several high-quality suitors to choose from because every great man will not be great for you. The richest man may not be most ideal for you. The most formally educated man might not be the person you need to partner with.

Men are competitive by **nature**.

They want to settle down with the best woman that they can win. If they feel they have absolutely no competition, they may begin to question why no other man wants you. If they feel like the only other men you have ever entertained are of a lower echelon, they could easily feel like you will be incapable of seeing the value they have to bring to your life, and you could potentially become a liability.

This whole fantasy that a man of means who has done the work is going to appear and dig you out of the mud is just unrealistic. Does it happen? Yes. But I am not here to sell you a unicorn of a dream. Most men pursue women within their social circles or tax brackets, no matter how beautiful that woman may be. Thus, when you are becoming a market maker, you need to be sure to implement a TROMP, *a top-tier rotation of marriageable prospects,* so that when he pursues you, he understands you have other great options, and when you choose him, he finds comfort in knowing you felt he was the absolute best choice among the top echelon of men. You did not make your choice based on surface-level attributes. Instead, you delved deep into understanding him (beyond the realm of physical intimacy) in a way that confirmed your shared alignment for the future you both envision together.

It is also important to note that when a man is looking for a wife, he should also date multiple high-quality women. You do not want to be the first or the only woman of high substance that he has ever had a chance with. You will need to learn that this is okay, and that part of his vetting process is not just to find the best woman, but to find the best woman for him.

Now, dating does not mean sex. Just because you are dating multiple people does not mean you need to sleep with any or all of them. You should be clear that you are courting for marriage, honest with him that you are considering multiple prospects if he asks, and comfortable telling him, "May the best man win," if he ever asks you certain questions.

This does a few things for you. It positions you to be fully pursued properly because they know that they are competing for your time. They will need to become more intentional in the conversations they have with you instead of trying to focus on baseless or fleeting feelings that will ebb and flow throughout the relationship. It will also keep you safe. Instead of lying to men and telling them they are the only one who you are entertaining, they will know upfront your dating style, and if they move forward with you, they are agreeing to your terms of dating multiple people until you both have made a full commitment of exclusivity to each other to move to the next phase.

Having one good man in your life is not enough to learn who you are most compatible with. Market maker women are not saying "Yes" because we have no other viable options. Neither are we committing ourselves to men out of desperation. We are making a conscious decision to choose exactly who we want to create a future with.

Something equally important to understand is you cannot force a man's hand.

You **cannot force him**
to love you.

You cannot force him to enter an exclusive relationship with you. You cannot force him to openly claim you. You cannot force him to be there for a child if he has one with you. The same way you can choose the life you want to lead, so can he. It will always be the man's decision to live his life as he so pleases. This is why it is vital to date multiple men before accepting a marriage proposal. It could be your desire to enter an exclusive relationship with a man; however, he may have opposing views.

You could choose to try and manipulate, guilt trip, trick on, or nag him. However, there is nothing you can do to force a man to take you off the dating market who does not want to take you off the dating market. Because of this, it makes no sense for a woman to casually date only one man at a time, hoping and praying that he ends up on the same page as her in the end.

When men are not motivated to take the next step with a woman, they will not. When they are motivated, however, it is due to factors that have very little to do with you *wanting* him to. These motivating factors could be external or internal. Internally, he could believe that the intrinsic values that you bring are worth holding on to in order for him to reach his lifelong goals. Externally, he could be hearing his friends, peers, father, or mentor, encouraging him to solidify his role in your life. However, a woman's mere desire to be married to a man is at the back of the list of reasons that would compel a man to marry her.

Now that the benefits of rotational dating are clear, I am sure many of you may find it overwhelming when you envision yourself putting it into practice. But the reality of it is this. If a relationship does not work and you put all your eggs in one basket, you are now back at square one. If you are single, that means every romantic relationship you have ever entered has ended along the way. What are the odds that your very next relationship will result in a lifetime partnership? Yes, there are situations where a previous partner may have passed away or maybe you both decided it would be better to remain friends instead of lovers. However, you are single now, and it is time to make things much easier for you in the dating market.

One of the first things I do when coaching women is ask them about the number of men they are currently dating or are used to dating at the same time. They pretty much all tell me the same thing, "I only date one man at a time." When I inquire about their reasoning, their responses often revolve around wanting to demonstrate their seriousness to the man, finding the idea of dating multiple men too overwhelming, and emphasizing that their dating efforts are not merely for amusement, but are aimed at the ultimate goal of marriage.

I totally understand why many women think this way. They truly believe that providing exclusivity to men the moment they begin dating them will inherently lead the man to provide exclusivity to them, leading them to a long-lasting marriage. But I am here to tell you right now, that is the absolute worst thing to do when you are aspiring for marriage. Just because you are not dating anyone else does not mean that man is now required to only date you. Men do not respond well to manipulation, and they do a horrible job at reading between the lines. You're setting yourself up for failure if you think that you can make a man commit himself to you because you are ready to commit to him, which brings me to the main idea of this section.

You need to be prepared to date multiple men. I know it may sound scary and maybe even reckless, depending on the way you were raised and how much you have bought into the unwritten rules of your society, but it is the quickest path to getting what you want in the end. How exactly can you date multiple men at once without feeling overwhelmed?

First, be honest with the men you choose to entertain. Causing yourself unnecessary anxiety around lying to them and keeping up with those lies is a sure way to become overwhelmed. Secondly, do not merely tell them you are dating other people. You must be clear about your intentions for dating. Telling a man that you plan on dating other men because you are single and you have that right, is completely different than telling a man that you are dating multiple people with the goal of finding the best partner for yourself in the end. Here is a quick example of two ways to do this.

Option 1: I am dating multiple men because I am a single woman and refuse to allow any man to dictate what I do with my body. My body. My choice.

Option 2: I am dating with the intent of marriage. Therefore, I leave my options open and date multiple men until I find the one who is ready to court me exclusively. And of course, I would need to feel the same way. I refuse to ever pressure a man to settle down with me. It would not make me feel good nor would it make him feel good.

Secondly, your goal of dating multiple men is not to see how many men you can squeeze into your schedule. Remember, it is always quality over quantity. This means, for some women, you may only be dating two men at the same time. Your goal is to have as many options as you need but you do not have to regularly date them all. Realistically, not every option will pass your vetting process.

Thirdly, keep a journal. Trying to remember every little thing about multiple men may be difficult. After spending time with someone or even talking on the phone, journal some of your thoughts about the experience. What is interesting about this person? What would you like to know more about them? What are some of the patterns in their behavior you have noticed? Before going on another date with them, be sure to review what you wrote so that you can easily pick back up where you left off. Whenever I am dating multiple men, especially in the beginning stages, I keep notes in my notepad for each guy so that I do not confuse myself. Work smarter, not harder. You will thank yourself later.

Lastly, make sure you are spending time with yourself. You do not want to fill every calendar day up with a date just because you are dating multiple people. Be sure to date yourself as well. It is always okay to decline a date when you need to rest or simply have time to yourself. It is also okay to ask to reschedule if you truly do want to spend more time with them but it is just inconvenient. This is especially important for introverts and house bodies. Having to leave the house so often in pursuit of a relationship can be exhausting in itself. So, do not work against who you truly are. Pace yourself. You do not need to find multiple men just for the sake of dating multiple people. Simply allow yourself to be open. As the men come, slowly weave them into your rotation.

Now, to put everything together, I will provide you with two case studies of how the TROMP method has played out in real-life scenarios.

Case Study 1:

A woman, let's call her Janet, has been actively dating for several months but has not found someone she feels compatible with. She employs the TROMP method and begins dating three men simultaneously: John, Michael, and David. John is a successful businessman, who is also highly educated and well-traveled. Michael is a kind and caring man, who works in the nonprofit sector. David is a talented artist and musician.

As she continues to date each of them, she notices that John is a bit too focused on his career and does not seem to have much time for her. Michael is a great listener, and they have deep conversations, but she does not feel a strong physical attraction to him. David is creative and exciting, but he is not as reliable and consistent as she would like.

Janet evaluates her feelings and decides that while all three men have positive qualities, David is not the best match for her long-term goals, and she decides to end things with him. She continues to date John and Michael, but with the understanding that they are both still part of her TROMP and she is keeping her options open. Eventually, she decides that Michael is the best fit for her, and they become exclusive because he also believed that she was the best fit for him and offered exclusivity to her as well.

Case Study 2:

Meet Britney, a thirty-two-year-old woman who is ready to settle down and start a family. She has been in a few long-term relationships in the past but has not found the right person yet. She decides to employ the TROMP method and begins dating three men who she believes are high-quality prospects for marriage. The first prospect is a successful businessman named Byran, who is financially stable and has similar career aspirations as Britney. The second prospect is a kind-hearted teacher named Dallas, who is a great listener and values family. The third prospect is a fitness trainer named Emmanuel, who is ambitious and has a similar lifestyle as Britney.

Britney spends several months getting to know each of the prospects on a deeper level and evaluates them based on their compatibility with her own values and goals. However, after several months, she realizes that none of the prospects are the right fit for her. Byran is too focused on his career and does not have enough time for a family. Dallas does not have the same level of ambition as Britney and does not align with her career goals. Emmanuel is not ready for a serious commitment and is not ready to start a family.

In this scenario, Britney may feel disappointed and may even question if she will ever find the right person. However, she reminds herself that the TROMP method is not a guarantee of finding the perfect partner, but rather it is a tool to increase her chances of finding a compatible partner. She also reminds herself that the process of finding a partner is not linear and that it may take longer than the three months she gave herself.

In the end, she does not give up hope and keeps an open mind. After reviewing her journals from the previous three months of dating, she learns to appreciate the TROMP method even more and sees it as a learning experience. She has gained valuable insights into what she is looking for in a partner and the time that it would have usually taken her to amass that level of awareness has been truncated significantly. She decides to take a break and focus on self-discovery and self-improvement before starting the process again.

In each of these scenarios, the TROMP method was a success. Not because both ladies found their life-long partner because Britney did not. However, both women were able to shorten their learning time of what it was they were looking for in a partner, date on their own terms, and walk away when they realized that the prospect was not good for them before any unnecessary damage took place.

A Moment to Reflect

As we conclude Part 3, let's take a moment to reflect on the key takeaways and engage in some introspective journaling. This will help consolidate your understanding and facilitate a deeper personal connection with the material.

Key Takeaways:

1. Design the Relationship: Understand your needs and wants in a relationship. This is the foundation of your dating market.

2. Establish Barriers of Entry: Set standards and expectations for potential partners. This will help filter out those who do not align with your values.

3. Create Rules of Engagement: Define how you will interact with potential partners. This includes communication, boundaries, and the pace of the relationship.

4. Identify Entry Signals: Learn to recognize signs that a potential partner is a good fit for your dating market. This could be their behavior, values, or how they treat you.

5. Develop an Exit Strategy: Have a plan for ending relationships that are not working. This helps protect your emotional wellbeing and keeps your dating market healthy.

6. Employ a TROMP (Top-tier Rotation of Marriageable Prospects): Keep your options open by dating multiple people at once. This allows you to compare and contrast potential partners, and ensures you do not settle for less than what you deserve.

Journaling/Reflection Prompts:

Remember, the goal of this section is not to dictate your dating life, but to equip you with the knowledge and tools to make informed decisions that align with your personal values and goals. Reflect on these takeaways and prompts, and consider how you can apply them to your own dating life.

Patterns in Past Relationships: Reflect on your past relationships. What patterns do you notice, and how can you use these insights to shape your future dating experiences?

Non-negotiables in Relationships: What are your non-negotiables in a relationship? How can you ensure these standards are met in your future relationships?

Creating a Safe Space for Communication: How can you create a safe and respectful space for communication in your relationships? What rules of engagement would you like to establish?

Understanding the TROMP Concept: Consider the concept of a TROMP (Top-tier Rotation of Marriageable Prospects). How can dating multiple people at once help you make more informed decisions about who is the best fit for you?

PART 4

THE MAKING
OF A WOMAN

Definitions from Shawdrism Language

hab·its \ ˈha-bəts *noun*

the defining factors of your future

self-a·ware·ness \ ˌself-ə-ˈwer-nəs *noun*

knowing who the hell you are, never will be, and ain't never been

sha·dow \ ˈsha-(ˌ)dō *noun*

half of who you are and everything you don't want to be, the repressed side of the beautiful you!

The Poor Tax \ thə ˈpȯr ˈtaks *noun*

the hidden costs women must pay when they are pursuing relationships while insolvent

The Rich Reward \ thə ˈrich ri-ˈwȯrd *noun*

the benefits and incentives that wealthy women receive when they are dating; a powerful advantage in the dating market

wealth \ ˈwelth *noun*

passport to freedom

Part 4: The Making of a Woman

The Market Maker Method™ Component 4: Maker
4th Rule: Develop yourself holistically.
Framework: The SHAW Self-Development Model™

In the first half of this book, it was vital to me that you learned the meaning of 'Market Maker', understood the type of woman you should not be or become influenced by, as well as debunked some popular beliefs that could prevent you from landing your ideal relationship. But now, the question is: How do you become that authentic woman I spoke about? How do you develop yourself internally so that you can reap the benefits externally? How do you learn to overcome your past and fully own your truth?

In this section of the book, we delve into the process of becoming the best version of yourself. We will explore practical tools and strategies for self-development and personal growth. This includes understanding and overcoming your past, developing healthy habits, and working on your appearance and wealth. This section, titled "The Making of a Woman," focuses on the principle of holistic development and how it relates to building successful relationships.

We will explore the practical steps you can take to become the authentic, confident woman you want to be, and how to overcome past traumas and negative patterns that may be holding you back.

To guide you in this process, I have developed *The SHAW Self-Development Model™*, which is a holistic approach to personal growth and self-improvement. It comprises four key elements: your shadow, habits, appearance, and wealth. By examining and strengthening yourself in these areas, you can increase the effectiveness of *The Market Maker Method™* and improve your overall life experiences. This system is designed to help you identify and overcome any internal barriers that may be preventing you from reaching your full potential, and to empower you to confidently make decisions that align with your authentic self.

Before You Begin

Welcome to Part 4 of this transformative journey. This is not a fleeting moment where you read a few chapters, make minor adjustments, and expect a miraculous shift. Just as a butterfly undergoes a significant metamorphosis, this journey requires consistent effort and dedication. In a world where many women find themselves stuck in disadvantageous relationships and patterns, it is not always straightforward to break free and start dating on your own terms. But the good news is, you are not alone. You're part of a community of women on the same path, and together, we can support each other and evolve.

To maximize the benefits of this section, I recommend the following steps:

1. Read each chapter slowly and thoroughly.
2. Pause and reflect on the information being presented.
3. Take note of any personal experiences or insights that come to mind.
4. Trust the process and be open to the transformation that is possible through this journey.

Part 4 is designed to delve into the depths of who you are. This can be uncomfortable, so I want to assure you that my intention is to guide from a place of compassion and understanding, not judgment. I, too, have grappled with the challenges discussed in these chapters. As such, I understand the initial instinct to deny certain behaviors and the struggle it takes to change them.

My goal for you is to use Part 4 as a tool for personal growth and transformation. So be gentle with yourself, embrace the process, and prepare to explore the depths of your habits, perceptions, and the power you hold in shaping your dating life.

Questions That Might Arise

What if I find Shadow work too challenging or uncomfortable?

It is natural to feel uncomfortable when confronting past traumas or insecurities. Remember, this process is about personal growth and healing. Take your time, and if necessary, seek professional help such as a therapist or counselor. You're not alone in this journey.

How can I change my habits when they are so deeply ingrained?

Changing habits is a gradual process. Start by identifying the habits you want to change and understanding their triggers. Then, replace them with healthier alternatives. Consistency is key, and over time, you will notice a shift in your behavior.

What if I am not comfortable with changing my appearance?

The focus on appearance is not about conforming to societal standards of beauty but about presenting yourself in a way that makes you feel confident and aligns with your personal values. It is about self-expression and feeling good in your own skin.

What if I am struggling with financial stability?

Financial stability is a journey, and it is okay to start where you are. This section provides tools and strategies to help you understand your financial situation and make informed decisions. If necessary, consider seeking advice from a financial advisor.

What if I do not see immediate changes or progress?

Self-development is a journey, not a destination. Changes may not be immediate, but with consistent effort, you will notice progress over time. Celebrate small victories and be patient with yourself.

The SHAW Self-Development Model ™

A Holistic Approach to Personal Growth and Self-improvement

Unlocking your hidden aspects, emotions, and subconscious patterns

Defining factors of your future

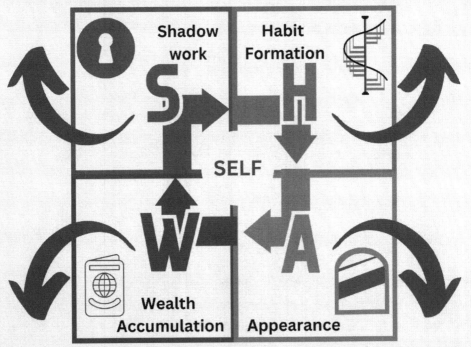

Shadow work

Habit Formation

SELF

Wealth Accumulation

Appearance

Your passport to Freedom

How you present yourself to the world

SHADOW WORK

CHAPTER 17

WHEN I FIRST HEARD OF SHADOW WORK, I thought it meant I would have to sit down, burn candles, evoke spirits from my ancestors, and chant affirmations from dawn to dusk. There is nothing wrong with doing any of those practices if that is your thing, but that is totally not what shadow work is all about. If you have ever gone to therapy and were asked questions about your childhood, your traumas, your fears, or why you held certain beliefs, you were simply being facilitated in a healing process that *some* call shadow work. It is possible for you to do this on your own. Disclaimer: Do not fire your therapist, sis!

In essence, your shadow is half of who you are, and often, everything you do not want to be. It is the part of us we subconsciously repress but regularly see in others. It is the part of us that reminds us we are human when it creeps out unexpectedly and forces us see there is more work to be done. This is not a negative thing because while a shadow is dark, it is not bad. Your shadow can also encompass positive traits that you've dismissed or overlooked because of external influences.

If you begin shadow work, you can strengthen your self-efficacy, reduce shame around your shortcomings, and learn to see yourself in a more holistic view, instead of limiting yourself to your *ego*, which is simply how you consciously view yourself. And ultimately, shadow work can lead you to a personal awakening. It can help you understand who you are at your core and why you are that way. It can help you to become more compassionate with yourself and empathetic toward others. You will learn that every conscious decision you make is a reflection of your subconsciousness. Until you can recognize, accept, and love yourself in whatever state you are in, you will not be able to fully accept and love others in their state of imperfection, which we all are always in.

It is important that you understand that the precursor to shadow work is self-awareness. You may not know how you would like to make the greatest impact on humanity just yet, but at a minimum, you should become aware of who you are and who you would like to become.

When dating on your own terms, you should consider your goals in life and where you would like to see yourself in the future before you dive headfirst into these long-term relationships with men for the sake of building. Most people do not take the time to get to know themselves but are constantly trying to get to know others. Study you. Gift yourself with the time it takes to develop your skills, increase your knowledge, and improve self-efficacy in the areas that will serve you most in the future. Get to know yourself intimately. Until you understand the woman you are, you cannot possibly fathom the type of man who would partner well with you. This is not a onetime thing. You are ever evolving, your mind is constantly growing, and your ideas are always expanding. This should be done regularly.

Truly understanding yourself is a journey that should involve introspection, self-awareness, and confronting your own biases and beliefs. Sometimes, the most profound lessons come from unexpected sources, pushing us to confront our shadows in ways we never anticipated. Such moments of clarity can arise in the most mundane of activities, revealing deeper truths about ourselves. So, as you embark on this journey of self-discovery, the tools and exercises provided in this chapter will guide you. And to be as transparent as possible, I will also share a few experiences that not only challenged my perceptions but also highlighted the importance of shadow work in my own life.

On the next page, there is a chart to help you become more self-aware and this section should not be taken lightly. Be sure to ask yourself these questions and sit with the answers. Do not judge yourself for how you feel. We are taking it step-by-step and this exercise is meant only to help you to become more aware of yourself.

When asking these questions, make sure you are always digging deeper. If you ask yourself, "Who am I?" The next question you could ask yourself is, "Who was I and when did I transition from being that woman to the woman I am today?" If you ask yourself, "Is travel important to me?" Your follow-up question could be, "Why is travel important? What positive feelings do I attach to traveling and is there anything else I can do to feel the same emotions that I do when I travel to a new place?" Make sure you are as thorough as possible.

01 THE PAST

What was your happiest moment?

Do you have unhealed traumas?

How do you describe your childhood?

What are your fears?

Who's let you down the most in your life?

Is that person yourself?

03 THE FUTURE

What are your long term goals?

What are your short term goals?

Where can your passions take you?

Do you aspire to motherhood?

How does the woman you want to become live, act, look, think?

02 THE PRESENT

Who are you?

What are some lies you've previously told yourself?

What are your core values?

How do you learn best?

Are you an effective communicator?

Are you happy with yourself overall?

How does your inner dialogue sound?

When was the last time you self-sabotaged?

What brings you peace?

> Never confuse the women you were and are with the woman you are to become. They are not the same.
>
> SHAW DRAKE

Childhood Trauma

One day, I went shopping with my daughter, who was eight years old at the time. We were specifically looking for shoes she would need for an upcoming wedding in which she was a flower girl. We found so many pretty shoes, but each time we asked for her size, they were out of stock or they did not make that shoe in the size she needed at all. Eventually, we realized the majority of shoes that fit her had some form of heel on it and decided to just work with the options we were given.

I remember seeing her put on her first pair of heels. Let me tell you, she looked like a baby giraffe walking for the first time! I laughed hysterically as she joined in. She felt just as funny as she looked as she struggled to walk in those heels. Now, this is where things took a turn.

I said to her, "Girl, you look like a little boy walking in those heels."

She stopped dead in her tracks, looked me in the eye, and said, "I do not look like a little boy walking in heels. I look like an eight-year-old girl who has never worn heels before." The sheer embarrassment and shame I felt in that moment was indescribable.

My daughter, who is wise beyond her years and very articulate, has always taught me things in life. So that was no surprise, but this time was different. This time, she was not simply teaching me; she was exposing me. She was challenging my beliefs and the way I viewed the world. She was forcing me to become aware of negative perceptions I had, and she immediately set a boundary that I knew I would never cross again. I apologized and we continued our shopping.

When I got home that night, however, I couldn't shake off that encounter. *Why would I say that to my daughter? Why did I think that was okay? When did I associate not being able to wear heels gracefully with looking like a boy?* That night, I had to do a lot of soul searching. I had to figure out the source of my negative perceptions, and I had to learn how to rewire my brain to no longer see things the way I saw them. By the end of the night, I realized that growing up, I was often told by family and friends that I walked like a boy, especially when I was just learning how to wear heels.

I do not remember feeling offended when those kinds of statements were made to me, but I remember accepting the notion that if a girl cannot gracefully walk in heels, she is essentially walking like a boy. When I saw my daughter that morning, I began to project. I repeated the cycle, and I got checked by an eight-year-old girl who refused to allow even her own mother to speak negatively over her.

On the next page, I want you to take the time to figure out some of the ideas that were planted in your mind that were negative and have impacted the way you view the world and interact with others. It can be anything from the way you speak, the way you look, your personality traits, the size of your goals, literally, anything. Dig deep. The space is limited, but feel free to do this exercise as many times as you need in your personal journal. The work is necessary. Not just for you, but for those whose lives you are impacting as well.

Journal: Unraveling Childhood Imprints

The Idea

What is a negative idea that was implanted in your mind at a young age and by whom?

What is the role they had in your life and did that affect the level of impact?

Your Projection

How are you projecting this belief onto others?

How has this affected your relationships with those dear to you?

The Goal

What would you like to replace this belief with?

What can you do to achieve this goal?

Transferring Belief Systems in Adulthood

For years, I taught women how to be sugar babies without giving sugar. That's a separate book, so I will not go into too much detail here. But I will share with you a personal story that truly affected me along that journey.

I was twenty-three years old, recently divorced, and I received a call from one of my younger cousins, where she told me about this new site that had sugar daddies. She explained to me what a sugar daddy was and told me to check out the site because I could get a lot of money from them. I was instantly intrigued. She never mentioned sex and me being the naive, young woman that I was, assumed that I would be able to receive money from men by just showing up on dates. Fortunately for me, this turned out to be true.

During this time, there were not many forums to actually seek advice on how to become a successful sugar baby, but I stumbled across one that had a little more information than the others. I quickly learned that sugaring was considered sex work and there was a hierarchy within the sex industry. White women earned more, black women earned the least, and everyone else fell somewhere between the highest and lowest earners. Also, you needed to have sex with these men to earn a lot of money.

I remember feeling pissed; I could not believe that everything I thought about being a sugar baby was completely wrong. However, I was so intrigued by this secret world that I decided I would still attempt it, even though I would only make a few dollars here and there since I would not be sleeping with them. If I am being honest, it was not my great moral compass that prevented me from sleeping with strange men for money. It also was not because of safety reasons. It was simply the idea that I could do the exact same thing, perform the exact acts as another woman and be paid less for it because of the color of my skin. That alone was enough to vow to myself I'd never sleep with a stranger for money. It just did not sit well with me.

Yet, I was excited that I could simply date high income earners who I would not organically cross paths with. When I started dating, I never requested or expected compensation above $150. I went on a few paid dates over the next couple of years and was satisfied with whatever I received. I was making six figures by the time I was twenty-three and wasn't struggling for money. But there was just something about being paid to attend luxurious dates. But how quickly can things change? A few years later, my income dropped by 60 percent. I began seeking work from home opportunities and was reminded of my previous dating experiences from a few years back.

I decided to give it a go again. Though this time, I was in need. I could not afford to go on dates with men for such little compensation, so I taught myself how to sugar without "sugar" successfully, to the tune of thousands for one date at a time. Some weeks, I had eight to ten dates lined up between lunch and dinner. I could not believe how much more I was being compensated in my thirties compared to when I was in my twenties.

After I did some introspection, I realized that I could have done the same thing when I was younger had I not allowed a stranger on the internet to influence me into believing that my dating market value in the sugar world would be extremely low because I was a black woman.

This led me to digging even deeper. *What other internal beliefs existed within me that prevented me from reaching my goals? Was I an angry black woman because I was divorced? Was I worthless because I had children? Did my lack of formal education at that time mean that I was not intelligent? What was it inside of me that made me easily accept and adopt someone else's belief system that did not serve me?*

On the next page, I want you to explore some of the ideas planted in your mind that you accepted as truth. I want you to be as introspective as possible and not write down the first answer that comes to your mind. If you do this enough, you will be able to recognize your areas of weakness that allow you to adopt beliefs solely designed to harm you.

Journal: Reevaluating Adult Beliefs

The Belief

What is a belief that you accepted in adulthood that affected you in a negative way?

What information did you use to determine this new, adopted belief made the most sense for your life?

The Effect

What was the effect?

How did this affect you in other areas of your life?

The Replacement

What new belief can you replace your old belief with?

What new, measurable goal can you attach to your new belief system?

No is a complete Sentence.

Reflecting on our internal beliefs reveals their profound influence not just on our self-perception, but also on our interactions with the world. One clear manifestation of this is in our ability to assert boundaries and make firm decisions. This becomes especially evident in the seemingly simple, yet often challenging act of saying "NO".

Many women have a problem saying, "NO," and we do not realize the root of the issue. But oftentimes, it starts in early childhood when you are being forced to give an adult a hug or speak to someone you do not know because your parents are telling you to. It starts when you are not afforded the autonomy as a girl child to make decisions for yourself, decisions that would make you feel good.

Subconsciously, you start to believe that what you want is secondary to everything and everyone else. In dating, this plays out in really unhealthy ways; not being able to walk away from the dinner table when you are ready to leave or not being able to tell someone "No, I do not want that" or "No, I would prefer this instead," without having that sense of guilt to follow.

Once you learn that your NO is valid without permission or explanation, you empower yourself that much more.

Dating does not come with obligations **and Love does not come with a** Life Sentence!

Therefore, walking away from or choosing to stay in a relationship with anyone does not determine your love for them, although it could serve as an indicator of the love you have for yourself. Confront your shadow. Do the work

---◆---

> ## IF YOU CAN'T CHANGE IT,
> ## CHANGE YOUR ATTITUDE.
>
> *—Maya Angelou*

HABIT
FORMATION
CHAPTER 18

WE SEE IT ALL THE TIME—women choosing the same types of men over and over again, despite these men repeatedly causing them harm, truly lacking in emotional intelligence, or blatantly stating that they are anti-marriage. These women constantly aspire to have healthy, loving, and committed relationships that ultimately lead to marriage (for some). Yet, they keep finding themselves in new relationships with men that perpetuate the same undesirable behaviors of the previous men they were involved with. Here is the thing—these women do not even understand why they are so committed to remaining in disadvantageous relationships.

They make promises to themselves that they can never keep, swearing to never date those types of men again. Even when they realize they are capable of attracting all types of men, they habitually choose the lowest value of them all. The worst part about this is that their poor habits are not only revealed through the men they choose, but in many other areas of their lives. This is because we are all creatures of habit. Once a habit is created, the brain requires greater effort and energy to replace that old habit than it does to maintain it.

Habits, which are most visible through routine, are known to be predictive measurements of a person's success or failures in life, thereby garnering more attention than the actual formations of those habits. When you look beyond the surface and take a more microscopic approach at understanding habits, you will see that habits are merely the outward manifestation of a multilayered assemblage of our identity. Therefore, it is not the habits themselves that are creating our futures, but rather an aggregate of all that which precedes it. For that reason, it is important to understand the six levels of habit formation, their relationships with each other, and the importance of intentionality at each level. Only then will we be able to explore common practices that are preventing women from successfully dating on their own terms.

The six levels of habit formation are thoughts, beliefs, choices, decisions, actions, and behavioral patterns. Our thoughts shape our beliefs. Our beliefs generate our choices. Our choices enable our decisions. Our decisions guide our actions. Our actions determine our behavior patterns. And lastly, our behavioral patterns create our habits. Let's discuss each level of habit formation at a time.

Habit Hacking
Understanding the 6 Levels of Habit Formation

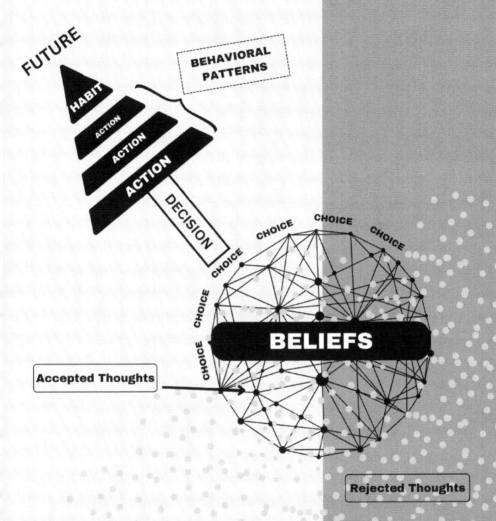

Our thoughts make up the first layer of habit formation. Right now, scientists still do not agree on exactly where every thought originates. However, they do agree that many of our thoughts are influenced by the things, people, and experiences we are exposed to. On average, humans experience thousands of thoughts per day, so while we cannot control every thought that enters our mind, we can generally control what we allow ourselves to be exposed to and manage the thoughts that accompany those things. The thoughts that most resonate with us are the ones that will become a part of our belief system, whereas all other thoughts are rejected, having no lasting impact on us.

Our beliefs are shaped by the thoughts that we accept, making them the second layer of habit formation. We have many beliefs, and they are extremely powerful because they are so deep rooted in the core of who we are. However, some are far more important than others. For instance, our beliefs about ourselves, money, and spirituality or religion will have greater effects on our future than our beliefs about the best band in the 1990s era. While beliefs are the second layer of habit formation, they are often the first level that people acknowledge and try to change if they are not serving them. This is why many people will engage in useful practices like affirmations, which we will discuss more in later chapters. Once our thoughts have been accepted and our beliefs have been created, we now move to our choices and decisions.

Although many people use choice and decision interchangeably, there is a distinct difference between the two. Whereas choices, the third layer of habit formation, aim to separate, decisions, the fourth layer of habit formation, aim to navigate. This is because choices are lateral and suggest multiple options, while decisions are successive and indicate one specific direction. As such, it is our choices that enable our decisions. People make choices based upon their emotions and decisions based upon rationality. If we feel that something is better, more pleasurable, useful, highly satisfying, etc., we would more often choose that over the things we feel are unfulfilling, difficult, harmful, useless. But there are also times when the choices we are given are similar in nature and still we choose the option that is most desirable to us at that moment. When we use rationale instead of emotions (decision-making), it is because we are no longer in a field, but instead, at a crossroad.

Actions are the fifth layer of habit formation and are simply recognized as things that we do. Actions can create instant gratification or displeasure as well as delayed gratification or displeasure. If a person believes that the action was rewarding in some way, they will be more likely to repeat that action again, especially if the reward was instant. If they do not like the results of their action, they are less likely to repeat that action again. What makes studying actions so difficult is that they are layered on top of each other. Sometimes, the reward of an action may lead us to another action that is not pleasurable for us. Even when we recognize that the aftermath of the second action is not desirable in any way, we find ourselves struggling to deny ourselves the reward of the first action. This is how vicious cycles are created. Since we take so many actions each day, it is sometimes difficult to notice and analyze our actions until we do them multiple times. By that point, the actions have become behavior patterns.

Behavioral patterns, the final stage of habit formation, are the routines we consciously engage in. These behaviors only come into fruition when multiple, instantaneous rewards are attached to them. Otherwise, there would be no motivation to take the same action again and again. This does not mean that the only actions people repeatedly take are the ones with favorable results. This just indicates that there are multiple positive benefits a person must receive in order to keep doing something over and over.

The difference between behavioral patterns and habits is the state in which each occurs. Behavioral patterns exist within our consciousness, whereas habits exist within our subconsciousness. For instance, if you start a new job in a location you had to use your GPS for, it may take you a week or two to learn how to navigate there on your own. However, after driving the same route after a month or so, you may find yourself pulling into the parking lot without fully remembering how you got there. Initially, you created the pattern of driving to your new job, but it took much more effort and concentration than it did to habitually drive there after a couple of months.

So now that we have an in-depth understanding of habit formation, let's explore six common practices at different stages of habit formation that are preventing women from successfully dating on their own terms.

Thoughts: Minimizing the Media

Because we do not know where every thought originates from, it is crucial for us to only focus on the ones that we do. These specific thoughts are derived from the things, people, and experiences we are exposed to. One of the most common ways for our minds to be influenced these days is through the media. When it comes to dating on your own terms, you want to make sure that you are not constantly exposing yourself to ideas that will work against you.

A few years back, I was a member of a group of women who were all successful with either high paying jobs or beyond the beginning stages of entrepreneurship. They were major divestors and conservative. In no way was this group a dating or level-up group. I joined because the leader of the group was a brilliant woman who I truly admired—and still do 'til this day. I would sit back and absorb all the content that was floating around the group. There was so much to learn and so many ideas being shared that I had never heard of at the point. I absolutely loved this group of women.

So, what was the issue? Well, the problem arose when I noticed that slowly over time, the content of the group was becoming more male centered in a nonpositive way. At first, it was about black men, then it was about other ethnicities of men who were adjacent to them. Then, it became about any and every negative thing a woman could find about a man. A few women in the group were in long-term, healthy relationships, but most of the women in the group were single and embittered by their previous relationships or dating experiences.

Instead of focusing on ways to position themselves in a space where they could meet a man whom they felt were worthy of their companionship, they would complain about all the things that men were doing wrong. Now, here me out. Their grievances were valid-many of which I could even relate to. But when you log into social media and the majority of the content you are ingesting is bashing men, how is it possible that your thoughts when you are alone will not be affected by them?

I finally spoke up and asked a couple women why they were so hellbent on finding and sharing the worst news about men that they would never even consider for marriage in the first place. It did not make sense to me. Before I came to the realization of what was happening, I had already been exposed to so many negative opinions about men, some of which I had accepted as my own.

The same things happen outside of groups. It does not matter if you are regularly ingesting content from TikTok, IG, or YouTube. It does not matter if you ever post or add value to the conversation. What matters is the type of content you are receiving and the frequency in which you are receiving it. Pretending that the content we are purposely exposing ourselves to daily has no bearing on us is foolish. Too often, by the time you recognize it, it has already spread throughout your mind in subtle ways.

Also, the music we listen to and the videos we watch are just as important as the things that we read. If you are regularly ingesting things that promote struggle-love, toxic relationships, or misogynistic or misandrist content, do not be surprised when you find yourself living out those same experiences.

Our thoughts are powerful, and it is critical that we treat them as such. Not everything deserves your attention. Some songs should not be played, and some movies should not be watched. Some people should not be followed, and some groups should not have your participation. So always remember, a haphazard consumption does not prevent the internalization and eventual manifestation of what is within you, for what is within you will surely become you.

Beliefs: Miscalculating Their Power

One of the common things women do that prevent them from dating on their own terms is miscalculate their power. This is seen in two ways. First, they believe they have the power to change other people. Second, they believe they do not have enough power to change themselves. Together, these beliefs are keeping them employed in a build-a-man factory while singing woe is me to the heavens. Neither are helpful in their journey of acquiring healthy, long-lasting love. Let's understand why these things are happening.

While it is not impossible, intentionally changing deep rooted beliefs about yourself is difficult. If it were not so, everyone would become exactly who they wanted overnight, but if we look at change from a psychological perspective, we can better understand why this is. First, our bodies strive to always maintain homeostasis. If we are hungry, our brain is signaled to eat. If we are hot, our body will begin to sweat to try and cool us down. If we are cold, we will shiver to try and warm up. If we are tired, we will fall asleep. These are all basic examples of how our bodies maintain homeostasis.

However, homeostasis is much deeper than those things and the concept does not solely address physiological responses, but psychological responses as well. Homeostasis from a psychological perspective is essentially the proclivity to maintain balance and equilibrium within us. Thus, it takes little effort, if any at all, to remain unchanged, which is interesting because you hear more people bragging about being who they always were—as if it requires more effort to remain the same than to change themselves. Regardless, it all starts within your belief system about yourself.

I am sure we have all been told at some point that we cannot control others; we can only control ourselves, though, it is easier said than understood for many people. Why is this the case? When we look at our belief system, we know that it consists of the thoughts that we have accepted, whether good or bad. When a woman believes that she does not have the power to change herself, she then looks for something or someone else that she believes she can control. This can be her children, friends, or even her man. It is much easier for her to accept that her life is not going the way that she desires if she believes that the lack of obedience of others is the cause. So, she justifies her inadequacies by placing the onus on others to behave in ways that would make her life easier.

Once a woman takes ownership of herself, her belief system, and the roles she has played in certain unfavorable situations, she gives herself permission to change. She learns that the only way she can blame other people for the way her life looks right now is to admit that she has less power over her own life than them. That no longer sits well with her. She also realizes that while the effort it takes to change herself is not easy, it is impossible to change anyone else. So, she stops wasting her time trying to convince others to live their life in a way that is more accommodating for her and starts living her own life in a way that is more conducive to the future she desires.

Choices: Making Poor Selections

A lot of women complain about always attracting the wrong types of men. But we learned in earlier chapters that who a woman attracts is never actually the problem. We are magnetic creatures. Therefore, we attract all types of people into our lives. Women who say they attract the wrong type of men are simply trying to justify their poor choices. However, the truth is they are doing two things: chasing unicorns and overlooking quality men. When you continue to do these things, you will constantly find yourself getting the short end of the stick while convincing yourself that nothing is your fault.

Imagine for a moment that you are searching online for a new gown to wear to an upcoming gala. After a few days, you give yourself a break and stop looking because you cannot find what you are looking for. Later, you open Instagram like you usually do, and one after the next, you see six different sponsored posts from companies you do not follow that are all advertising formal wear. This was the last thing on your mind, but you are excited.

You go through each post one by one. The first leads you to a site that has amazing gowns, but the price point is well above your paygrade. The next leads you to a site with amazing gowns and decent prices, but you think to yourself, if I can stumble across this with no effort, what else can I find? So, you pass. The third advertisement leads you to a site with horrible gowns—so bad that you cannot even remember why the initial post caught your attention. The fourth has seemingly good products in your price range, but the shipping will take two weeks. Although your event is not until six weeks down the line, you are anxious and do not want to wait that long. The fifth ad leads you to a site where it is obvious that the garments are too cheaply made so you exit as fast as you can. You know you can do better than that. The final ad leads you to a site that has the absolute most amazing gowns you have ever seen, at a far cheaper price than you were willing to pay, with the fastest shipping time possible. Additionally, you have the option of customizing the gown for a small price without any delay in the original shipping time.

You do not understand how you can be so lucky. You do not even bother to look for reviews. If others knew about this site, it would be everywhere on social media, but you are one of the few people who stumbled across this lucky gem. You do not care that the price seems too good to be true. You do not care that you have never heard of this brand before. You are sold.

You have found your dream dress despite it feeling like the dress found you. After all, it all started with an Instagram post belonging to a page that you did not even follow. You see this as your sign, pull out your card, purchase it, and share your excitement with your closest friends about the most incredible dress you found today. You feel fantastic and cannot wait to wear it at your upcoming big event.

While waiting for this purchase to arrive, you shop around at a few local boutiques for shoes and accessories that you believe would go extremely well with the outfit. Because you saved so much on the gown, you spare no costs on the shoes and accessories, despite all these additional purchases being nonrefundable. You will be the talk of the event and you cannot wait for all eyes to be on you.

A few days later, the company emails you that your package has been shipped and that the tracking number will be available within twenty-four hours. However, twenty-four hours pass, and you receive an email stating that there has been a delay but not to worry because it will be shipped the next day. You do not care. You are still basking in your glory of finding such a sweet deal, but the delays keep happening. Weeks go by and it is getting closer and closer to your event. Your friends suggest that perhaps you should just find another dress. You refuse.

You have never seen anything like this, and you will wait for as long as you possibly can for it to arrive. The event is now two days away and you are finally accepting that what you purchased is never going to come. You mention to one of your friends what is going on and they refer you to a store that is known for having wonderful gowns at fair prices. So, you swallow your pride and go to see what the hype is about. You see a dress, try it on, and realize that it is a perfect fit. It hugs your every curve, while maintaining the perfect balance of classiness and sexiness. It completely matches the shoes and the accessories you already have, and it is in the price range that you can afford. However, you are so upset about the previous dress never arriving that you take the dress off, hang it back on the rack, and head back home.

The gala comes and goes but you do not attend. Your friends call you and ask why they did not see you at the gala, and you explain that you did not have any good options. You explain how you are so frustrated because you started prepping for this, months in advance, and you wasted your money on a dress that never showed up, causing you to lose more money because you paid for shoes and accessories you did not need after all. You are confused about how everything went wrong.

Your friends bring up all the red flags and remind you that you had two quality options: the second website that you imagined could be topped, and the last dress you found at the storefront but chose not to purchase. You convince yourself that your friends just do not understand and end the conversation. Very similar situations keep happening. You purchase gowns that are too unbelievable to be true online. They never show up. You overlook other great options and continue the lie to yourself that you only really run into scamming companies.

This scenario that I have given is a metaphor for what many women do when they are choosing their partners. They are regularly chasing these unicorns. They often allow these men to sweep them off their feet just by the words that they are telling them in the beginning stages of dating, but these men never show up for them in the ways they should. They never come through emotionally, physically, or in any way that matters to you, despite them advertising themselves as a man who does all the above.

Instead of women seeing these men for exactly who they are, they buy into the hype every time. It would not be as bad if they would at least give the other qualified men the time of day. But time and time again, they insist that it is only one type of man that they attract, and that man just so happens to be bad for them.

The truth is, no one solely attracts one type of person to their life, whether good or bad. If we do not learn a lesson the first time, we must repeat that lesson before moving on. The lesson here is that better men are available, but you will never truly see them if you continue chasing these unicorns, overlooking quality, and choosing partners using the same metrics that have failed you every time.

Decisions: Being Counterproductive

Relationships can be complex and difficult even in the best of circumstances. For women, it can be especially difficult to make wise decisions about their relationships because of the added pressures of social norms. All too often women prioritize their partners desires over their own or diminish the importance of their own mental and emotional needs. This can lead to situations where women are making counterproductive decisions in their relationships, such as prioritizing their partner's career ambitions over their own and putting themselves last or being passive aggressive in the things they do and speak.

Women can inadvertently put themselves in positions where they are submissively accepting bad behavior. This can lead to women becoming reluctant victims of chronic manipulation in their relationships, and hesitant to voice their opinions or stand up for themselves. It is imperative that women are aware of the potential dangers of these counterproductive behaviors and make conscious decisions about their relationships that put their well-being first.

Putting yourself last is a recurring problem for many women. Not only does it prevent you from developing healthy relationships, but it can also lead to feelings of stress and resentment. This can cause a cycle of low confidence and self-worth, which has the potential to derail any progress that you have made to empower yourself. When you put yourself last, you are investing your resources and time in someone else to the detriment of your own well-being.

In addition to the immediate effects of putting yourself last, there are more serious long-term consequences. It might eventually lead to burnout and a range of physical and mental health problems. Since women are often pressured to presume other people needs are more important than our own, building a sense of self-worth can be difficult. This can lead to feelings of being undervalued and insufficiently appreciated, which can manifest itself in a range of emotional issues.

It becomes a slippery slope because when you do not make it a habit to prioritize yourself, you start to develop distorted views about what is important in life. Instead of valuing yourself and your own needs, you can begin to obsess over pleasing your partner. This, in turn, causes feelings of resentment and unhappiness. You also can inadvertently increase your self-doubt. When you are constantly missing out on opportunities for growth and learning experiences, it can be easy to start questioning your worth and your abilities. This self-doubt can then have a huge impact on your mental health and your ability to push yourself and reach your full potential.

When your needs are not met and your lack of time for self-care becomes a daily practice, it can become increasingly difficult to manage your stress levels and maintain a healthy lifestyle. This can take a significant toll on your physical health, leading to a lack of energy, burnout, and poor sleep quality. As a woman dating on her own terms, it is important to remember that taking care of yourself is just as important as taking care of others. Taking the right steps to prioritize your needs can lead to improved mental and physical health, increased self-confidence, and healthier relationships overall.

The second most common thing that I have seen women do in relationships besides putting themselves last is being passive aggressive with their partners. I do not care how well you expect your partner to know you, you must always take a proactive approach in relationships because being passive aggressive can lead to more issues down the line. This is especially true if the other person does not realize how you are feeling and does not understand why you are being passive aggressive, and this behavior can turn even the most understanding partner into feeling resentment, leading to a breakdown of trust and communication within the relationship.

By being passive aggressive, it can be difficult to have an open, honest dialogue with your partner. As communication is essential in a relationship, it can be difficult to express yourself if you are not being straightforward with your feelings. This can lead to both you and your partner feeling frustrated and confused and can create an unnecessary divide between the two of you which could have been avoided by talking openly with each other. Not stating exactly what it is that you want can create feelings of powerlessness and cause you to be stuck in a one-sided relationship where you feel like you are not able to voice your opinion. But the truth is the relationship could have gone very differently had you done your part. While it may feel uncomfortable at times to continuously make your needs clear, it is counterproductive to the relationship to expect your partner to be a mind reader. Speak up, prioritize yourself, and give yourself the opportunity to be part of a healthy relationship.

Actions: Mismanaging Your Time

One of the greatest indicators of a woman's time management skills in life is the time she spends in relationships. Women make a habit of either doing one of two things: staying in relationships too long or leaving relationships too quickly. Both are equally bad because the first implies that there was a lot of wasted time during the relationship and the latter implies that the time a woman gave herself to get to know a man was not utilized properly and will not increase her chances of a better relationship in the future. Let's look at each situation more closely.

Women who stay in relationships too long do so for many reasons. It all leads to wasted time that you can never get back. You might tell yourself that you are simply focused on making a relationship work, and while this is important, it should never happen at the expense of working on yourself. Unfortunately, this is what usually happens. When you overstay in a relationship, you tend to make concessions and compromises that ultimately do not serve you or help you grow as a person. You also can significantly reduce the amount of time available to manage other aspects of your life. While there are some relationships that can be saved, for many, the time and emotional energy spent trying to fix the relationship or force it to work is often mismanaged and not utilized to its highest potential.

Women can mismanage their time in a variety of ways when they stay in a relationship too long. For starters, they could be spending a large amount of time trying to resolve issues within the relationship and working toward making it last, while sidelining other priorities and activities. Another way in which women may be mismanaging their time while in a relationship is by overriding her own needs to tend to their partner's. If a woman is consistently choosing to take care of her partner first, then this can severely limit the amount of time available to take care of herself.

On the flip side, many women who leave relationships too soon can also be mismanaging their time by not taking the time to really get to know someone and see if the relationship has potential for growth. When people enter a relationship, it is vital to give it a chance, but it is also crucial to be honest with yourself about what you want and what type of relationship you are looking for. It is better to leave if the relationship is not going in the right direction, rather than wasting time on a relationship that is not going anywhere.

However, leaving too quickly robs you of the opportunity to figure out what you have a problem with exactly. This is particularly true when a woman leaves in the midst of displaying strong emotions and is not able to work through these feelings to make a balanced, thoughtful decision. Rather than taking the time to evaluate and reflect on the relationship, she may choose to stay in the relationship to gain closure. Learning from a relationship is far more important than seeking closure from a relationship. When you learn exactly what you did not like or would never live with again, closure becomes inevitable. Otherwise, you are more prone to finding yourself in the same situation again and again.

Though leaving a relationship quickly can often feel like the right decision in the heat of the moment, it can be difficult to look back and determine if the right action was taken. This is because the emotions associated with a breakup can be confusing and complicated, and an individual may not have the necessary perspective needed to make a fully informed decision. Therefore, women must be careful not to rush into the decision to end a relationship too quickly. Instead, take the time to sit with your feelings and think critically about the relationship and the decisions you are making. Doing so will provide you with the necessary context you need to make a sound, reasonable decision that is based on more than just emotions.

Behavioral Patterns: Living in Delusion

I absolutely hate when men call women delusional. Often-times, it is being said to attack rather than to facilitate dialogue about the self-sabotaging behavior the woman may be exhibiting. But after coaching many women, I have concluded that the ultimate negative behavioral pattern women exhibit when trying to date on their own terms is disregarding her dating history and her current dating market feedback. If you want to be a market maker, you simply cannot be delusional about where you come from and where you are currently. Let's explore these two patterns more.

Women are often inclined to downplay their negative dating history, preferring to forget about unpleasant situations and focus on the good moments. Unfortunately, this tendency to sweep things under the rug can leave them living in a state of delusion rather than fully understanding the world in which they navigate. The real issue here is that these negative experiences have a larger impact on them than they may want to admit, and without that admission, they are unable to heal and move past them.

Ruthlessly ignoring negative dating history can lead to unhealthy patterns of behavior. Many women find themselves in similar positions, attracted to the same type of person and ending up in the same way without realizing what is happening. Twisting the narrative around bad experiences and refusing to recognize and confront them can create a false sense of security in believing it will not happen again, not understanding that the same thing has happened before. So, being able to recognize patterns and reflect on experiences is paramount. This requires a level of honesty and self-reflection that might be uncomfortable. But if you avoid accountability and instead focus solely on positive experiences, you become unable to make any meaningful changes in your life, leaving you in a dangerous state of delusion, and a dangerous cycle of unhealthy relationships.

One of the most important aspects of dating market feedback is understanding what kind of relationship you are looking for. Are you attempting to find a long-term partner, spouse, or are you looking for something more casual? Whatever your answer may be, you should always strive to be conscious of your current dating market feedback and glean information from it to develop realistic expectations. Ignoring the messages present in these experiences can lead to a lack of awareness and an inability to take control of your romantic destiny.

Another beneficial type of dating market feedback women should pay attention to is learning more about what they desire in a potential partner. Making the effort to observe how people you have been with or interacted with react to your wants and needs can provide insight into what sort of qualities you want in a relationship. We will talk more about this in the next section of this book. However, this saves time in the long run as you can use the feedback you gather to better filter out those who do not meet your standards.

As you can see, habits are imperative. Each stage of habit formation affects another and when identifying what your habits actually look like, you will see an overlap of the stages depending on the angle you take. When you are dating on your own terms, you want to set yourself up for success, so making sure you are not engaging in these six common habits can make a world of a difference for your dating life.

APPEARANCE

CHAPTER 19

I was getting ready to leave the house one day looking like a hot mess when my 86-year-old grandmother stopped me in my tracks and questioned me about what I was doing. I told her that I was running to the store to pick up a few things and I'd be back shortly.

She said, "You will not leave the house looking like that. Comb your hair and put on something nice." I cannot remember exactly what my response was at that time, but I tried my best to quickly explain to her why my appearance was not a big deal.

She then said, "You don't have a man, and you won't get one if you keep leaving the house looking like that." I reminded her that I wasn't looking for a man and was simply going to the grocery store. To which she replied, "The grocery store is exactly where I met my man."

I realized I was not going to win that battle. So, I shut my mouth, fixed myself up, came back to receive the approval of the matriarch of my family, and went grocery shopping. Shortly after I left the house, I took selfies, made videos, and Facetimed a few friends while I was walking the aisles of the store. I felt absolutely amazing. Before I fixed myself up, I was not having a bad day. However, I was not experiencing a great day either. I would be remiss if I did not acknowledge that my entire mood shifted in a positive way the moment I looked in the mirror and saw my reflection.

Initially, I took great offense to my grandmother telling me that I was not going to get a man if I did not keep myself up. It sounded like such an outdated, sexist way of thinking. I did not want a man who would only concern himself with my aesthetics or attire. I did not want to allow the opinion of a man I did not even know existed to dictate how and when I groomed myself. I did not care to appeal to the male gaze, nor did I care to fish for their compliments.

I was above that—an evolved woman, worthy of being judged by more than just my looks. I wasn't going to be swayed by a woman from a generation that just did not understand this new age way of living. I had it all figured out.

Eventually, this situation taught me that although I was more formally educated than my grandmother, her wisdom superseded mine. Yes, I was well read, but she exuded a level of intelligence that a book could not offer me. My initial understanding of her statements was a result of my surface-level thinking. I needed to dig deeper, think more intuitively, and expand myself beyond the millennial rhetoric that condemns a lot of traditional ways of courtship.

In doing so, I learned that my grandmother was not actually warning me about not winning the heart of a man. On the contrary, she was cautioning me about devaluing the essence of myself. She was trying to teach me the importance of showing up for myself in even the most miniscule decisions that I made on a daily basis. And let's be honest. She absolutely knew I wanted a man.

My grandfather passed away decades ago and she never remarried. Clearly, her life's goal was not to keep a man, but she took the time to teach her know-it-all granddaughter that the less I cared for myself, the less I could expect others to care for me. If I were not intentional about giving the world the best version of me, I'd inadvertently make space for those who don't deserve that best version.

It sounds great in 2023 for a woman to say she does not need a man; but the truth is, many women still want them no matter how much cognitive dissonance they may exhibit at times. Many women, especially those without children with hopes of becoming mothers, are wanting to partner with a man to procreate and share a life together. AI hasn't completely taken over yet.

I took pride in telling my grandmother that I was not man-hunting, but I was also being dishonest because I wanted one. I wanted a man. Had I not learned that lesson that day, I would have eventually married a man who was okay with accepting the lesser version of myself. I would have continued to create space for people who and situations that did not require me to invest in myself daily. I would have settled for mediocrity in so many areas, all to prove a moot point that a man must accept me as I am.

Even though I put extra effort into my appearance that day, I still did not meet my husband. Actually, I did not even get approached by a potential suitor, but that experience taught me three important things. First, I did not have the wisdom of an eighty-six-year-old woman and sometimes it is best to just shut the hell up. Secondly, how I presented myself to the world, not just men, was important and should not be taken lightly. Lastly, the effort I put into my appearance, or the lack thereof, affected my energy and reflected the way I felt about myself.

So, in this chapter, we will discuss four things that women should pay close attention to when entering the dating market: attire, posture, exercise routine, and home.

Attire

One of the most common misconceptions in life is that motivation precedes action. The truth is motivation is simply a feeling. It is a desire or a longing to do something. When a person feels most motivated to do something, it is typically after they have already started. Think about it. Have you ever wanted to lose weight, write a book, or simply start a new hobby? You probably did not look forward to your first day in the gym or the first smoothie you tried. You most likely dreaded writing the first word of your novel and maybe never even started a new hobby out of fear of failure.

People can have a desire to do something for years but never start it because they are waiting for motivation that they feel they need, and they know they do not have. But after you have taken the step to improve your health, write that book, or start your new hobby, you find yourself more easily deciding to do it again and again. This is what motivation looks like. Sometimes, the task does not become easier, you simply become better and more motivated to do it.

What does this have to do with your attire as it pertains to your dating goals? Well, the same concept applies. Like the situation I described with my grandmother, many women are leaving the house looking any kind of way.

They are waiting for something good or grand to happen to them to give them a reason to put on something nice. They are waiting to lose weight. They are waiting to find a man. They are waiting to get enough money to fund a whole new wardrobe.

They are waiting to land that new job. They are waiting until their kids grow up and they have more time to do the activities they want and go to the places they desire. They are waiting until they simply feel better about themselves, their situations, and their future. They are finding a million reasons to not make their appearance a priority.

What we choose to wear has a lot to do with how we feel about ourselves, and how we feel about ourselves has a lot to do with whether different types of people want to remain in our lives after we have attracted them. Every woman remembers a time where she got a new hairstyle, put on a new outfit, or even an old faithful dress from her closet that always makes her feel extra beautiful and sexy, and her mood and energy instantly change.

We have all been there. But we try to convince ourselves that what we wear is not a big deal. We hear phrases like "The clothes do not make the person; the person makes the clothes." While that is true, it is also true that when people look good to themselves, they feel better, even if that boost of pride is short-lived. This is why it is necessary to regularly practice adorning yourself. It's important to make sure you put as much effort as you can into your appearance. It is not because you are shallow; it is because not caring about how you look can eventually affect how you feel about yourself.

Have you ever had a man approach you when you were feeling and looking your best? Have you ever had a man approach you when you were feeling and looking your worst? I am sure those two experiences were different for you. There will always be men who will approach you even when you are out in these streets looking crazy, but as a rule of thumb, I do not suggest that you give these men your attention.

There is always going to be that one woman who says she met her husband while she looked like she had just been run over by a truck. Let me be very clear, we do not care about your unicorn, sis! Men who approach women when they're not dressed up often assume these women are low-maintenance and don't invest much in their personal upkeep.

They usually expect for her to look like that the majority of her days and will praise her for not engaging in certain beauty practices while simultaneously fawning over every woman on social media who does. Put forth as much effort into your appearance as possible because that is how they will view you moving forward. That is the standard that you will set for yourself.

So yes, there is a direct correlation between what you wear and what you think of your potential. Looking good and dressing nicely is a powerful way to boost self-confidence. This little bit of effort goes a long way and as you notice the difference, you can bring this newfound confidence into other areas of your life. Also, feeling good about yourself and being well kept also encourages others to take you seriously.

Being intentional with your appearance can help you land the job or deals you want, the recognition you deserve, and even your ideal partner. This does not mean to overdraw your checking account to buy the latest designer. It means dressing for the occasion or better. Above all, it means showing up as much as possible as your best self for you!

Dressing well is much more than donning the trendiest clothes. It is all about looking poised and feeling self-assured in any situation. When put together, you send a positive message to others around you.

Lastly, when you are alone in your home, it is never a bad idea to put effort into how you look as well. I used to find old T-shirts or oversized clothes that I could lounge around the house in because they felt comfortable. I mean, who does not want to feel comfortable in their own home. But when I began adding comfortable and beautiful loungewear to my wardrobe collection, I noticed that my energy remained lighter in my home than usual. It created a ripple effect.

After I purchased a few new sexy and comfortable pajamas, I then decided I wanted the most comfortable slippers. I later created a full bedtime routine for my skin because I could not have crusty legs in nice pajamas. I purchased perfume and oils that I wore only to bed. I did not make these changes overnight, but one small decision to put effort in my appearance resulted in me having a much better experience in my alone time. This set the tone for what I required of others that wanted to date me. If my time spent with them did not feel better than my time spent alone, there was no incentive for me to continue pursuing that relationship.

In addition to your attire, a large percentage of how others perceive you also comes from your body language. This can include posture, gestures, facial expressions and eye movement. Let's discuss posture.

Posture

There is a lot of power in posture. If you tend to slouch, straighten up. If you tend to fold your arms out of habit, open them up. You want to appear welcoming to the people you are hoping to welcome into your life.

Also, your posture and body language say a lot about your confidence. Have you ever paid attention to the way a confident woman works a room? One of the first things you will notice is her walk. She has a commanding stride, and she stands in her femininity and power. It does not matter if she is short-legged and pigeon-toed. It does not matter if she is not the best dressed in the room. It does not matter whether she is conventionally attractive in the society she lives in. She somehow still finds a way to command attention just by the way she stands, walks, and carries herself.

You want to be able to always express your confidence through your body language. Make a conscious effort to stand tall, talk with your hands, make eye contact, and practice active listening. Engaged body language also uses open gestures, nodding, and smiling. It may even involve mirroring the movements and expressions of others. Although these things might sound silly and seem inconsequential, they will help you to appear more approachable and more confident as you engage in dialogue.

On the other hand, actions like slouching, fidgeting, avoiding eye contact, tapping your foot, or biting your nails are all tell-tale signs of nervousness and uneasy body language. These are big nos. You may not always feel confident, but there is beauty and strength in learning to push through your discomfort or uncertainty. On the surface, no one will be able to tell the difference because the appearance will be the same, and you will see it becoming more natural over time. So, stand tall, take up space, and act like you deserve to be in whatever room you are occupying.

Physical exercise

I have helped a lot of women learn to date on their own terms. Some of the more prominent concerns I hear during their consultations are whether they need to lose weight, become a size six, spend five hours in the gym a week, or have a salad every day for lunch. The honest response I give most women is a whopping, "NO." Your dress size alone will never dictate whether you can partner with your ideal guy.

We all have different body types. Being a woman who is thin does not mean she does not have health issues, and being a woman who is bigger does not mean she does have health issues. So then, why is taking control of your health important when it comes to finding your ideal partner?

When I think about health, I think about it from a holistic point of view. Health is not just your BMI. Health is about your overall physical, mental, emotional, and spiritual state at any given time. Let's briefly discuss these four aspects of health.

Exercise can benefit you in many ways. It can decrease your anxiety; help manage depression; rid your skin of toxins; improve your sleep; increase energy, flexibility, and mobility; strengthen bones, muscles, and will power; and improve your overall mood. More specifically as it pertains to dating, it can serve as a conversation starter, position you in the pathway of potential suitors who also prioritize their physical fitness, increase sexual stamina, boost your libido, and foster greater self-esteem.

If you only exercise to lose or gain weight and to show off your latest fitness outfit, you risk developing an unhealthy relationship with working out. The moment you find yourself unable to lose or gain weight despite putting forth reasonable effort, you might start feeling that exercise is futile. And if you're not getting the attention you desire from your latest fitness wear, you might lose the motivation to hit the gym altogether.

Therefore, it's crucial not to confuse the superficial benefits of exercise (like appearance or attention) with its deeper, long-term health benefits. Relying solely on the former can set you up for disappointment. Physical exercise should be approached as a long-term preventative measure, ensuring you reap all its holistic benefits.

While it's essential to understand that health is multifaceted and not solely determined by one's weight, it's also crucial to recognize that, for some, weight loss is a necessary step towards better health. Many metrics and studies used to determine obesity often don't account for the diverse builds of different ethnic groups, which can lead to misconceptions. However, it's essential to consult with healthcare professionals to understand what's best for your individual health needs. It's not about fitting into a societal mold but about ensuring your body is at its optimal health for your unique circumstances.

Also, for women who are planning to have children in the future, preparing your body before you conceive can go a long way. Carrying a child for nine months is not easy on the body. You want to give yourself every opportunity to ensure that your pregnancy goes as smoothly as possible, as well as your postpartum months.

Home

A woman's personal appearance is not the only thing that should be considered when she is learning to date on her own terms. The appearance of her home is also essential. After all, it is not unlikely that you will invite your partner over someday. Having a clean, uncluttered house truly goes a long way. I know this may seem completely unrelated to dating, however, it can help improve your dating life significantly.

There are four main reasons why you would want to keep a clean home:

1. It is an outward reflection of our human design.
2. It reduces anxiety and stress and improves your sleep.
3. It reduces shame when inviting your partner over.
4. It sets the tone for cohabitation.

Every living organism, whether human or not, needs systems to operate properly and remain functional. Systems are vital in our bodies and our homes. Every living thing works with a system of different parts that interact together and make up its whole. In fact, this concept is so intertwined in life, that there is a well-known saying inspired by it: "The whole is greater than the sum of its parts."

Our bodies have many systems like the circulatory system to keep it supplied with oxygen and the digestive system to break down food. In the same way, a home also needs systems to function freely. When you take the extra time to make sure that your home is decluttered, clean, and functioning optimally, you make your life so much easier, which leads us to the next point.

A well-maintained home is antithetical to an unhealthy body system. Exposure to dirt, dust, and allergens can trigger many inflammatory symptoms in the body and is the main culprit behind chronic respiratory issues. Keeping the home free of dust, grime, and other debris is not only beneficial for your physical health, but psychological health as well. Having a well-maintained and organized environment reduces stress and improves sleep which helps keep the body's hormones in balance.

Also, maintaining a good appearance for your home is crucial to your dating life because not only does it show pride in your living space, but it also helps to eliminate any embarrassment or shame when it comes to having your partner over. Keeping your home in good condition allows you to feel more at ease and comfortable when you open your door and saves you from having to rush to get things clean before they arrive. You can simply relax knowing that the warm ambiance you created within your home and benefit from regularly will now benefit you in additional ways with your partner.

Finally, maintaining an inviting and well-kept home sets the tone for future cohabitation. A clean and organized living space not only demonstrates self-respect but also conveys respect towards others. It showcases your ability to fulfill the role of a home manager, should you desire it, and assures a potential partner that you value cleanliness and order. Moreover, creating a welcoming environment fosters bonding and relaxation, signaling your openness to nurturing personal growth within the shared space.

Keeping your home presentable and inviting is helpful in creating a successful and healthy relationship. By doing so, you are demonstrating that you are serious about building a relationship and allowing your partner to be a part of your everyday life.

WEALTH ACCUMULATION

CHAPTER 20

As a woman entering the dating market, it is essential that you are conscious of your financial well-being. Many women do not want to hear this, but entering a relationship while poor is entering a relationship without power. You must be able to accumulate wealth to truly control your life. When I say, "wealth," I do not simply mean having money and material possessions, but I am also referring to having access to an abundance of opportunities and experiences that would not otherwise be available to you.

In this chapter, we will discuss the dangers that emerge from a lack of wealth and the life you can live due to the power of wealth. We will also explore the ways in which you can access wealth to achieve the level of control and influence that is necessary for you to become the market maker you are designed to be.

The Dangers that Emerge from a Lack of Wealth

The Poor Tax

The Poor Tax - It is not something you will find on your bill or written in any government document, but make no mistake, it is a very real thing. It is the invisible cost that comes with not having enough money. It is the toll that poverty takes on your mind, body, and soul. It is the weight of constantly worrying about how you are going to pay for basic necessities, and the emotional toll of feeling like you are constantly scrambling just to survive.

This "tax" manifests in various ways. It is the extra money you must spend on subpar goods and services because you cannot afford the higher-quality options. It is the higher interest rates and fees that come with being financially unstable. It is the stress and anxiety that come with living paycheck to paycheck, never knowing when a financial emergency might happen, and not having enough money to cover it.

But it's not just about money. *The Poor Tax* also exacts a psychological price. It's the feeling of being trapped in a cycle of poverty, the nagging sense of inadequacy, and the belief that no matter how hard you work, escaping this cycle seems impossible.

The Poor Tax is a heavy burden to bear, and it is one that many women are all too familiar with. It is a harsh reality that those without wealth, have less power and control over their lives. Essentially, And let me tell this: In the realm of dating, *The Poor Tax* has its own set of implications. *The Poor Tax* is a term used to describe the hidden costs that people must pay when they are pursuing relationships while financially insolvent. When financial stability is elusive, it can feel like you're wearing a target. You become more vulnerable, not just to financial opportunists but also to settling for less than what you deserve in a relationship.

It is not just predatory men that you must worry about. *The Poor Tax* affects all your relationships, not just the romantic ones. When you are struggling to make ends meet, you are less likely to have the energy or resources to build and maintain healthy relationships. Not only are you more likely to be taken advantage of, but you are also less likely to have a strong support system to fall back on.

Let's be real, as women, we already have enough to worry about. For women, these challenges are especially pronounced. We already navigate a myriad of societal expectations. Adding financial worries, like whether we can afford essential medical care or pay rent, only compounds the stress. It's tough to focus on cultivating meaningful relationships when you're drowning in financial concerns.

In this section, we will be talking about how to avoid falling victim to *The Poor Tax* and how to build wealth so that you can have the power and autonomy to create the relationships you desire. Trust me, being financially secure will change everything. You'll have the freedom to choose who you want to be with and how you want to be with them. It is time to take control of your financial future, so that you can have control over your dating future too.

The Perils of Pursuing Wealthy Men and the Vulnerability of Poor Women

When women set financial standards for the men they choose to date, they are often told that "rich men are dangerous." As we learned in Chapter 7, this warning is often used as a scare tactic to keep women available to noncompetitive men, but it is not necessarily supported by the facts. While there can be disadvantages to entering a relationship with a significant financial disparity between two people, these dangers or disadvantages can be mitigated when both people have accumulated individual financial wealth.

In other words, the danger of rich men is often overstated, while the vulnerability of poor women is often understated. When poor women enter relationships without financial resources of their own, they may be more prone to financial vulnerability and the negative consequences that come with it. This can include anxiety and stress about money, the risk of making poor decisions based on financial considerations, and a loss of personal autonomy in the relationship. Without a financial cushion to fall back on, these women may be more likely to stay in unhealthy or unfulfilling relationships out of financial necessity, rather than being able to walk away and invest in themselves.

On the other hand, when both partners have accumulated individual financial wealth, these dangers or disadvantages are less likely to be present. Wealthy men are not inherently "dangerous," and relationships between wealthy partners can be healthy and fulfilling. Instead, the real danger lies in financial vulnerability and the lack of resources that can create it. That's why it is important for women to focus on building their own wealth and financial stability, rather than relying solely on a partner to provide for them. By taking control of their own financial future and striving for financial independence, women can reduce their vulnerability and create the foundation of security and stability they need to build healthy and fulfilling relationships.

The Dangers of Money as a Primary Factor in Decision-Making

As a woman, you have many crucial decisions to make in your life. Whether it is choosing a career, a partner, or a place to call home, these choices have the power to shape your future and determine your level of happiness and fulfillment.

Unfortunately, one of the worst mistakes you can make when making these decisions is allowing money to be the primary factor. When you prioritize financial considerations above all else, you risk sacrificing your values, your passions, and your long-term goals. You may find yourself in a situation that does not align with your desires or your sense of purpose, simply because you felt like you had no other choice.

While the immediate effects are concerning, making decisions based primarily on money can have lasting consequences. Staying in a job or relationship that doesn't align with your values or fulfill you can lead to long-term unhappiness, depression, and a gradual erosion of self-worth.

On the other hand, when you have the financial resources and stability to support your choices, you are able to focus on what truly matters to you. You can make decisions based on your values, your passions, and your long-term goals, rather than being constrained by financial considerations. You have the freedom to pursue your dreams and to create the life and relationships you desire.

If you want to live a happy and fulfilling life, it is essential that you focus on building wealth and financial stability. By doing so, you can reduce the influence of money as a primary factor in your decision-making and give yourself the freedom to choose the path that is right for you. Remember, your worth is not determined by your financial resources. You have the power to create the life you desire, regardless of your current financial situation. With determination and hard work, you can build the wealth and stability you need to pursue your passions and live a happy and fulfilling life.

The Importance of Financial Security in Relationships

In the realm of relationships, being a market maker means you strive for a partnership where commitment transcends mere financial support. Yet, many women find themselves tethered to relationships where their partner's primary role is that of a financial provider. Such dynamics can become especially precarious if children are involved. Should the relationship end, the woman might face the daunting prospect of single motherhood without adequate financial support.

To safeguard against such vulnerabilities, it's imperative to cultivate your own financial independence. When you stand on firm financial ground, you not only elevate your own self-worth but also attract partners who offer more than just monetary support. A relationship should be a union of equals, where both parties bring emotional, intellectual, and financial contributions to the table.

This isn't to downplay the significance of financial stability in a relationship. Indeed, a strong financial foundation can be the bedrock upon which couples build a harmonious life. But it's essential that both partners contribute to this foundation, ensuring that their bond is about more than just money.

By prioritizing your own financial security, you empower yourself to select partners who value you holistically. Don't shortchange yourself by settling for anything less. Invest in your financial future, and in doing so, pave the way for relationships that are rich in commitment, understanding, and mutual respect.

The Power of Wealth

The Rich Reward

While lack of wealth can be a hindrance in the dating world, wealth can be a powerful advantage. This is what we might call "The Rich Reward." The benefits and incentives that wealthy women receive when they are dating. *The Rich Reward* is an important concept to consider when analyzing wealth and the dating scene because those with money have access to the luxuries and extravagances associated with dating wealthy partners, which can significantly enhance their experiences in the arena of love. This includes exclusive restaurants, access to exclusive events, such as a private ballroom party or special trips together. Those who come from wealth have access to these opportunities and many more, which provide them with a dating experience unlike any other. It is clear to see that wealth plays a prominent role in the realm of dating, and in many cases, those with the most money can reap the greatest benefits.

If we dig beyond the surface level, we see that it is not just trips, restaurants, and exclusive events. With financial stability, women are able to focus on their personal and professional goals, and not have to divert time and energy to worrying about their financial situation. This allows them to pursue their passions and purpose, and they can enter relationships with more clarity and intention, which leads to more meaningful connections. One additional advantage of wealth in the dating scene is the ability to connect with a wider range of people and opportunities. When you have financial resources, you can easily expand your social circle and network by joining exclusive clubs, attending high-end events, and connecting with other successful and influential individuals. This can open doors to new career opportunities, personal growth, and potential romantic partners.

Another benefit of wealth in dating is the ability to create a more stable and secure future for yourself and your family. When you have financial stability, you can plan and make investments that will help to secure your financial future. This includes things like saving for retirement, buying a home, or starting a business. Having a sense of financial security can also provide peace of mind and allow you to focus on building a fulfilling and meaningful life.

In addition to these advantages, wealth also allows for greater freedom and flexibility in relationships. When you have financial resources, you can make choices based on what is important to you and your partner, rather than being constrained by financial considerations. This can include things like choosing to live in a specific location, pursuing your passions and interests, or starting a family. Overall, wealth can be a powerful tool that provides a wide range of benefits and advantages in the dating scene. From increased access to resources and opportunities to greater control, self-esteem, and financial security, the rich rewards of wealth are numerous and impactful.

The Impact of Wealth on Attraction and Relationships

When it comes to attraction and relationships, wealth can have a significant impact on how women are perceived and treated. Research has shown that people with more financial resources tend to be viewed as more attractive and desirable partners. This is because wealth is often associated with success, power, and status, all of which can be highly attractive qualities.

However, it is important to note that the impact of wealth on attraction is not solely a function of the wealth itself. Rather, it is the confidence and security that comes with having financial resources that is truly attractive. Wealthy women who possess this sense of confidence and security can project a sense of self-assurance and independence that is highly attractive to potential partners.

Moreover, when it comes to relationships, wealth can also have a positive impact on the dynamics of the partnership. Women who are financially stable can be more assertive in their relationships, setting boundaries and expectations in a way that allows for more equality and mutual respect. They also have the resources to invest in the relationship, be it by planning vacations, buying a house, or taking care of their loved ones.

Wealth is not the only factor in attraction and successful relationships. Shared values, interests, and communication are also crucial components. However, by having a certain level of financial security, women are able to feel more in control of their life and able to attract and build relationships on more equal footing. With wealth, they have the power to set the standard for the type of relationship they want, and more readily attract partners who align with their values and goals.

The Importance of Not Fearing Wealth

As a woman, it is easy to fall into the trap of fearing wealth. Society often tells us that accumulating wealth and financial success is not a feminine pursuit, and that by pursuing wealth, we will become unattractive, intimidating, or even emasculating to men. This is not true. Wealth is not something to be feared, but something to be embraced. When you have financial resources and stability, you gain the freedom and autonomy to make choices that align with your values, your passions, and your long-term goals.

However, as you strive for financial success, be aware that there may be people around you who feel uncomfortable or even jealous of your growth. Men may feel intimidated if you make more money than them or women may resent you for "having it all." It is not just strangers, friends and family members may make you feel guilty for chasing wealth.

It is important to not let these insecurities hold you back from reaching your goals. Remember that your financial success is not a reflection of your worth as a person and it is not a measure of your femininity. Focus on building a life that aligns with your values and your desires, no matter what anyone else thinks.

Keep in mind that as you strive for wealth, you will encounter those who have already achieved it and will have the privilege to learn and gain access to their networks and opportunities, ultimately helping you in your journey. Embrace the idea of wealth, not fear it. Be proud of your achievements and what you have accomplished financially. And most importantly, do not let anyone make you feel guilty for pursuing the life you want.

Modernity, Women and Wealth

As women, we are often taught to view wealth as something to be feared or ashamed of. We're told that being too successful or making too much money can be intimidating to men, or that it can cause us to lose friends or alienate ourselves from our community. However, this belief is a relic of the past and does not align with the modern reality of women and wealth.

In today's world, women are taking charge of their financial futures and building wealth at unprecedented rates. According to a recent study, women own more than eleven million businesses in the United States and control $14 trillion in wealth.[8] This trend is only set to continue, with women projected to hold two-thirds of the nation's wealth in a few years.

However, despite these advances, many women still struggle with self-doubt and internalized beliefs that they do not deserve wealth or that they will be judged for their success. This is unfortunate for several reasons.

Wealth can give women the freedom to **create the life** they want, **pursue their passions**, and **build the relationships** they desire!

It is important to remember that wealth is not something to be feared or ashamed of. It is a tool that can be used to create a better life for us and those around us. We should also strive to break down the limiting stereotypes that still exist in our society, that women should not be wealthy.

Therefore, let's stop fearing wealth and start embracing it. Let's celebrate the success of women in business and recognize that our wealth is a powerful force for good in the world. By doing so, we will be able to build the lives we want and the relationships we deserve.

How to Access Wealth

As a woman, you have the right to abundance and financial stability. It is your birthright to have access to the resources and opportunities that allow you to build the life and relationships you desire. In order to claim this birthright, it is essential that you focus on building your own wealth and financial stability. By following these steps I will list below and committing to building your wealth and financial stability, you can claim your birthright of abundance and create the life and relationships you desire. Do not let anyone tell you that you cannot have it all. With determination and hard work, you can achieve financial success and create the foundation of security and stability you deserve. Here are a few key steps to access wealth and create a foundation of financial security.

Increase your financial knowledge:
The importance of increasing your financial knowledge as a woman cannot be overstated. It is essential to understand money and how it works in order to make sound financial decisions that will benefit you in the long term. Whether you are looking to enter a relationship or simply want to take control of your own financial well-being, a solid understanding of budgeting, saving, investing, and other financial topics is crucial.

As a woman, it is important not to rely solely on a partner to manage your finances or make financial decisions for you. Instead, take charge of your own financial planning, and set goals for yourself. Do not be intimidated by the complexity of financial concepts and the jargon that surrounds it. Start by educating yourself about the basics and gradually build your knowledge and understanding over time. There are plenty of free resources available online, such as tutorials, articles, and videos that can help you get started.

Additionally, consider attending seminars or workshops to gain a deeper understanding of specific financial topics. This can include creating a budget, saving for the future, and investing in assets that have the potential to appreciate over time. It is particularly important to increase your financial knowledge before entering a relationship as it will give you the tools to be able to make informed decisions about the financial aspects of the relationship, ensuring that you are in a stable and secure position. Always be open to learning and continuously improving your financial knowledge.

Seek out opportunities for financial growth:

As a market maker, you must constantly be on the lookout for opportunities to grow your wealth. Of course, when it comes to seeking out opportunities for financial growth, every woman's situation is unique. Some may find that they are able to increase their income through education or career advancement, while others may find that starting a side hustle or investing in assets is the best path for them. Be open to different possibilities and do your own research to determine which opportunities are the best fit for you.

One effective way to find opportunities for financial growth is to network with other women in similar situations. Joining groups or clubs in your community, attending conferences, or even just talking to other women who are working to build their wealth can provide valuable information and connections that can help you find opportunities for growth. Additionally, considering starting your own small business or investing in low-cost investment opportunities as other ways for those who have time and resources.

Another important consideration when seeking out opportunities for financial growth is the importance of setting and working toward specific financial goals. This means taking the time to evaluate your current financial situation, and then determining what you would like to achieve in the future. It could be something like paying off a credit card debt, or saving up for a down payment on a house. You can then start working on a plan to achieve these goals.

It is also crucial to remember that financial growth is not only about increasing your income but about decreasing your expenses and learning how to manage your money better. Building wealth takes time and effort, and it is vital to be patient and consistent with your financial habits. The most important thing is not to give up on your goals and to keep learning from your experiences.

Finally, there is no single path to financial growth, and what works for one person may not work for another. Be open to new ideas and opportunities, and do not be afraid to take calculated risks when the opportunity arises. By being proactive and seeking out opportunities, you can increase your chances of achieving financial growth and building the life you desire.

Remember that your greatest asset is yourself:
Your greatest asset is yourself, and investing in yourself is one of the most important steps you can take to build wealth. This can include investing in your education, your skills, and your career. When you invest in yourself, you increase your earning potential and open yourself up to new opportunities for growth and advancement.

It is essential to recognize your own worth and to take ownership of your professional and personal development. This means seeking out new opportunities for growth, whether it is through education, professional training, or other forms of self-improvement. It also means being open to new experiences and taking risks, even when they may be uncomfortable or unfamiliar. The more you invest in yourself, the more valuable you will become to yourself, your partners, and the world around you.

Investing in yourself is not just about acquiring new skills or qualifications. It is also about taking care of your physical, emotional, and mental well-being. This can include things like regular exercise, healthy eating, therapy, or mindfulness practices. When you take care of yourself, you increase your overall productivity and effectiveness in your personal and professional life.

Moreover, by investing in yourself you will increase your worth, not just in the dating market, but also in the job market. You can negotiate for higher pay, better working conditions, etc. You will feel more confident in your own skin and that will be reflected in your dating choices, the way you treat yourself, and the way you let others treat you. Remember, investing in yourself is a lifelong endeavor, and the more you invest, the more you will gain in return.

Remember that money is a tool, not an end in itself:

As a woman, especially in these modern times, it can be easy to get caught up in the idea that accumulating wealth is the ultimate goal. After all, society often equates success and happiness with having financial security and the ability to purchase material possessions. However, money is only a tool and not the end goal itself.

When you focus too much on accumulating wealth, you risk losing sight of what is important in life. Your relationships, health, and overall well-being can all suffer when you become overly consumed with chasing money. It is important to remember that money is simply a means to an end, and not the end itself.

Additionally, building wealth and achieving financial success is not an overnight process, it requires time and effort. Be patient and give yourself grace as you work toward your financial goals. Also, not everyone starts at the same place financially, and some people may have more resources and support than others. Be mindful of these inequalities and understand that accumulating wealth may be a slower process for some.

It is also crucial to remember that wealth should not be the sole measure of success or self-worth. You are more than your net worth and your achievements should not be defined by your bank account.

Find other sources of fulfillment and meaning in your life, such as your relationships, hobbies, and personal growth, and remember that true success and happiness cannot be quantified by wealth alone. Building wealth takes time and effort and should be viewed as a means to an end, not the ultimate goal. So, always remember to show yourself grace in the process.

A Moment to Reflect

As we conclude Part 4, let's take a moment to reflect on the key takeaways and engage in some introspective journaling. This will help consolidate your understanding and facilitate a deeper personal connection with the material.

Key Takeaways

1. Shadow Work: Confronting and understanding our unconscious aspects is crucial for personal growth and healthier relationships. Unresolved issues can affect our relationships, and addressing these issues can lead to personal transformation.

2. Habit Formation: Our habits shape our lives, and changing them can lead to significant improvements. Understanding the habit loop, setting clear intentions, and creating a conducive environment are key strategies for forming healthy habits.

3. Appearance: While physical attractiveness can influence initial impressions, it is the inner qualities that sustain a relationship. Self-care and maintaining a healthy lifestyle are essential not just for aesthetics, but for overall well-being.

4. Wealth Accumulation: Financial independence and wealth accumulation are important for women. Wealth provides access to more opportunities and experiences, impacts attraction and relationships, and should not be feared. Strategies to access wealth include increasing financial knowledge, seeking opportunities for financial growth, investing in oneself, and viewing money as a tool rather than an end in itself.

Journaling/Reflection Prompts:

Remember, the purpose of this section is not to prescribe a rigid path towards personal growth and wealth accumulation, but to empower you with the knowledge and tools to make informed decisions that align with your personal values and aspirations. Reflect on these takeaways and prompts, and consider how they can be applied to your own journey towards self-improvement and financial independence.

Shadow Work: Reflect on any unresolved issues or unconscious aspects of your personality that you feel may be affecting your relationships. How can you address these issues and what steps can you take towards personal transformation?

Habit Formation: Identify one habit that you would like to change. What is the habit loop associated with this habit? What clear intentions can you set to change this habit, and how can you modify your environment to support this change?

Appearance: How do you view the role of physical appearance in your life and relationships? How can you incorporate self-care and a healthy lifestyle into your daily routine, not just for aesthetic purposes, but for overall well-being?

Wealth Accumulation: Reflect on your relationship with money. How can you increase your financial knowledge and seek opportunities for financial growth? How can you invest in yourself and view money as a tool rather than an end in itself?

PART 5

ALL THINGS MEN

Definitions from Shawdrism Language

a wo·man's place \ ə ˈwu̇-mənz ˈplās *noun*

The designated area for women to sit back, relax, and let men figure things out on their own or with the help of other men; a place where women thrive by letting the man 'MAN'.

an·chor·ing \ ˈaŋ-kər-iŋ *verb*

the process of establishing how you should be treated by associating your reputation with positive experiences from your past

de·cen·ter men \ dē-ˈsen-tər ˈmen *verb*

The liberating act of shifting the focus from pleasing men to prioritizing oneself; a radical reorientation towards self-love and empowerment.

edge \ ˈej *noun*

The unique blend of characteristics and qualities that set a woman apart, making her irresistibly attractive and intriguing in her own distinct way.

high val·ue traits \ ˈhī ˈval-(ˌ)yü ˈtrāts *noun*

The golden threads woven into one's character that elevate their worth beyond the superficial, radiating an irresistible allure that's more than just skin deep.

W2W con·vo \ ˈdə-bəl-ˈyü-tə-ˈdə-bəl-ˈyü ˈkän-(ˌ)vō *noun*

(Woman to Woman) A bad decision; the result of displaced fault from the culprit to a contender.

Part 5: All Things Men

The Market Maker Method™ Component 5: Man
5th Rule: Recognize and Strategize.
Framework: The DRAKE Diamond Model™

In Part 5 of the book, we delve into the world of men and the ways in which we can navigate it more effectively. This section, titled "All Things Men," focuses on the principle of recognizing and strategizing when it comes to building meaningful connections with the opposite sex.

We will explore common misconceptions and self-sabotaging behaviors that women often engage in when pursuing romantic relationships with men. This includes things like centering men, ignoring our own needs, and focusing on negative traits in potential partners.

To combat these issues, I have developed *The DRAKE Diamond Model™*, which is a set of strategies that improve your interpersonal skills in dating and enhances the effectiveness of *The Market Maker Method™*. *The DRAKE Diamond Model™* comprises five key areas: decentering men, redefining high-value traits, anchoring your reputation, knowing your market, and examining your edge.

By focusing on these five elements, you will be able to adopt a more positive and productive outlook when it comes to choosing men in your life. By the end of this section, you will have a better understanding of how to position yourself in a way that attracts your ideal partner, and how to avoid common pitfalls in the dating world.

Before you Begin

Welcome to Part 5 of this transformative journey. In this part, we delve into the world of men and the ways in which we can navigate it more effectively. This is not a quick fix or a magic formula, but a thoughtful exploration of how we can build meaningful connections with the opposite sex.

To maximize the benefits of this section, I recommend the following steps:

1. Read each chapter slowly and thoroughly.
2. Pause and reflect on the information being presented.
3. Take note of any personal experiences or insights that come to mind.
4. Trust the process and be open to the transformation that is possible through this journey.

Part 5 is designed to help you understand and strategize when it comes to building meaningful connections with the "right" men. It is about breaking free from self-sabotaging behaviors and adopting a more positive and productive outlook when it comes to choosing men in your life. So be gentle with yourself, embrace the process, and prepare to explore the depths of your habits, perceptions, and the power you hold in shaping your dating life.

Questions That Might Arise

What if I find it difficult to change my approach to dating?

It is natural to find change challenging, especially when it comes to deeply ingrained habits and behaviors. Remember, this process is about personal growth and transformation. Take your time, and if necessary, seek professional help such as a therapist or counselor. You're not alone in this journey.

What if I am not comfortable with the idea of "decentering men"?

The concept of "decentering men" is not about disregarding or disrespecting men, but about ensuring that you are not ignoring your own needs or focusing too much on negative traits in potential partners. It is about finding balance and ensuring that your relationships are mutually beneficial.

What if I struggle with the concept of "knowing my market"?

Understanding your "market" in the dating world is about understanding what you are looking for in a partner and what you bring to a relationship. It is not about commodifying yourself or others, but about having a clear understanding of your values, needs, and desires.

What if I do not see immediate changes or progress?

Self-development is a journey, not a destination. Changes may not be immediate, but with consistent effort, you will notice progress over time. Celebrate small victories and be patient with yourself.

The DRAKE Diamond Model^{TM}

A 5-Step Process to Increasing Your Dating IQ

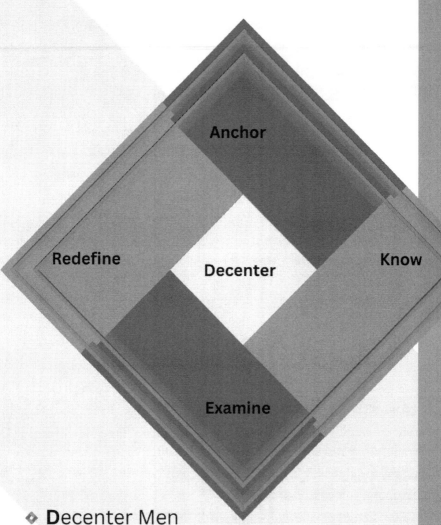

- **D**ecenter Men
- **R**edefine High Value Traits
- **A**nchor Your Reputation
- **K**now Your Audience
- **E**xamine Your Edge

> **" I DON'T WANT TO BE THE WOMAN WHO'S WAITING FOR SOMEONE TO LOVE ME. I AM A WHOLE PERSON ON MY OWN. "**
>
> *- Beyonce*

DECENTER MEN
CHAPTER 21

IN PART 1, WE DISCUSSED THREE pick-me archetypes and learned that the main thing they had in common was centering men. I get it. From a young age, girls have been fed this lie that men should be the center of our universe. From Disney films to chick flicks, we have been conditioned to believe that our ultimate goal in life should be to secure a man; that it is okay to sacrifice ourselves, our families, our belief system, and anything else in order to win the heart and the approval of a man whether or not they are worthy of our companionship.

Even in today's times where women in America have much easier access to higher education, you will often hear, "Women go to college for a B.S., and leave college with a MRS," all to insinuate that the most important thing to leave college with is not actually the degree she worked so hard on, but a decree of marriage. No matter how much women try to elevate themselves, there seems to always be the notion that getting a man is and should always be the most important thing and the highlight of a woman's life.

Because of this, I do not blame women for holding certain views, but it is my desire to help women wake up and see the truth for what it is. Men are not the prize, and neither are the women who continually give up their authenticity, sacrifice themselves, and center men to enter a relationship. It must stop now; it is time to start prioritizing ourselves and stop giving a damn about what every man thinks of or wants from us. Thus, in this chapter, we will focus on five common ways you can decenter men:

1. Show up as your most authentic self
2. Stop blaming "the other woman"
3. Stop being an intentional side chick
4. Require consistency in his character
5. Stop making excuses for his failures

Show Up as Your Most Authentic Self

Nothing saddens me more than to know a woman showed up to a first date pretending to be someone she was not. Not only is she robbing her suitor of the opportunity to get to know the real her, but she is robbing herself of the pleasure she would receive from basking in her authenticity. In Chapter 4, we discussed the various reasons a woman misrepresents who she is in order to land a man; and it is painfully clear that it all boils down to the woman not believing she is enough.

When you go on a first date, oftentimes, you know little about a man. Sure, you may know what field he works in, a few of his hobbies, whether he has children, and maybe even his height, however, you do not know a lot. So, why is it that you feel the need to pose as someone to get to the second date? You might find that the man is not even good enough for you. You may find you two have nothing in common. You may learn that your core values are so different that you would never even want to see him again.

There are only two reasons a woman would show up as a representative of herself. Either she believes that the man is inherently better than her and she needs to pretend she is on his level, or she inevitably believes that this stranger deserves exactly what he is looking for although she does not. She is being presumptuous that she cannot receive her heart's desires because she is operating out of fear. Even if you are able to secure a ring, you will never be truly happy in that relationship. Acting will become exhausting when you are never able to step outside of that character. So, you must become comfortable showing up as yourself, flaws and all. I can guarantee you that the man sitting across from you at the table also has them.

Stop Blaming The Other Woman

Too many times, when a woman finds out her husband or partner is cheating on her, she instantly blames the other woman. It does not matter to her that it is the man who has dishonored his vows or broken the promises he made to her. Instead of accepting the fact that she is with a disloyal man, she directs all her anger toward the woman, absolving the man from any responsibility. Throughout the duration of her relationship, she considered her man to be strong, decisive, and intelligent. Yet, she lies to herself that he suddenly became weak, confused, and naive to the decisions he made. She convinces herself that it was a mistake and chooses to believe the other woman is the culprit.

When women do this, it is because they know that they will never leave. They cannot reconcile in their minds that the person they are in love with can purposely hurt them in this way. Whether they have built a full life together, raised children for fifteen years, or just started out in the relationship, they feel like their investment into that relationship is not worth dissolving over infidelity. They convince themselves that the man is still worthy of being in their life and that the other woman is a mere bump in the road that she needs to remove. Now, here's the thing. It is a woman's prerogative to stay. It is a woman's choice to forgive. It is a woman's right to try and fix things in her relationship if she wants to remain in it.

But it is **never** the other woman's fault.

The standard by which women uphold other women is far greater than the standard many of them uphold for the men in their life. This is why it is so easy for women to end friendships with their female friends than to end a romantic relationship with their male partners. A woman will forgive her partner a million times over but will end a friendship over a simple misunderstanding. Men know this; they are not dumb. They do not accidentally fall into another woman's vagina, and they do not ever really believe they will be let go if their woman finds out they have cheated.

However, the lengths some men will go to have their cake and eat it too is immeasurable. Many women who find themselves being the other woman had no idea that the man had committed himself to someone else because men will lie, lie, lie. So, checking or blaming another woman will never stop the behaviors of a cheating partner. Having a woman-to-woman conversation (w2w convo) will not stop a man from pursuing the next woman. When you decenter men, you learn to recognize them for exactly who they are. It is not your fault if a man lies to you, but it is your responsibility to hold him accountable once the lie is exposed. When you learn to center yourself, you stop accepting less than you deserve. You stop blaming anyone outside of your marriage or relationship for its failure. You stop trying to hurt or destroy a woman that your husband or partner chose to engage. You stop making excuses for the harm the man you are with has caused you. He is a homewrecker. It is never the other woman.

Stop Being an Intentional Side Chick

A woman who centers herself would not purposely place herself in dangerous situations. I am not just talking about the idea that some women in relationships will fight or even try to kill another woman over her deceitful man. I am talking about sexual, financial, and emotional safety.

Men are simply not worth **risking everything** over.

It is often a woman's ego that makes her believe that a man who admittedly lies to his partner will choose to be completely honest with her.

Many women who choose to engage with men in committed, monogamous relationships claim that they are with him because of financial gain and good sex, without having to involve themselves with the mundane day-to-day tasks of his life. These women do not want to play house. They do not want to budget shared finances. They do not want to deal with rowdy kids that are not theirs. They do not want to commit themselves to that man because they prefer a more transactional relationship in that season of their life. Knowing that, let me be the first to say, there is absolutely nothing wrong with having those preferences.

If a woman does not want to cook and clean for a man, tend to his kids, regularly deal with his baby-mama drama, consider his expenses before receiving or asking for money, provide emotional support, or feel compelled to engage in as much sex as possible and whenever he wants it, she does not have to. She should not have to. But pretending that it is generally easier to deal with a man who is leading a double life over one who does not have to look over his shoulder daily is simply foolish. If you know a man has demonstrated horrible character, how is it possible to think you are the one person who he is being honest with?

Do not operate out of ego. Do not delude yourself into thinking that a man who is willing to cheat on his partner with you is worthy of your time, energy, or body. A woman who centers men can easily justify why it is okay to intentionally be a side piece to him, regardless of whether she is receiving very little or great benefits from him. Let's be honest. Most men today can barely afford to financially support one household, let alone two.

Most **intentional** side chicks are not dating men with a **large amount** of disposable income.

We all know the statistics. Women are selling themselves short and convincing themselves that the little financial gain and community peen they are receiving is for their benefit alone. They are claiming that it has nothing to do with the man or his relationship status. But the truth is these women are rewarding deviant behavior from men who are only willing to give them the leftovers from another woman's house. Let's just call a spade a spade.

When you stop centering men, you also stop forming alliances with men who you know are actively hurting other women. You transition from operating out of lack to operating from a place of abundance. You stop believing that the only available men who can give you what you desire are men with horrible character. We all know that if not you, there's always another willing participant. So no, it is not your responsibility to prevent a woman from being cheated on by her partner. It is your responsibility to manage your own personal relationships and to only reserve space for people who are not regularly putting you in a compromising position.

Many women are pushing back against the patriarchy, maintaining autonomy over their bodies, and not caring about the backlash they are receiving from the greater society. I get it. For so long, women have been ostracized for being sexually liberated. Women have been judged by their ability to remain faithful and kept, despite men not having the same judgments made against them. Women are simply tired of the double standards and have begun taking a stand against them.

However, I do not care what anyone tells you. Men and women are not equal. There are unfair advantages that both genders receive in the dating world. For instance, physical beauty is a clear social currency for women. If you were born conventionally attractive, there is little you need to do to gain the attention of a man. Women can even build a sizable amount of wealth based upon their looks alone. How many men can do that? It is a double standard. On the flip side, men rarely judge women by how much money they make or their earning potential. We can argue that it is because women generally make less than men in their same fields, but we also know that men will date women with far less earning potential regardless of the field she has chosen.

When it comes to relationships, it is far less beneficial for women to intentionally date a man who is in a relationship than it is for a man to intentionally date a woman who is in a relationship. Why is that? Well, it is said that women hold access to sex and men hold access to relationships. By that logic, it is easy to see why that is the case. If a man dates a woman who is already in a relationship, he can essentially take her from her man because he is the one who offers the relationship to that woman. But rarely can a woman take a man from another woman. We all know that it is not common for men to leave their wives for their side chick, no matter how agreeable, fun, young, vibrant, fit, and great in bed she is. They will stay with their wives until their wives become fed up and leave them. And usually, that man still does not marry the side chick if that is what she wants.

Ask yourself, if the goal is to challenge patriarchy, why are not the men suffering the majority of the consequences? Why would not the goal be to create a society where dishonorable men suffer for deliberately bringing harm to women instead of further rewarding them for it? If you believe that patriarchy has stifled the sexual liberation of women unfavorably, why participate in making it less taboo for men to commit sexual transgressions against other women in their life? Let's make it make sense, sis!"

Require Consistency in His Character

I do not judge a man's character by how well he treats me. Instead, I judge him by how well he treats other women who he is not attracted to or who can never benefit him in any way. I refuse to date men who appear to only treat women good if he has access to her sexually, if he finds her aesthetically pleasing, or if she is benefitting him in some way. If his goodness toward women starts and stops with his penis, I refuse to give him access to myself.

Treating me well is **not enough**. Treating women well **collectively** is key.

When you learn to center yourself, you stop allowing men to convince you that you are special, and therefore deserve his special treatment, which oftentimes is basic human decency. You are special with or without the approval of a man or the validation of a man. You are special whether you are chosen or not, proposed to or not, seen, heard, or understood, or not. Allowing men to measure your specialness by the kindness he is willing to show you, in contrast to other women, is a sure way to set yourself up to receive the poor treatment from him the moment the two of you have issues.

A man will not always be happy with you. He will not always support every decision you make. He may have some traumas and triggers that make it easier for him to be offended by you. Then what? Do you expect a man who has demonstrated he has little regard for women collectively to still show you love, grace, and understanding during those times? Have you bought into the lie that he treats you differently because he loves you? Do you think he will still treat you well when you find yourself in a season with little to offer him?

His character should be consistent, and his commitment should be distinct. It is that commitment that will allow him to prioritize you over others. You should not desire to be with a man who treats you well while mistreating other women. That's not a brag. Instead, open yourself to men who consistently demonstrate respect towards women, who act as protectors to the women in his life and community, and show empathy and understanding in their interactions with others.

Stop Making Excuses for His Failure

Men will fail. That is not a bad thing. When you find yourself in a relationship with a man who is failing at a goal he has set in life, it is not your job to try and bail him out. Men are made stronger men during their times of adversity. Each time you bail a man out of a situation, you are robbing him of the chance to sharpen the tools he needs to succeed in life. This does not mean you should not be a supportive partner. This does not mean you cannot be a listening ear. This does not mean you cannot offer your perspective or give insight into a situation that you may be better at. This does not mean you should not carry your own weight with projects you two are working toward together.

It does mean, however, that you must be able to sit back and let that man "man". Let him use his brain and resources outside of you to work through his hardships. If you are in a relationship and your man loses his job, you need to sit back and continue living your life and working toward your goals. Stopping what you are doing to help him job hunt, submit resumes, buy him new suits, or simply decrease your household spending by 70 percent for things to be easy for him will rarely serve you or your family in the long run. Most importantly, it will hurt him the most. Now, if you or someone you know has bailed their man out time and time again and the man and family are now living their best lives, Great! Remember, I do not care about your unicorn, sis!

As a woman, you can be understanding in his hardships, especially because you will experience them as well, and as a couple, you can learn to work through certain things together. But if you find yourself in a situation where your partner is constantly pursuing bad situations because he knows you are going to always bail him out, you need to step back and relieve yourself of the responsibility to make sure he stays afloat.

If your man has fathered children before your relationship, and he has convinced you that he has no relationship with his children because of the child's mother, your job is not to go in and try to force him to be a better father. You must recognize something very quickly. If you choose to have a man in your life who is an absentee father to his children, and you have his child, you can easily find yourself in that same situation. Either be okay with that from the beginning or deny him access to you. Regardless, holding him accountable for the way his life is playing out is imperative.

Does this mean that men cannot grow beyond their past mistakes? No, it does not. But it does mean that they will not experience as much growth as necessary if you constantly try to be their mom, therapist, or get out of jail free card. Most of the issues that men have can be solved with the help of other men. If he has no role models or no male connections that can help redirect him or uplift him in low times, you must consider this fully.

Good men have
other good men
in their life to rely on.

As such, learn to stay in a woman's place and let that man man! What exactly is a woman's place? Well, it is the designated area for women to sit back and let men figure things out on their own or with other men. Why is this important?

Women have traditionally been socialized to accept the shortcomings of their partners and make excuses for them, despite having no responsibility for the situation at hand. This dynamic is not in the best interests of either party, as it fails to address the underlying issues and can undermine the trust between partners. Women should stop making excuses for their partners' failures, as it shields them from taking responsibility for their actions and perpetuates a cycle of negative behavior.

When women make excuses for their partners' failures, they are essentially ignoring the root cause of these issues. They may tell themselves that their partner was having a hard day, or that they did not mean to let them down, but this does not address the actual problem. If a partner consistently fails to meet expectations, it is important to talk about it directly, instead of glossing it over with an excuse.

Making excuses also reinforces blame-shifting in the relationship dynamic. Women might find themselves saying that their partners' mistake is really their fault, when in fact this is not the case. Blame-shifting creates an unhealthy power dynamic and can lead to bitterness and resentment, both of which are destructive to any kind of relationship.

By not making excuses for your partner's failures, you can help create an environment of accountability and responsibility in the relationship. This helps build trust, open lines of communication, and promote mutual respect.

> ❝ SEXINESS WEARS THIN AFTER
> A WHILE AND BEAUTY FADES,
> BUT TO BE MARRIED TO A MAN
> WHO MAKES YOU LAUGH
> EVERY DAY, AH, NOW THAT'S
> A REAL TREAT. ❞
>
> *- Joanne Woodward*

REDEFINE HIGH VALUE TRAITS

CHAPTER 22

WHAT MAKES A MAN TRULY VALUABLE? Is it the size of his bank account, the car he drives, or the job title he holds? Society often equates high value with high earning, leading many women to believe that a man's worth is synonymous with his wealth; however, I have turned down wealthy men who were low-value because money alone is never enough.

True value is not found in a man's wallet; it is found in his character. It is reflected in how he invests in himself, how he treats his family, and how he interacts with those who cannot offer him anything in return. It is about his authenticity, his bravery, his ability to communicate and comprehend effectively, and his sense of direction. It is about his emotional intelligence, his family orientation, his generosity, and his honesty.

In this chapter, we will delve into these high-value traits, providing you with a comprehensive guide to help you redefine what you should look for in a man. This list is not exhaustive, but it serves as a starting point to help you distinguish between superficial characteristics and true value.

An important thing to note is depending on the age of the man, there are practical expectations that you can have. For instance, if a man is in his mid-forties, he needs to have proven leadership in different areas of his life, especially if you are looking for him to be a leader in your home. His communication and comprehension skills should be high, and he should already be living purposefully. An older man should especially have higher emotional intelligence in comparison to a younger man, but young men should still be honest, useful, and well-balanced.

High-value men does not mean **old and decrepit.**

High-value men in their forties and fifties were often just as valuable in their twenties and thirties. Many relationship coaches caution younger women against dating their peers, suggesting that youth and high value are incompatible. While it is true that maturity often comes with age, it is a misconception to believe that younger men cannot also possess high value. If you are young and seeking a high-value man close to your age, rest assured, it is entirely possible.

A high-value man at twenty-five might still be in graduate school, perhaps with limited financial resources, but remember, it is his traits that matter most. Take stock of where you are in life and what you desire. If you are comfortable dating a high-value man who is just starting his journey, do not feel as though you are making a mistake. Do not let youth be a deterrent to recognizing good men. After all, age is just a number, and value is about character, not the number of years lived.

Upon reviewing the list, you will observe that none of the traits are tied to a man's physical appearance, level of formal education, height, skin color, or parental status. Why?

There is no specific **net worth** that a man must possess.

High-value traits delve deeper, enabling you to discern a person's true essence. The most significant factor determining a man's value is how he invests in himself, cares for his family, and treats those he perceives as unable to offer him any benefits.

As you craft your own list of desired traits, ensure you do not conflate preferences with high value. It is perfectly fine to prefer a man of a certain height, within a specific age range or income bracket, or one who has never been married or does not have children. However, these preferences do not dictate whether a man is of high value. They can, however, help you determine if a man is an ideal match for you. Now, let's explore the list. While it is not exhaustive, it can serve as a guide for traits you might want to consider:

◊ **Authentic** - High-value men are genuine, attracting the right women by being true to themselves.

◊ **Brave** - They have the courage to face uncertain and uncomfortable situations, crucial for building a family.

◊ **Communicates and Comprehends Effectively** - They can articulate their needs and understand yours, fostering healthy communication.

◊ **Direction** - They have a clear sense of direction, providing stability in their lives and relationships.

◊ **Emotionally Intelligent** - They can recognize, regulate, and interpret their own emotions and those of others, contributing to a healthier relationship.

◊ **Family-Oriented** - They prioritize family, preparing methodically for their future families.

◊ **Generous** - They are generous with their resources, including money, time, and affection, without jeopardizing their stability.

◊ **Honest** - They uphold their promises and align their actions with their words, fostering trust in the relationship.

◊ **Influential** - They positively impact those around them, demonstrating true leadership.

◊ **Joyful** - They find joy in life and share it with those around them, contributing to a positive relationship environment.

◊ **Kind** - They treat others with kindness and respect, reflecting their high value.

◊ **Loyal** - They are committed and faithful, providing security in a relationship.

◊ **Motivated** - They are self-driven, reducing the need for external motivation.

◊ **Nurturing** - They care for and support their partners, contributing to a loving relationship.

◊ **Open-Minded** - They are receptive to new ideas and perspectives, fostering growth in the relationship.

◊ **Patient** - They exhibit patience, essential for navigating the ups and downs of a relationship.

◊ **Quality Time** - They value and prioritize quality time with their partners, strengthening the bond.

◊ **Reliable** - They are dependable, providing security and trust in the relationship.

◊ **Self-Disciplined** - They have control over their actions and decisions, contributing to a balanced life.

◊ **Tolerant** - They respect differences and can cope with difficult situations, fostering harmony in the relationship.

◊ **Useful** - They serve a clear purpose in your life, providing practical tools and information.

◊ **Values-Driven** - They live according to their values, providing a strong foundation for their actions.

◊ **Wise** - They make decisions based on wisdom and understanding, contributing to a stable life.

◊ **Xenial** - They are hospitable and friendly, fostering positive interactions with others.

◊ **Yearning for Growth** - They have a desire for personal and professional growth, contributing to a fulfilling life.

◊ **Zealous** - They are passionate and enthusiastic, bringing energy and excitement to the relationship.

As we conclude this chapter, it is crucial to remember that the process of redefining high-value traits is a deeply personal and transformative process. It is about shifting your focus from the external to the internal, from the superficial to the substantial. It is about recognizing the value in authenticity, emotional intelligence, generosity, and other such traits that truly enrich a relationship. It is about understanding what truly matters to you in a partner and aligning these traits with your values and aspirations.

It would also be helpful for you to reflect on your past experiences, consider what you have learned, and use these insights to shape your definition of high-value traits. This process is not about conforming to societal expectations or norms, but about identifying what resonates with you on a personal level. As you move forward, prioritize these traits and let them guide you in your dating journey. Remember, you deserve a partner who is high-value in the truest sense, one who complements you and contributes to your growth and happiness.

ANCHOR YOUR REPUTATION

CHAPTER 23

IN THE ROLE OF A MARKET MAKER, you must never underestimate the power of your reputation. While some may argue that character holds greater importance, a tarnished reputation can hinder opportunities to demonstrate character. When I refer to reputation, I am focusing more on how others perceive you rather than the actions you have undertaken. Therefore, when getting to know a man, it is crucial to set the tone for how you should be treated by anchoring your reputation to positive past experiences.

But what does anchoring mean in this context? Anchoring is the process of establishing how you should be treated by associating your reputation with positive experiences from your past. This process communicates to others that you are accustomed to and deserving of the standard you have set for yourself. Anchoring can help a potential partner understand that you are high-value and should be treated as such. It also sets clear expectations for your behavior and treatment.

As a woman, you can hold yourself in high regard, exuding self-esteem and confidence, even bordering on arrogance. However, men are still men. Many have learned to gauge a woman's value based on how much he believes she was valued by her previous partners or how much he thinks she would be valued by the next man.

Men often use their male counterparts as benchmarks for how well they need to treat a woman. This is why they ask numerous questions at the beginning, such as:

"How many children do you have?"

"How many fathers do your children have?"

"Have you ever been married?"

"Why are you single?"

It's not that they inherently have something against dating women with children, wish you were an innocent virgin, or even care if you're a recent divorcee.These men are probing because they want to understand how well you have upheld your standards with the men who have had gained access to your life for a significant period. Sure, you will share your future expectations, but he is curious to see if your actions align with your words.

If you are the type of woman who forgives countless times when a man disrespects you, he will wonder if you are accustomed to being mistreated, neglected, or overlooked, and if you think it is reasonable to stay in a toxic relationship. He's interested in knowing how readily other men gained access to you, as he gauges his own worth by how easy or challenging it was for him to win you over compared to other men. He's particularly keen to know if you have committed to a man of low caliber who might become a burden to him in the future.

It is not necessarily because he intends to repeat the hurtful things done to you. Indeed, there are men who seek out the most vulnerable, unhealed women to inflict further harm. More often, it is because they want to feel they have chosen the best woman possible, and one of the determining factors is how other men perceive and treat you. This is crucial to them. Men genuinely care about other men's opinions of their woman.

So, how can you ensure from the start that he feels you are worth all that you expect from him?

You use another man's **validation to reinforce** your self-portrayal.

This might sound sexist, and it may even make you uncomfortable. But consider this: people generally prefer hearing praise about a person from someone else, rather than hearing that person self-praise without any external confirmation. With men, the more he believes another man has valued you, the more he will strive to do the same. He understands your standards. He knows what you are accustomed to. And he is going to make sure he surpasses your past experiences.

When you meet a new guy and you begin to talk about your past, you do not want to indulge into too much detail, whether good or bad. You want to always come across as a bit mysterious, giving him just enough information to want to keep getting to know you. But when the time comes where he asks about your past relationships, no matter how horrible, toxic, damaging, or unfulfilling it was, you do not need to overshare.

This man is not your therapist. He is not a neutral party, and he should not be listening to the worst things that have ever happened to you when you are getting to know each other. Many women find maintaining privacy to be difficult. They want to spend five hours on the phone or a date discussing all that has happened to them and why they all of a sudden realize they deserve better and now expect the new man to make up for everything the past men did to hurt them.

If you go to a job interview, you do not use that time to talk about why your last job was so horrible. Perhaps your co-workers treated

247

you poorly. Perhaps you were required to do mandatory overtime even though the overtime pay was less than the overtime fee for your childcare. Perhaps the work environment was toxic or limiting. All those things could be true, but when you go to the interview, your goal is to let them know your current skill level, express how you could be an asset to the company, and paint a clear picture of what your expectations are for your future growth, if offered the job.

With your relationship, this analogy applies. We will cover this more in later Chapter 25, but it is important to note that your reputation is what is going to secure the position. If you are repetitively making poor relationship choices, it is going to be difficult to develop the reputation you want no matter how you try and sell your story.

Instead of saying "I was in a toxic relationship, and he emotionally abused me, cheated on me, and spent all of my money," you can say things like "We spoke different love languages. No matter how hard we wanted to love and honor one another, we just could not make it work. We realized at some point that it was just better for us to move on so that we did not walk away jaded and unable to receive real love when the opportunity presented itself again."

This lets the man know that you are mature, levelheaded, and a woman who still believes in love. You do not come across as bitter, angry, or even the cause for the breakup. You give no indicators that you have willfully accepted mistreatment from a man, and you do not come across as if you lack accountability, blaming everything on the ex. You seem ready to move forward. You have done the work! And you have kept your reputation intact.

———————————◆———————————

> KNOWING YOUR AUDIENCE IS THE
> KEY TO EFFECTIVE COMMUNICATION
> AND UNDERSTANDING. TAKE THE
> TIME TO LEARN ABOUT THE PEOPLE
> YOU'RE TRYING TO REACH, AND
> YOU'LL BE ABLE TO CONNECT WITH
> THEM ON A DEEPER LEVEL.
>
> - Sheryl Sandberg

KNOW YOUR MARKET

CHAPTER 24

There is nothing more disheartening than being unrealistic about the type of men you can attract. If the men in your current dating pool are not providing the feedback you desire, you are either fishing in the wrong pond or you have not yet developed the qualities that captivate their attention and motivate them to commit. If no one is interested in what you are offering, it is time to reassess. This is a fundamental principle of "How to Sell 101". It does not suggest you lack value. It does not mean you must lower your standards or settle. And it certainly does not imply that no man wants you. All it reflects is a consensus of how the men you are currently interested in are perceiving you at this moment, and that is okay.

Your history of unsuccessful or toxic relationships does not bar you from entering a new healthy one; however, maintaining a successful, long-lasting relationship will be emblematic of your willingness to embark upon a journey of healing, self-discovery, and self-development in a manner that may be uncomfortable and laborious for you. Instead of shirking responsibility for your past relationship failures, losing hope in romantic love altogether, or subscribing to the defeatist dogma that *all men ain't shit*, you can embrace the power that you have, elevate your thinking, develop an edge, and cultivate a pool of qualified contenders of your love. So, do the work anyway.

In this chapter, we will discover methods of discerning what men want. When I ask women what they want from a man, it is typically a relationship that leads to marriage. Within that relationship, they describe the man as one who has a lot of money, demonstrates loyalty, protects, is attractive and above certain height, etc. When I ask women what they believe men who fit that description are requiring from a woman, their response quickly places them into one of four categories:

Category 1

Women in this category typically do not have an answer because they genuinely believe that men are averse to relationships or commitment, even if they found all the desired qualities in a woman. The issue here is that many men are entering relationships and marriages every day. While men are not a monolith, they all have specific criteria that, when met, will prompt them to commit to a woman. When these women accept that men might actually desire a relationship or marriage, they realize they simply do not know what those men require.

Category 2

Women in this category believe that men primarily want sex. The problem with this belief is that many women are already offering men what they think they want - sex - but are still not receiving the relationship they desire in return. It is clear that sex alone is not what ultimately leads to a relationship. When these women accept that sex is not the key to securing a relationship, they often remove it from the equation. This is not necessarily a bad thing. However, they are then left unsure of what to offer these men.

Category 3

Women in this category believe that men want too much. They argue that men are looking for a woman who will be submissive, cook, clean, act as their therapist, bail them out of hard times, provide mind-blowing sex, and tolerate their infidelity. The issue with this belief is that many women are already doing these things and are still not being chosen as wives. When women accept that perhaps these are not the qualities that would lead a man to propose, they struggle to think of anything else that a man would value. So, once again, they realize they have no clear understanding of what men truly want.

Category 4

Women in this category do not really care what a man wants because they believe that men generally do not know what they are looking for in a wife. Even if a man ends up with a woman who is entirely different from his initial preference, it is usually because he got to know her better over time, or he disregarded his list of preferences (often to his detriment) because he found a woman irresistibly attractive. The point is, whether a man's preference aligns with his most compatible match or not, it is not a reason to dismiss what he is saying.

Category 5

Women in this category believe that being a woman is more than enough for any man to feel honored to be in her presence. These women are arguably the most delusional because they are out of touch with reality. It is implausible that a man of even average quality would have no standards for the woman he would choose to marry.

Let's be honest here. Most women today could be married if they so desired. There are plenty of men out there who would be thrilled to take you off the market and proudly declare you as his wife to the world. However, the stark reality is this: the majority of those men are not the ones to whom you would willingly give your time and attention. Women are seeking the cream of the crop. Women want men who are desired by other women. Women generally do not want to 'date down,' and even if they momentarily settle for a man they perceive as beneath them, we all know how those relationships typically end. They want the most desirable men.

The only way to understand what these desirable men are looking for is to ask them directly and be prepared to accept their answer. If the majority of men who are tall, fit, attractive, intelligent, and without children (or at least without issues with their children's mothers) are telling you that they want a woman who is above average in conventional attractiveness, of a certain weight, with no children - then that is what they want.

If the majority of men are saying, "I would marry a woman who has a lot of her own money, but she would still need to figure out how to manage the house and children we have," then that is what they want. It does not matter how unfair that may sound. Just as you have your preferences, they are allowed to have theirs. I am not suggesting that these are the answers you will receive from them. I am simply advising you to listen to the feedback you receive from men and believe them when they express their preferences.

Are there exceptions to these rules? Always! While both men and women have their preferences about what they believe makes a person worthy of their hand in marriage, these preferences can change. Nonetheless, if you do not fit a man's initial preference, and he does not perceive what you have to offer as more valuable than his preference, he simply will not choose you.

Now, if you find yourself not aligning with a man's initial

252

preferences, and still believe you two mught be a good fit longterm, what do you do? First, remember that everyone is entitled to their preferences, just as you have yours. But here's the thing: you can't take your children and stick them back into your womb, nor should you want to. Your life experiences, choices, and even challenges have shaped the incredible woman you are today. So, what can you do?

Self-Reflection: Take a moment to evaluate yourself. Are there areas you genuinely want to improve for your own well-being and growth, not just to fit someone's preference? If so, work on those.

Expand Your Horizons: If one man's preferences don't align with who you are, remember there are countless others out there. Broaden your dating pool and be open to meeting different types of people.

Value Yourself: Understand your worth. Just because you don't fit one person's mold doesn't mean you won't be the perfect fit for someone else.

Communication: Engage in open conversations. Sometimes, understanding the reasons behind preferences can lead to deeper connections and changed minds.

Seek Compatibility: Instead of trying to fit into someone's checklist, look for someone whose values, goals, and life vision align with yours.

At the end of the day, it's essential to find someone who appreciates you for who you are, not just for how well you fit into a preconceived box. While preferences are valid, genuine connection and mutual respect are the cornerstones of lasting relationships. Don't settle for anything less.

Now, here is how you can learn about the desires of the men you want. First, you must know what spaces they commonly occupy. Ask yourself, where would these types of men be? What are some of the activities they may enjoy doing in their spare time? Are they frequently at these social events? Do they shop in certain stores? Are they in Sunday morning church services? Do they volunteer at certain charity events? Are they playing basketball at their local basketball court? Are they members of Delta Sky Club? Are they participating in trail rides? Do they wine down at bars in high end restaurants or are they more commonly found at local hookah lounges? Do they have online dating profiles? If so, which sites do they use? Are they members of certain Facebook groups? You have to do your research based upon your preferences to know where these men are.

Second, you must put yourself in their line of sight. This means, if you are not already regularly frequenting those same places, you need to intentionally place yourself there. Can you organically meet a man outside of those settings? Yes, you can. Will you increase the probability of meeting those men if you are in those settings? Absolutely. When you are a market maker, you are not allowing life to just happen to you. You are taking control of your life and giving yourself the best opportunity to gain the things that you want.

Third, you actually have to talk to them. When I say this, I do not mean that you must begin to heavily pursue them. The majority of men want to feel wanted by women, but they do not want a woman to chase them. It is a turn off. Fortunately for women, we do not have to seek out men in an aggressive way. There are ways that women can signal to men that they are interested. It could be as simple as liking a pic or commenting on a status. Believe me, even when women are not shooting their shots, a lot of men who are interested take that as an invitation to converse with you one-on-one. In person, it could be you simply introducing yourself and sparking up a small conversation. The majority of the time, you will not have to make the first move. But if this man does not see you or know you exist, you must make yourself known.

Before I go to step four, let me be very clear. If you are sharing the same spaces with these men and have sparked conversations, winked, or did something to place yourself in their line of sight, but they are not showing interest in you, you need to understand why. There are a few reasons why a man would not show romantic interest in you.

First, he is not physically attracted to you. Men are visual. If you are not what he is looking for physically, and he does not already know your personality, he is not going to try to pursue you. You must accept that. Second, the space where you both are may not appropriate for him to shoot his shot. If you are in a working environment with him, it may be difficult for him to open himself to the idea of dating you, depending on his or your position. Now, we all know about male bosses dating their secretaries. Yes, it happens. But there are definitely certain instances where a man would not feel comfortable pursuing a woman who shares his same workspace, especially with all of the policies that exist today that could be disadvantageous toward him. Lastly, he could already be taken and not looking for a new woman.

Fourth, get to know him. Whether you exchange numbers, go on a first date or find yourself in a group setting that allows you to ask certain questions without coming across as creepy, you want to learn what he is looking for. You can do this by asking specific questions. If you never allow a man to tell you exactly what he is looking for, you can only make assumptions.

Fifth, rinse and repeat these steps until you have talked to enough men to gain greater perspective on what those men are looking for. The answers will not be the same. Some will be vague. Some men will tell you they are not sure what they are looking for in a wife. Some will cut the conversation short. Some will exhaust you with details. Some will give you very concise answers that are easy to understand. And some might sound like they are talking in code. However, this is all a part of the process, and you are simply using these experiences to collect data on the type of men you are interested in.

Once you have a general idea of what these men are looking for, you can decide if you are the type of woman that would meet those requirements. If you know you are not and never aspire to be, you need to figure out a different type of man that would be suitable for you and start the process over. The type of men you may want is not always the type of men who will want you. If you are determined that you do not want to change your preferences, you need to create an edge that will allow you to be considered despite not being what they would initially look for. If they have a preference for the woman you are already planning to become, even better. You know that they are men that you would allow into your dating market, but you just need to continue taking the time to develop yourself in a way that makes those men attracted to you in the future. Then, that world is your oyster.

What you do not want to do once you find out what they are looking for is to become upset that you are not that woman. Do not try and convince a man that you should be his type. You do not need to use spells, magic, manipulation, or whatever else you can think of to alter his perception of you. You simply need to be acceptant of his preferences whether they are in favor of you or not, and you need to be realistic about whether you truly are the type of woman he would choose.

Knowing the mind of your market can save you a lot of time and heartache down the line. I do not care how beautiful, successful, or funny you are, you are not every man's type, and you should not be. There are many men who will want to have sex with you, who do not mind spending time with you in a situationship, or who believe you are good enough to be a placeholder while they look for the woman they truly want to be with. Do not fall victim to this. Once a man tells you exactly what he is looking for, and confirms that you are exactly that woman, yet he is not being intentional in his pursuit of marriage with you, you need to address it. Notice, I said address it and not immediately walk away. You cannot blame a man for not considering you for marriage if you have never told him that you are dating with the intent of marriage. There should be distinct signs in your relationship with him that you both are leading toward marriage with each other.

EXAMINE YOUR EDGE

CHAPTER 25

As a woman of multiple children, I used to struggle with owning my truth and seeing my value in the dating market. I felt like I could not compete with childless women who had preserved their wombs for the love of their life. It did not matter to me that all of my children came from my marriage. It did not matter that I had seemingly made good decisions that resulted in unfavorable results. It did not matter to me that I was young and ignorant to life when I decided to become a mother to three children in the same year. The only thing that was in the forefront of my mind was the fact that my children would be seen as baggage to any man I would encounter.

Although this was far from the truth, I believed this for years and suffered from that belief. Although I never lied to potential romantic partners about being a mother, I also did not take pride in it. I did not own my truth and I did not view the uniqueness of my story and life experiences as something to be praised. As embarrassing as it might sound, it took me hearing someone else repackage my story and frame it into a positive way for me to discover the beauty in my uniqueness. It is how I was able to examine my life and discover my edge and I want you to learn how to do the same.

First, what exactly is an edge? Your edge in the dating market refers to the unique characteristics or qualities that set you apart from others and make you more desirable or attractive to potential partners. It is a way of positioning yourself as an asset in the dating market, by highlighting your positive experiences and qualities. Developing an edge involves being mindful of your past experiences and how they have shaped you and your perception and using that understanding to present yourself in the most attractive way possible to potential partners.

Let's look at two ways that I can frame my motherhood story. Please note, this is my motherhood story, not my overall story.

Option 1

Hi, I am Shaw. I just got out of a relationship, and I am now a single mother of four children. I am not jaded and still believe in love, but I need to make sure that a man will accept me and all my children as well. I do not really have drama in my life with my ex, but he cheated on me, and I knew I deserved better, so I left him. My children are my world, and they will always come first. They are good kids, and I am not looking for a new daddy for them, just a positive male role model in my home if I were to ever marry again. I do not need a man to take care of me financially because my children and I want for nothing.

In this scenario, it seems like the things that I stated are all positive, but the truth is it does not separate me from any other single mother out there. My motherhood story sounds very generic: failed relationship, infidelity, single mother, independent. What about that will look or sound alluring to a man I would be interested in? How do any of the things I stated entice him to learn more about me? Where is my edge? Let me repackage my story and show you a better way to set yourself apart and become more appealing.

Option 2

Hi, I am Shaw. I am a mom of four children. I married my college sweetheart at a very young age, joined the military, birthed two children and adopted one child all in the same year. Life was seemingly great until things fell apart when I realized we did not share the same core values as each other. We tried therapy and a lot of other strategies to salvage our marriage because I believe marriage is worth fighting for, but I realized it just could not be saved. Even though we did not have a day-to-day toxic relationship, I realized it would not be fair to either of us to continue in a marriage where we were unequally yoked. I do not regret marrying him because I made the best decisions I could with the knowledge I had as a nineteen-year-old woman. Years passed and I struggled to find and accept myself as a single mother and entered a relationship that I should not have, which once again resulted in a marriage and a child. That relationship served as the catalyst for change in my life and has helped me to become the woman you are speaking with today.

Since then, I have world schooled my children in many countries, exposing them to new cultures, people, and concepts that have helped shape them into the beautiful souls they are. My oldest son has been featured in a kids magazine chronicling his globetrotting experience. My daughter became a number one best-selling author at the young age of eight and was featured on The Fox Morning News and many other major news outlets, Radio Disney, and a host of other talk shows and podcasts around America. My youngest son has now reentered the public school system and tested several grade levels above his peers. My baby girl is growing up bilingual, having spent most of her life living abroad.

Life is great and I am so proud to be their mother. If I ever partner with a man again, my goal is to be with someone who can add value to what I have already established and who has the space, capacity, and desire to welcome us into his already established life as well. Family is important to me and biology does not trump blood. Although I am not looking for a man to come and rescue me or my children, I am looking for a man with shared principles who is willing to use his resources to edify the family we create together because I am ready to do the same. Throughout my single years, my children have been fully prepared for me to remarry someday and are not resistant to the thought of me finding new love. So, I am now ready to explore.

In this scenario, I take my truths and package them in a way that is easily digestible, alluring, and most importantly, truthful. I take accountability for the things and experiences in my life that did not end up in my favor and I show exactly how I have overcome those situations. I then focus the majority of my attention on the accomplishments my children and I have experienced after my failed marriages and create an image in his mind of what life could look like if he decided to enter a marriage with me, from a motherhood perspective. This, sis, is how you develop an edge. No, you are not actively competing with other women, but you are aiming to show yourself in the best light possible.

Examining your edge is similar to you **creating a resume**.

This is why many people now see the importance of hiring a professional resume writer. Sometimes, it is not that you do not have what it takes to get hired for the company of your dreams; you simply do not know how to stand out from the crowd and garner the attention of hiring managers because you have failed to develop an edge. You have failed to fully recognize your unique value proposition, understand what it is they are looking for and how you can be the best fit for that role, and view the lessons and experiences that gave you the skills you have now as necessary and pivotal to your growth.

The example I gave is to show you how one aspect of your life can be packaged in two different ways that will garner two different results. However, you need to learn how to do this in every area of your life. It may be difficult initially to view certain parts of your story in a positive light, but with the will and the work, it is possible. You may need someone else to help you with this. You may even find it helpful to invest in a coach, a mentor, or a course. But regardless of your path to getting there, it is vital that you reach a place of security in who you are no matter what your past looks like.

Since developing my edge, my dating life has been great. Men who thought they would never date a woman with one, two, or three kids, have found themselves swooning over a woman with four. It is not because I have big tits and a small waist. You can find that aesthetic of a woman almost anywhere these days. It is because I have learned to own my truths, accept my past, and sell my story in a way that makes the men I am interested in dating head over heels for me. Not only does this benefit me, but it sets the tone for other single mothers to have the opportunity to date great men who may not have otherwise been given the chance, simply because they were a mother.

In their minds, they are thinking, "If Shaw can accomplish all of this with four children, and without a partner, what else can she do with a partner? Shaw knows exactly how to turn her tragedy into triumph, pivot when necessary, and maintain a positive outlook in life. This is the type of woman I want to partner with."

On the next page, I want you to take the time to develop your edge in the dating market. The key is to take any losses or teachable moments that have shaped you into becoming the woman you are and package it in a way that makes your ideal partner see you as an asset and not a liability. You may discover at this moment that you need more personal development. You may realize that what you have to offer right now is not what your ideal guy would be interested in no matter how you reframe the narrative of your life. And that is okay. It gives you the opportunity to be real with yourself. It allows you to see the areas you need to work on, and it helps you to find beauty in where you are currently in your life. It is impossible to become the woman you desire if you refuse to acknowledge, love, and take pride in the woman you are today.

Journal: Repacking Past Adversities

The Adversity

What is an unpleasant situation or adversity from your past that has significantly affected you?

What beliefs or assumptions did you form about yourself or your life as a result of this adversity?

The Impact

How has this adversity and the beliefs formed from it affected your self-perception, relationships, or life choices?

Can you identify any patterns or recurring themes in your life that may stem from this adversity?

The Repackaging

How can you reframe this adversity as a learning experience or a source of strength?

What positive qualities or skills have you developed as a result of overcoming this adversity?

The Future

How does this new narrative align with your future goals and the person you want to become?

What steps can you take to ensure this new narrative guides your future decisions and actions?

Part 5: A Moment to Reflect

As we conclude Part 5, let's take a moment to reflect on the key takeaways and engage in some introspective journaling. This will help consolidate your understanding and facilitate a deeper personal connection with the material.

Key Takeaways

1. Decentering Men: Recognizing the importance of not centering men in our lives is crucial for personal growth and healthier relationships. This involves focusing on our own needs and desires, rather than prioritizing the needs of men.

2. Redefining High-Value Traits: Understanding what truly constitutes high-value traits can lead to significant improvements in our relationships. It is about recognizing the qualities that truly matter in a partner, rather than focusing on superficial traits.

3. Anchoring Your Reputation: The way we present ourselves to the world can have a significant impact on our relationships. By anchoring our reputation, we can ensure that we are seen in a positive light and attract the right kind of partners.

4. Knowing Your Market: Understanding the dating market and knowing what we are looking for in a partner is crucial. This involves having a clear understanding of our values, needs, and desires.

5. Examining Your Edge: Recognizing our unique qualities and experiences can help us stand out in the dating market. It is about presenting ourselves in a way that highlights our positive experiences and qualities.

Journaling/Reflection Prompts:

Remember, the purpose of this section is not to impose a fixed narrative on your past adversities, but to empower you to reframe these experiences in a way that fuels your growth and resilience. Use these reflections to explore your past, understand its impact on your present, and shape your future.

Decentering Men: Reflect on any instances where you may have centered men in your life. How can you shift your focus to your own needs and desires?

Redefining High-Value Traits: Identify the traits that you truly value in a partner. How do these traits align with your values, needs, and desires?

Anchoring Your Reputation: How do you present yourself to the world? How can you anchor your reputation to ensure that you are seen in a positive light?

Knowing Your Market: Reflect on your understanding of the dating market. What are you looking for in a partner and how does this align with your values, needs, and desires?

Examining Your Edge: What are your unique qualities and experiences? How can these help you stand out in the dating market?

PART 6

MASTERING THE MARKET

Definitions from Shawdrism Language

af·fir·ma·tion \ ˌafər-ˈmā-shən *noun*

A positive statement or belief that compels the universe to grant your desires. Affirmations empower and inspire action toward achieving dreams.

dec·la·ra·tion \ ˌde-klə-ˈrā-shən *noun*

A powerful statement or principle that guides life, influencing decisions and shaping one's path. Disregarding declarations can lead to negative consequences and disrupt harmony.

hy·per·ga·my \ hī-ˈpər-gə-mē *noun*

The audacious action of leaving dusties right where they had you all the way f¥%ked up.

hy·po·ga·my \ hī-ˈpä-gə-mē *noun*

The bold act of choosing violence by settling for low-hanging fruit.

i·sog·a·my \ ī-ˈsä-gə-mē *noun*

The blissful luxury of basking in the afterglow of success.

se·duc·tion \ si-ˈdək-shən *noun*

The enchanting art of evoking strong emotional attraction in another person through slow, subtle actions that stimulate as many senses as possible

Part 6: Master the Market

The Market Maker Method™ Component 6: Mastery
6th Rule: Master the market.
Framework: The Market Mastery Model™

CONGRATULATIONS! You have reached the pinnacle of *The Market Maker's Method™*—mastering the market. It is a common misconception that mastering a skill takes ten thousand hours of practice, as popularized by Malcolm Gladwell's book, *Outliers*. While it is one of my favorite books ever, Gladwell failed to emphasize the impact of quality guidance and teaching in mastering a skill[9]. Your teacher can either shorten or lengthen your learning curve. While it *will* take time for you to synthesize all the information you are learning, it will not take forever as you are learning from the best!

In this final section, you will use *The Market Mastery Model™* to discover the key metrics for mastering your market through six key areas: setting your intentions, seducing the man of your choice, short-circuiting the dating process, seizing setbacks, shutting the door on past relationships and negative thoughts, and shooting your shot toward the men you desire.

Each chapter is crafted to provide you with the tools and knowledge needed to navigate through the journey of mastering your market and creating the life of abundance and romance you want. You will learn how to set clear intentions for the relationships you desire, take control of your dating process, and effectively handle setbacks and negative thoughts.

Remember, the true measure of success is not the hardship you face, but how you navigate through it. With the guidance provided in this section, you will have the tools and knowledge to master your market and create the life of abundance and romance you desire.

Before you Begin

Welcome to Part 6, the final stage of your transformative journey where you will learn to assertively navigate the dating world. This is not a quick fix, but a significant shift in your approach to dating that requires consistent effort and dedication.

To maximize the benefits of this section, I recommend the following steps:

1. Read each chapter slowly and thoroughly.
2. Pause and reflect on the information being presented.
3. Take note of any personal experiences or insights that come to mind.
4. Trust the process and be open to the transformation that is possible through this journey.

Part 6 is your final leap towards becoming an empowered and assertive Market Maker in the dating world. This section is not just about learning new concepts, but about embodying a mindset that allows you to confidently navigate your romantic life.

My goal for you is to use Part 6 as a catalyst for your transformation into a woman who knows her worth, understands her desires, and is not afraid to pursue them. So, as you embark on this section, remember to be patient with yourself, embrace the process, and prepare for the ultimate shift in your approach to dating.

Questions That Might Arise

What if I am not comfortable with making the first move?
It is natural to feel uncomfortable when stepping out of your comfort zone. Remember, this process is about personal growth and gaining confidence. Take your time, practice, and gradually you will become more comfortable with it.

What if I am struggling with handling setbacks in dating?
Setbacks are a part of the dating process. This section provides tools and strategies to help you effectively handle setbacks and negative thoughts. If necessary, consider seeking advice from a professional, such as a therapist or counselor.

What if I am not ready to shut the door on past relationships?
Closing the door on past relationships is a personal journey and it is okay to take your time. This section provides guidance on how to do it when you are ready.

What if I do not see immediate changes or progress?
Self-development is a journey, not a destination. Changes may not be immediate, but with consistent effort, you will notice progress over time. Celebrate small victories and be patient with yourself.

The Market Mastery Model^{TM}

Six Concepts that Empower Women to Assertively
Navigate the Dating World

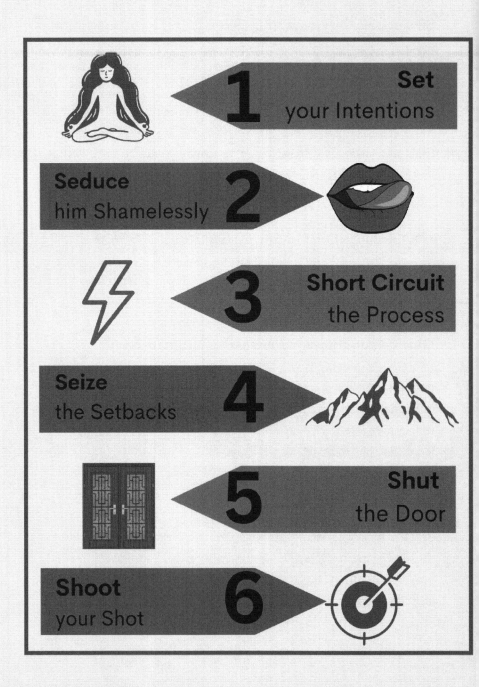

> **" YOU HAVE TO BE VERY, VERY CLEAR ABOUT WHAT IT IS YOU WANT TO ACCOMPLISH, AND YOU HAVE TO HAVE THE COURAGE OF YOUR CONVICTION. "**
>
> *—Mellody Hobson*

SET YOUR INTENTIONS

CHAPTER 26

AS I PROGRESSED IN MY ADULT LIFE, I became aware of a disparity between my active and passive vocabulary. Despite my frequent reading and diligent efforts to memorize new words, I found myself struggling with articulation in social settings. I could easily understand and participate in conversations but often found myself reflecting on how I could have better expressed my thoughts. This led to feelings of frustration and the belief that my speaking abilities did not align with my writing abilities, causing others to perceive my writing as inauthentic.

Through my research, I discovered that there was a simple explanation for my struggles with vocabulary retention. I found that the size of my active vocabulary was far greater than the size of my passive vocabulary. I learned that my passive vocabulary consisted of all the words I had been exposed to throughout my lifetime, which

I could understand in context but may struggle to define outside of it. My active vocabulary, on the other hand, were words that I could easily access in my mind and use in everyday conversation, as I fully understood their meaning without the need for context. With this newfound understanding, I was able to identify a clear path toward rectifying this issue and improving my verbal communication skills.

I also learned that I was able to write more efficiently than I spoke because I had far more time to process my thoughts. I also had the benefit of using thesauruses if I knew the word I had written was not exactly the word I was looking for. As we know, in spoken language, we do not have the option to do either of these things. Through further research, I found that the solution was to actively work on converting words from my passive vocabulary to my active vocabulary through the use of retention strategies and setting clear intentions. As a result, my verbal communication skills have greatly improved, leading to reduced anxiety in public speaking and increased confidence in everyday conversations. However, this is an ongoing journey, one that requires consistent effort to achieve mastery.

The process of converting passive vocabulary into active vocabulary is akin to the journey many individuals undertake to manifest their desires with greater ease. Though the path to accessing one's desires may seem arduous at first, with perseverance and determination, it need not remain so. The law of attraction, though often touted as a means to achieving success, may not always yield the desired results. Yet, it is not uncommon to find oneself pondering over the secret behind the ability of the highly successful to manifest their aspirations. It can seem as though they are part of an elite group privy to a code of silence, never revealing the keys to their success.

The truth is many successful individuals have mastered the art of manifestation through consistent and correct practice, allowing them to effortlessly manifest their desires. They figured out a way to close the gap between "I desire" and "I am". It is important to note, however, that manifestation does require a certain level of energy and focus, as we all have limited capacity. So, the more you practice, the better you become and the less effort required on your part.

My dating journey did not begin with ease and success. I did not always possess the self-assurance that allowed me to confidently hold out for the best partner. I did not always attract a plethora of high-quality men at such a rapid pace, which almost led me to believe that the majority of men I was meeting were unicorns. Yes, I have been there.

Dating has not always been a walk in the park for me. There have been moments of difficulty, frustration, and disappointment. As I allowed myself to engage in the dating process, reflect on my experiences, and actively choose to improve myself, the journey became increasingly smooth. It is not by luck or coincidence that I am where I am today. I do not have to possess the most striking features, hold the highest degree, or always be in agreement with men. Instead, my unwavering commitment to self-improvement and becoming the best version of myself has set me apart and brought me success in my dating life.

One of the key practices that I embraced in my journey toward success was that of consistent and deliberate manifestation. Having been exposed to the principles of faith and positive thinking from an early age, I had a foundational understanding of the power of manifesting one's desires. However, it was not until I began to actively and intentionally practice manifestation techniques that I truly began to see the benefits manifest in my life. Through regular exercises and a commitment to manifesting the best version of myself, I was able to attract the things and experiences I desired with greater ease and frequency.

Dating on your own terms may not always be a simple task to undertake. However, through purposeful exercises, you can become a market maker who has a plethora of potential partners at your disposal. In this chapter, we will delve into three exercises that will assist you in setting your intentions for the relationship of your choosing. Many individuals believe that they must wait an extended time to attain the things they desire, due to past experiences or lack thereof. They fail to comprehend that every word spoken throughout one's life has already been brought into existence, and their sole responsibility is to maneuver themselves from their present state to the manifestation of their desires.

When I decided to increase my active vocabulary, I did not close my eyes, wish for it, and watch my vocabulary increase by a thousand words overnight. Instead, I set my intentions which oriented my journey and informed me on the direction and action I needed to take to ensure my desire became a reality. I methodically shortened the gap between my starting point and my desired outcome.

The following three writing prompts will help you manifest the relationship you desire, assisting you to set your intentions and take the steps necessary to lead you to the relationship you have already spoken into existence. Desire is not enough. Once you have done these things, you will no longer stress about whether a man is the right one for you or not. You will no longer worry if you will ever meet your ideal guy.

Instead, you will close the gap between, "**I desire**" and "**I am**".

Personal Declaration

In the introduction of this book, I encouraged you to recite a declaration that would assist you in your market maker journey. I have noticed over the years with the women I have worked with, many of them believe that a declaration is the same as an affirmation. Because of this, I'd like to discuss the difference between the two before prompting you to create your own.

An affirmation is a tactic used to trick the universe into giving you what you desire. It can be powerful when used repetitively and followed by gratitude. Basically, you are stating things that have not fully come into fruition as if they already have, and then truly being grateful for those things. The subconscious mind cannot tell the difference between what is in reality or not, which means that you can state an affirmation, evoke massive feelings of gratitude, and attract those very things into your life more easily. Affirmations are a part of positive thinking and have no negative consequences attached to them if you miss your morning affirmation routine or if the things you are looking to manifest into your life have not happened yet.

A declaration is quite different. It is an order or principle that must be obeyed. Declarations are used to separate you from those very things that do not and will never serve you. It is meant to influence your decisions and act as a guiding principle for your life. But here is the kicker. Declarations are a part of our decision-making process and bear negative consequences when you do not adhere to what you have declared, whether immediate or in the distant future.

So why would a person choose to use declarations over affirmations? Well, they should not choose between the two because both are useful. We need something to lift us (affirmations), and we need something to ground us (declarations). Repeatedly affirming that you are a millionaire despite having $32 in your bank account is just as important as consistently declaring to honor your body. Affirming the love you have for yourself is important just as declaring to honor your intuition.

Now that you understand the difference between the two, take the time to develop your own set of affirmations and declarations that you will find useful for yourself through the lens of romantic relationships. Be sure to show gratitude with your affirmations and commitment toward your declarations. These are meant to be stated at least once a day so that you can take control of the things you want to manifest into your life as well as be reminded of who you are and what you will accept.

Possible Affirmations	
I am ...	
I have ...	
I feel ...	
I know ...	
Today is ...	
My husband is ...	
My partner is ...	
My life is ...	
My children are ...	
I love ...	

Possible Declarations	
I believe ...	
I speak ...	
I have ...	
I honor ...	
I adopt ...	
I accept ...	
I welcome ...	
I give myself ...	
My actions ...	
My thoughts ...	

Ideal Partner Generator

In earlier chapters, you learned how to separate men you would be interested in from men you would never give the time of day. To take it a step further, a helpful exercise that you can do is create a brief statement that will describe the man that you are looking for. You can use this as a reference over time to decide if the man you are interested in dating is indeed ideal for you. I attempted to do this in the past, and while my intentions were good, I did not take into account a few things. I will show you what my ideal partner statement was before, walk you through the reasons why it was not the best, and give you the steps to create an ideal partner statement for yourself.

"The man I would be interested in dating would totally prefer women who maintain high financial standards for their partner. He did not work as hard as he did to level up his life to be with a woman who does not understand the importance and value of having a man who can financially provide for her and their family without needing to rely on her income. He does not work against the divine feminine and masculine and is looking for a woman who enjoys being taken care of despite that she has also secured her own bag and is highly capable of taking great care of herself. This man understands he has great character, but he knows character alone does not pay bills. It is an absolute turn off for him to hear a woman say she does not want a lot from a guy because he wants to be wanted by her in many ways. He knows what he is looking for and is not willing to settle for a woman who accepts coffee dates from him or any other man. He is a high-value man waiting to connect with a woman who is equally high value."

This was nothing short of a disaster. First, including information about what you do not want for yourself or what you do not want him to be like is counterproductive. My statement included so many things that I did not want him to be and if I am regularly reciting this and putting this out into the universe, that is exactly the things that I will attract. Your focus should only be on what it is that you desire.

Second, the entire statement was talking about one topic, *money*. On the surface, it appears to be well thought out. However, the statement was extremely one dimensional and does not truly represent the totality of my desires. Your statement should be balanced and comprehensive.

Third, it is helpful to incorporate the five W's and H in your statement: who, what, when, where, why, and how.

Who	Who is he at his core? (values, beliefs, principles)
What	What benefits is he looking for?
When	When is a good time for you to meet?
Where	Where do you see the relationship taking you?
Why	Why would he choose you specifically?
How	How will he know you are the one?
WE	Final WE statement.

Now, let's put this all together:

My ideal partner is/believes/values **blank**. He is looking for/to **blank**. He will choose me because **blank**. I will choose him because **blank**. After/During/Before/When **blank**, we will cross paths. We are meant to be together because of **blank**. Our relationship will assist us in **blank**. We **blank**.

Here is an example: My ideal partner is highly attracted to my mind, body, and spirit. He is looking for a wife who shares his same core values of loyalty, honesty, and empathy. He feels honored to be my man because of the respect I show him as well as myself and he deliberately loves me through difficult times. He knew I was the one when he realized my vision for my future aligned with his and quickly chose me after picturing what his life would look like without me. I chose him because of his instinctive nature to protect, ability and willingness to provide, and his past performance of working well under pressure. We crossed paths after we both did the necessary work to heal our past traumas and make space for each other. For us, it is not about perfection, but progress, and because of that, we are truly winning.

Vows

Another great exercise you can do when preparing yourself for the possibility of newfound, romantic love is to write your wedding vows to your future husband. However, an even more powerful exercise would be for you to write vows to your present self. Both exercises are helpful, but doing them in the wrong order and without having done the work in your personal life is a sure way to set yourself up for failure.

A few years ago, I decided that it was time for me to open myself to romantic love again. I was not even in the dating market, but I took time to envision what I would say to him on our wedding day. Below I am going to share with you what those vows said. I want you to understand why I wrote them and why they were absolute trash. Let's check them out on the next page and discuss how you can engage in this exercise in a healthier way.

My Vows to my Husband

◊ I promise to love you with conditions and hold you accountable when you are struggling to remain faithful to your word in any area of your life.
◊ I promise to give you all the space you need to surprise me throughout the week with your modest monetary displays of affection.
◊ I promise to leave at the first sign of abuse (not harm).
◊ I promise to be direct, in control of my emotions, and logical when engaging in difficult situations.
◊ I promise to be a great friend so long as you clearly reciprocate.
◊ I promise to always encourage mentorship, counsel, and outside professional advice for the both of us.
◊ I promise to never allow you to think I would not walk away.
◊ I promise I will love you, challenge you, sex you down real good, and give you kisses in the rain.
◊ I promise to be all in, unless your actions show you are out.
◊ I promise to never allow you to be less than the man or father figure you can be while simultaneously being my husband. This is my vow!

My intention was good. However, I was writing from a place of brokenness, trauma, and fear. Each vow was a reactionary response to things I had dealt with in previous relationships that I never wanted to happen again, but saying these vows would have never prevented me from experiencing these same issues. I had not done the necessary work to speak from a place of healing, wholeness, and love. So, I want to help you first create your vows to yourself, then help you create your vows to your ideal partner. Your vows are a representation of the things you deeply desire for yourself and your partner.

Journal: Writing Your Vows

To Yourself

What are three promises you can make to yourself?

How will those promises serve you and the relationship?

To Your Husband

What are three promises you can make to your husband?

How will those promises serve him and the relationship?

SEDUCE HIM SHAMELESSLY

CHAPTER 27

I AM SURE MANY OF YOU WERE worried that we made it to the end of this book without talking about the art of seduction. Do not worry, sis. I got you! Seducing a man is one of the most powerful things a woman can do, and when done to the wrong man or at the wrong time, you could potentially create a disastrous situation for yourself. So, an important topic we will discuss using *The Market Mastery Model*™ is the art of seduction, a key area a woman should master when she is in the dating market. The most important thing to know about the art of seduction is this:

Seduction is always slow,
often subtle,
and stimulates all five senses.

In this chapter, we will explore exactly how we can use this art to our advantage by focusing on the speed in which we do things, the subtleness of our actions, and strategies to stimulate all five of his senses. It gets a little risqué, but I guarantee you this; when you master seduction and apply it to the correct person during the appropriate times, you will be saying "yes" to your last first date sooner than you know it.

But first, I want to be sure you understand the difference between being sexual and being seductive. Whereas sex is the physical expression of connectedness and desire, seduction is the evocation of strong emotional attraction. Thus, seduction could, but does not always lead to sex, and sex does not require seduction, but can be greatly enhanced by it.

Seduction Stimulates All Five Senses

Stimulating his five senses is the easiest way to make sure you leave him wanting more. It is been said that our eyes are by far the most important organs of sense as we receive up to 80 percent of all impressions through sight. Next comes hearing, touch, smell, and taste, respectively. We will discuss each sense according to its importance.

Sight: Your appearance is the first thing a man will notice. This is everything from your attire, physique, and the way you style your hair, to your nail color choice, smile, and the eyeshadow above your eyes. Yes, men notice these seemingly small things. Therefore, ensuring that you are detail oriented in your overall aesthetics is extremely important when it comes to seducing a man on sight. Beyond your aesthetics, it also includes your body movements, posture, and even your energy. So, desiring a man to disregard 80 percent of his impressions of you to get to know you for who you are on the inside is counterintuitive to who he is as a human. When you first make your presence known to your potential suitor, know that 80 percent of the work is already done just by focusing on sight.

Hearing: Second on the list is sound. When you are seducing a man using sound, you want to speak in your lower register when possible. The sultrier the voice, the more seductive you become. Speaking in a cadence, deeping your tone, whispering certain sounds, and extending the length of your words will stimulate him in a way that he was not even ready for. Of course, we all have unique voices. So, the goal is not to speak like another woman, but to strategically utilize your own voice to captivate your audience. In addition to the sound of your voice, the choices of your words are also vital. You want to be able to communicate with him in a way that makes him feel like you want him, without having to say those words, especially in the beginning stage.

Touch: Seducing a man through touch is one of my favorite things to do. But beware, this can stimulate you just as easily as it does him. Touch is the first sense to develop, and it is crucial to feel a sense of connection to other people and things around us. Physical touch is so powerful that it can reduce a person's blood pressure as well as their heart rate. So, you can imagine how little effort it really takes to seduce a man using touch alone.

Now, of course there are levels to touching. When you are just getting to know a potential suitor, your goal should not be to physically rock his world in the bedroom. However, you can still stimulate him with a handshake, hug, or kiss on the cheek. You can also touch his chest, his biceps, beard, or even his knee if you are sitting next to each other. One of my favorite things to do is to lean in closely and whisper sweet nothings into his ear, so close that he can feel the vibrations of the sound of my voice. My body gently connects with his as my hands smoothly glide over his chest and shoulders. All of this to tell him something as simple as, "Soon." Men love this.

Something even more incredible to note is this. You do not even have to physically touch him to seduce him through touch. You can merely touch yourself and drive him wild. Of course, as your relationship elevates, so does your physical touch. But touching yourself seductively can send the most vivid imaginations through his mind even when the only thing you actually did was stroke your neck downward.

Smell: The ability to seduce through smell is powerful and is both a short-term and long-term play. A pleasing scent can captivate a man's attention and can also leave a lasting impression, even when you are no longer around. This is because odors are closely related to emotion and memory. If a distinct scent can trigger a childhood memory or emotion, it can surely trigger recent experiences as well. This is why you want to be sure you are intentionally incorporating smell in your seductive ways.

Your natural body scent in conjunction with whatever perfumes, lotions, and oils you adorn yourself with can be quite alluring for a man. If you have yet to discover your signature fragrance, or better yet, your fragrance for the season, make a mental note to test out a few to see which compliments your natural scent best. Not every fragrance is for every woman. You want your scent to be memorable, but not overbearing, wearing just enough to make an impression. Men always love a good smelling woman. And I must add, your breath and hair are just as important. So be sure that your overall hygiene is on point.

Taste: I know you might be asking how it is possible to seduce a man through taste, especially when you are first getting to know him. And the truth is there are very few times you will be able to do this if you are first meeting a potential suitor. It is okay; you have so many opportunities with the other four senses. However, if you find yourself in a situation where finger food or appetizers are being served, you can always feed him a small taste of what is available. And of course, as you dive deeper into the relationship, you can allow him to eat off your body in whatever way you both are comfortable with.

Seduction Is Always Slow

An important aspect of mastering the art of seduction is learning how to pace yourself. Seductive women walk slower. They speak slower. They respond slower. They kiss slower. And most importantly, they move more slowly in their relationships. I know some of these things may sound like they are arbitrarily done, but they are not.

Imagine rushing into a room of potential suitors, speaking at a fast pace, answering every question hastily, and demanding a man to enter an exclusive relationship with you after one week of interacting with each other. It sounds ridiculous, but this is how many men view women who have not mastered the art of seduction. When you move too fast, you appear anxious, easy, and desperate, as if your only goal in life is to get a man.

Now, imagine entering a room full of potential suitors. You stand near the doorway and pause, while slowly gazing from side to side to get a better view of those standing before you. You stride slowly from the door to an area far enough away to garner as much attention as possible without you needing to say one word or dress provocatively.

A handsome man walks up to you and asks for your name. Before you reply, you slowly look at him from head to toe, then back up to his eyes, give a slight smile, and slowly state your name. The two of you have a full conversation, and instead of you answering every question like you are trying to get as many words in as possible before he gets away, you balance the cadence of your responses, speaking at a normal tempo at times, and noticeably slower when you want him to hang onto your words.

You both show genuine interest in one another, and he asks for your number. Instead of quickly telling him, you pause again and respond with something clever like "Feeling daring tonight, I see … I can give you my number, but you may just fall in love." It sounds corny, and truthfully, it is. But believe me, when you make him wait a little longer and speak a little slower, while ensuring you are being perceived as confident instead of coy, you will indeed create a lasting impression and make him want to get to know you even more.

This is a simple idea of what it looks like to use seduction with a stranger. It is so powerful that it did not require any physical touches. There was no kissing (or even hugging in this instance) involved, no sexual conversation in any way, and no need to drop something in front of him to show him what you are working with. Yet, you have aroused his emotions. You have managed to permeate his thoughts so that when you walk away, you are all that he will be able to think about. After doing this, I can assure you that a coffee date will be the furthest thing from this man's mind.

Seduction Is Often Subtle

Seduction may have a lot to do with speed, but it definitely does not end there. Subtleness is also important. Your goal is to layer your efforts on top of each other to create the most seductive experience for the man of your choosing. Do not worry, this is just as much for you as it is him. Watching a man become putty in your hands is incredibly satisfying to say the least. So, using the above scenario, let's explore how you can incorporate subtleness to your seductiveness.

After making it to your chosen destination in the room and giving yourself time to absorb what is going on around you, you decide that you are ready to shoot your shot. Instead of walking over to him (you could if you desire), you could wait until the two of you connect eyes, softly smile, wink, then turn away slightly, glancing every so often to confirm your interest. If a man is interested in you after noticing you, believe me, he is definitely going to approach you after you do this, if he has not done so already.

While you are conversing, make sure you are not being so serious the entire time. Otherwise, you could appear disinterested, pretentious, or like you are trying to play hard to get. A way you could do this is by being playful throughout your interactions with him. No, this does not mean pulling out all your funniest jokes (unless comedy is truly an authentic part of your personality) or propositioning him to a drinking match.

Let's say he asks you the infamous question, "What do you do for a living?" You can respond with something like "What do I do for a living? I am sorry, but it is not polite to talk about sex in the first conversation," or "I give murderers alibis. The best part, most of my work is from repeat customers," or "I scam banks and other large institutions. Do not worry. I have only been to prison twice." Okay. Okay. Perhaps none of those are actually suitable responses. But being appropriately funny can be seductive to a man. Being able to effortlessly put a smile on his face will cause him to lower his guards, become more comfortable, and desire more time with you in the future.

It could be as simple as asking a man, "Have you chosen the numbers?" After he inquires about what you are asking, you respond with something similar to, "You have manifested the woman of your dreams. If you are not already a betting man, I'd imagine tonight would be the exception." Again, another corny line. However, it is simple and cute enough to make a man smile without doing or saying the absolute most. You're subtly implanting the idea in his mind that you are the physical manifestation of his dreams. Even if he cannot remember your exact words the next day, the inception of his desire to make you his has been subconsciously ingrained in the deepest parts of his mind.

Earlier, we spoke about taking pauses in between your statements, but when you are seducing a man, you do not always need to do so using words. Your body language is just as important, if not more. Depending on your comfort level, you could gently caress your neck, softly bite your lip, or rub his chest as if he has a piece of lint on it. Subtle movements and gestures will pull him deeper into the moment without you needing to physically decrease the space between the two of you.

If that is outside of your comfort level initially, you could simply smile with your eyes, laugh at his jokes, or even touch his hand. The key thing to note here is that you do not need to make big gestures, cause a scene, or give him everything you have got to woo him. Just know that subtleness goes a long way.

The examples I have given to seduce men were mostly appropriate for the meeting phase because I did not want this chapter to turn the entire book into an erotica. However, knowing how to seduce men shamelessly is important at every level of courtship, from the first interaction (as long as it is not in a professional or inappropriate setting), throughout the duration of your courtship and beyond. As your relationship progresses, so would the manner in which you seduce him.

Furthermore, the importance of seduction goes beyond stealing the attention of a man or sexually arousing him. You can also use your seductiveness to relieve your partner's stress, reduce tension within the home, or entice your man to give you exactly what your heart desires. When you are seductive, you are able to make him feel like he is the one with the ideas to do the things you want because you have planted the perfect seeds at the most opportune times. You have targeted each of his five senses, subtly and slowly, and although he is fully satisfied, you have left him wanting more each and every time.

> "TO SHORTEN THE PROCESS OF TRANSFORMATION, IT IS ESSENTIAL TO BE CONSISTENT AND TO TAKE ACTION EVERY DAY."
>
> —Marie Forleo

SHORT CIRCUIT YOUR PROCESS

CHAPTER 28

HYPERGAMY AND HYPOGAMY ARE TWO TERMS that have been gaining popularity in the level-up social circles for women, both on and offline. *Hypergamy* is the act of marrying or dating someone who is a member of a higher social or socioeconomic class. Conversely, *hypogamy* is the act of marrying or dating someone who is a member of a lower social or socioeconomic class. Simply put, hypergamy means marrying or dating up while hypogamy is marrying or dating down.

A less common term used in these social circles that is equally important is *isogamy*, which is the act of marrying or dating someone who is a member of the same social or socioeconomic status as you. This simply means you are dating someone at your current level. In this chapter, we will focus on the benefits of becoming a hypergamous woman in order to short circuit your journey to becoming a market maker, explore the disadvantages of entering hypogamous relationships, and learn if isogamous relationships are right for you.

There are many benefits of practicing hypergamy. When people think of a woman entering a hypergamous relationship, they typically consider the most common one, which is to reap financially. While this is extremely important, it is surely not the only benefit there is, and it is definitely not the only one that should be considered. This type of relationship can serve you in multiple ways and if you choose not to explore the many ways possible, you are doing yourself and your future a great disservice.

Hypergamy Benefits

The purpose of a woman entering a hypergamous relationship is to elevate herself from her current social or socioeconomic class to a higher one to create better opportunities for herself and children than those originally afforded to her. This does not mean every woman should begin pursuing relationships with billionaires or multimillionaires. The richest, most powerful men are not always the most ideal candidates for you depending on your current circumstances and future goals.

In America, there are four classes: upper, middle, working, and lower. You would technically be practicing hypergamy if you are from and still a member of the lower class and you date or marry someone from the working class. This one step up would render you many benefits if you are strategic with it. Furthermore, the likelihood of you being born into a working-class family and having the innate ability to successfully navigate upper-class circles is low. You have to truly work to feel like you belong.

This is not about classism or elitism either. I can guarantee you a third-generation upper class woman would have a difficult time navigating common lower-class situations and circles just the same. Therefore, it behooves you to understand that if you jump classes unprepared, it could potentially cause other issues. This is why you need to level up regularly.

It is NOT to get a man.
It is to feel comfortable in the spaces
YOU want to occupy.

Consequently, the most strategic way to successfully increase your socioeconomic or social status through hypergamy is to pursue relationships with men who are one step above your class until you are comfortable dating higher.

This does not mean you are selling yourself short. It is being calculated in your movements, as there is no such thing as only being able to change your socioeconomic or social class once.

The practice of hypergamy is believed to have originally started in India where a very defined caste system existed. From an evolutionary-psychology perspective, women began having higher expectations for the men they chose to mate with after realizing the men were not sticking around after birth to ensure the well-being of the child and the mother. Women learned quickly that their initial investment into parenthood came at a greater cost than the men they would mate with, so they began to look for men who had the will and capability to make the greatest investments into their child and themselves long term.

Also, women in early American history did not have the advantages that we have today, where we are able to become educated and earn a livable wage on our own merits. Marriage, for many women in the past, was often the only way to guarantee that her status and finances in life would improve if she was born into poverty. The woman's future literally depended upon whether her father could find a suitor from a higher socioeconomic status than his. Or else, she would die with the same amount of wealth as she had been born into, if not less.

Today, in America at least, this is clearly not the case. Women have the freedom to find their own partners, date multiple men before marrying, and elevate themselves financially and socially through many different avenues, such as education, entrepreneurship, investing, and so many more. Practicing hypergamy today does not hold all the same implications as it once did for women, but there are still many reasons for a woman to intentionally practice it.

There are many studies that show the latest trends of women now becoming more educated than her male counterparts. A lot of marriages today consist of men being less formally educated than their brides. It is now more likely for a woman to practice educational hypogamy in her relationships. But here's the thing. Despite this new trend of women dominating in academia, their male counterparts still out earn them collectively. So, how is it that while women are now more educated in America than men, they are still earning less?

We could discuss this comprehensively, but I'll focus on the wage gap that yet exists between gender in the workforce. This is one of the main reasons it is still beneficial for women to practice hypergamy. Until the wage gap closes and unless a person's education level can directly correlate to their earnings, regardless of gender or race, women will always have a reason to intentionally date and marry up.

Practicing hypergamy can short-circuit your journey of dating on your own terms because it can alleviate some of the apprehensiveness in choosing a partner who is incapable of financially supporting you and your children while you nurture your skills to fulfill your purpose. When you are open to dating a man regardless of his financial status, you have more considerations to make:

1. Does he have the earning potential he claims?

2. How long will it take for him to earn more?

3. Will he expect me to contribute 50/50 until he is able to support the family completely on his own?

4. If I have a child with him, will we take a financial hit that is difficult to recover from

When you choose to only date men with a higher income than you, you simply must consider whether he is generous with his resources and wise in his investments.

Also, hypergamous dating instantly places you in a network of higher-earning individuals. If your relationship with your higher-earning partner does not work, and you have intentionally created relationships within those circles, it is much easier for you to have other equally qualified suitors. This may seem treacherous, but it is not. Again, people tend to date within their same social circles or tax bracket because the access is much easier and the probability of your lifestyle standards being similar are much higher.

Suited for Isogamy

What happens if you choose not to practice hypergamy? Does this mean you are now doomed to a life of loneliness, heartache, and poverty? Will you have no other options of leveling up in life, both socially and financially? Is this indicative of low self-esteem? Of course not!

While I am a strong advocate for women making a conscious decision to practice hypergamy, I understand that not every woman will or even needs to. Some women excel in life and relationships dating at the level in which they currently are. But even still, this option is just not conducive to everyone. I know on the surface it appears to be a safe option for women, considering it is not dating down, but it is much more complicated than that. Hence, our goal for this section—to understand what kind of woman actually is suited for isogamy.

In the past, I believed every woman needed to practice hypergamy. I did not consider how unrealistic that was and I failed to take into account the woman's current status and personal objectives.

This all changed for me one day when I was having a conversation with a woman on social media who shared many different views from me. She made a statement that stood out the most in my mind: "I can afford to sleep with whoever I want because I have money."

At the time, I could not look past her situation, which I will not go into detail about, to realize there was some truth to it. Albeit money alone is not enough. But that conversation quickly created curiosity in my mind. I began to wonder if there were ever good reasons for a woman to not practice hypergamy, and if so, under what circumstances would they apply?

We have discussed several benefits that a woman receives when dating up, but if we are being honest, there are some women who simply do not need those same financial securities that other women are looking for. If a woman has already amassed a level of wealth that would afford her, as well as her current or future children, the lifestyle that she desires for them, she does not have to limit herself to choosing a partner based upon how well he can elevate her life financially. She has the luxury of prioritizing nonfinancial preferences over financial considerations for her potential suitors. Remember *The Poor Tax* vs *The Rich Reward*?

If their relationship ends, she does not have to worry about whether she will be financially destitute. If she bears his children and they divorce, she does not have to rely on the consistency or amount of his financial child support to continue living a life of financial abundance. She can afford to hire help for her children, her home, and her businesses. She has the funds to pay for therapy to heal, vacations to rejuvenate, top-tier education for her children, and her philanthropic ambitions. She is truly financially solvent and has the option and power to find use in men in less conspicuous ways than most. Women with wealth are most suited for isogamy if they so choose.

> COWS RUN AWAY FROM THE
> STORM WHILE THE BUFFALO
> CHARGES TOWARD IT — AND GETS
> THROUGH IT QUICKER. WHENEVER
> I'M CONFRONTED WITH A TOUGH
> CHALLENGE, I DO NOT PROLONG
> THE TORMENT, I BECOME THE
> BUFFALO.
> — *Wilma Mankiller*

SEIZE
THE SETBACK
CHAPTER 29

AS I WATCHED A DOCUMENTARY about a professional mountain climber and his novice son, I was struck by the realization that the road to the summit is never a straight line. The documentary detailed the equipment and strategies used by the climbers, as well as the physical and mental challenges they faced. It was then that I truly understood the adage that the journey to the top is filled with obstacles and difficulties.

One aspect of mountain climbing that stood out to me was the process of acclimatization. According to *The Wilderness Medicine Society*, it is recommended for climbers to take a night to acclimate for every one thousand feet gained above ten thousand feet, and an additional rest day for every three thousand feet gained.[10] This process, known as climbing high and sleeping low, is crucial for success as it allows the body to adapt to the thinning air and lack of oxygen at higher altitudes.

As I delved deeper into my research on mountain climbing, I realized that the process of climbing a mountain can be used as a metaphor to many aspects of life. Just like a mountain climber must climb high and descend to acclimate, we too must be intentional in our journey to success. We must be willing to take risks, face challenges, and push ourselves to new heights. We must also be willing to take a step back, rest, and regroup before pushing on to the summit. The more intentional and strategic we are in our journey, the greater our chances of achieving our goals.

This was the most profound lesson I learned from the show. The climbers were not judging their success by how fast they reached the summit, nor were they being forced by anyone to go back down the mountain after climbing so high. Instead, they were methodical in their steps, intentionally climbing high and sleeping low to ensure that they were as prepared as possible to continue their journey and to preserve their greatest asset: themselves. Because the truth is, being reactionary could cost them their lives in certain instances. Therefore, they took an offensive climbing approach to increase the probability of their success.

When I began trading in the forex market, I was reminded of this lesson—mountain climbers methodically climbing high and sleeping low to ensure that they were as prepared as possible for their journey. Whenever you open any chart, you will always notice that the price never only moves in one direction. No matter whether the market is trending upward or downward, it is always making short moves in the opposite direction. This is not done by happenstance. The forex market is the largest market that exists, and it moves over seven trillion dollars a day. Because the market makers are moving so much money at a time, they intentionally drive the market in the opposite direction to receive more favorable entries and to assist them in reaching their overall targets.

Seize the Setback

To clarify, if the market makers want to move the market higher, instead of continuously entering "buy" positions to raise the price, they will reach a certain price point, enter a "sell" position to lower the value, then proceed to buy again. They are not doing this without reason. Every decision the market makers make is done so intentionally. When they make these short-term moves in the opposite direction the market is trending in, they are doing so to create protection for themselves. In forex, this term is called "mitigation."

When retail traders enter a position and lose that trade, oftentimes they become disheartened. They believe that the market is playing tricks on them, and they did not execute their trade properly. They become dismayed and end up making an unnecessarily unfavorable decision afterwards. Instead of looking at the loss they took optimistically, they see it as a sign that they have failed once again. But the truth is the first entry in every trade is designed to give you feedback. They did not simply lose their money to the market. Instead, they paid the market for more information to enter a more highly probable trade the next time around. However, without knowing how to take control of their trading, they saw no benefits of their losing trades.

From the examples of mountain climbing and the forex market, I realized that there are two types of people in this world: those who take a proactive or offensive approach in life and those who take a reactive or defensive approach. Whether you are climbing a mountain or the corporate ladder, navigating the forex market or the dating market, the concept remains the same.

At twenty-four years old, my monthly income was around $8,700 dollars. I just knew that I was on my way to earning more. However, it did not happen that way. Over the next three years, I lost over 60 percent of my monthly income. I did not know exactly what I was going to do, but after quitting my last job, I promised myself to never work harder on someone else's dream than I did my own. As you can imagine, this came with a price, but no matter how difficult things became, I never stopped believing that I was on the right path. I never pitied myself, justified my poor decisions, or blamed myself for things that were outside of my control. I understood that I was simply paying the price for the life I was going to experience in the future.

When it comes to dating, your market maker's journey is trending upward, and just as you intentionally climb high, so should you intentionally sleep low. Each time you raise your price, you must be sure that the last price paid created a solid barrier of entry that will protect you when moving higher. Your path to the top will never be a straight line. This does not mean you are doing something wrong. It simply means that you are preparing yourself for greater heights.

You are positioning yourself for the best this life has to offer. Stop feeling defeated in every setback you experience. Instead, seize the setbacks and use them as ways to protect yourself and propel yourself to higher heights.

The Market Maker Method™ is strategically designed for winners. Once you reach mastery level, you will understand that there are decisions you will make that many other women will not. You will sacrifice temporary comfort for long-term companionship. You will learn that your mind is more powerful than you ever imagined, and you will appreciate the dark times as much as the light. You will welcome difficult times because you know that better times are ahead. You will show gratitude for the men who were not right for you, making it easier to recognize and appreciate the man who is.

Seize the setback, prepare for the setup, and never sacrifice your future by settling for today.

◆

SHUT THE DOOR

CHAPTER 30

WHENEVER I HEAR A WOMAN TRY to convince others that all her exes still want her, I instantly know that she is either delusional or stagnant in life. I am certain that most of my exes do not want me. Do they know that I am an amazing woman? YES! Will they sometimes miss what we had? Maybe, maybe not! But are they aware that we are not a good fit despite what we thought we had in the past? YES! As you level up in your journey, you will not continue to grant access to the same types of men, and you definitely should not be familiar enough with the ones from your past to even know that they miss you in that way, even if you have children with them.

The more you come back to reality and get to know who you are and what is required of you to fulfill your purpose, the more you will realize that not everybody wants you back. And that is a good thing. I will be damned if I ever brag about how all my exes still want me like

I have not experienced a level of growth that will make the majority of them experience discomfort while in my presence. You do not need your exes to miss you to validate your dating market value.

You are not one to be missed!
However, you will always be the one that is remembered!

While it may initially hurt to accept that your options in dating have reduced, it is actually the most positive awakening you can have when desiring a relationship. Instead of being disillusioned into thinking that every man out there would love to wife you, you will become fully aware that most men would not consider you for marriage. That is not a bad thing. Because it is that very knowledge and acceptance that will allow you to no longer place yourself in positions to feel undervalued, undesirable, or unloved. You are no longer in the business of convincing men that you should be valuable to them. Relationships should be beneficial to both parties, and each party should feel and believe that they are winning.

If a man does not habitually find value in the things that you have to offer but chooses to enter a relationship with you, he will always struggle to treat you as if you are valuable to him. I see it all the time. So many ladies are settling for crumbs. They are settling in their marriages. They are settling in their friendships. They are settling in their finances. They are settling in their goals. They are settling in almost every facet of their life. They are settling for any man that would pick them. When that happens, they are essentially sacrificing the greatest version of themselves and forfeiting their ability to achieve their fullest potential.

You must always remember that having no partner is better than having one that will take from your legacy. So, I am here to tell you this today. You do not get what you desire. You do not get what you dream about. And you most certainly do not get what you deserve.

You get what you accept,
settle for,
and believe to be true.

If you believe the only men that will marry you are subpar to what you truly desire, get ready to be a settling wife with a subpar life.

Besides, getting a man to marry you is not difficult. It is not a flex. They are not this scarce commodity. Many men do want to marry even if they do not want to do right within that marriage. They are not dumb. They see the benefits of having a wife, and they simply try to see how little they can offer while receiving the most as possible.

Shut the door to men that are not good for you, do not want you, and would never claim you or build anything for you or themselves. Shut the door to past or present relationships that have damaged you, stagnated you, or positioned you to live a life of mediocrity. Shut the door to the people who were familiar with the unrefined version of yourself but refuse to accept and acknowledge the new and cultivated woman you are becoming. Shut the door to the opinions of others whose life experiences are not what you would choose for yourself. And shut the door to pipe dreams, potential in others, limiting beliefs, and all the things that do not serve you.

When you do this, you will not always be supported. You will not always be liked. You will not always be understood. You will not always be praised. You will not always be recognized. You will not always be what other people want you to be. And that is okay.

You are not obligated to remain open, trying to fix what has been irreparably broken. You are not required to give second, third, and tenth chances. You are not bound to remain the same person you were ten years ago, six months ago, or even yesterday. You are not responsible for anyone else's happiness but your own, and you will never be able to experience all that this life has to offer if you continue prioritizing other people's desires for you above your desires for yourself. We are all living on borrowed time. The more time you use on the wrong men, the less time you have to cultivate what is within you.

To drive the point home, let's take a look at human conception. Female babies are born with all the eggs they will ever have during their lifetime. Every egg inside of a woman has existed within her before she was ever conceived. More specifically, each person living today was carried not just in the wombs of their mothers, but their grandmothers as well.

As a woman ages, the quantity of her eggs is reduced. Once she has reached a menopausal state where she no longer has the ability to release eggs, even though they still exist within her, it is extremely unlikely for her to get pregnant naturally [11]. While it is not impossible for a healthy child to be born to an older woman, the odds of giving birth naturally are less in her favor if that is her goal.

Age is not only a factor for women who desire to create a child, but it is also a factor for men. The quality of the sperm is highly important to the conception of a healthy child, and it can be impacted by medical issues, environmental factors, as well as lifestyle choices[12]. Obesity, erectile dysfunction, exposure to radiation, alcoholism, and drug use are examples of this.

A woman's eggs can be high in quantity and quality but may never get the opportunity to be fertilized if her partner is experiencing male infertility.

Human conception is symbolic of the process we all go through when we are trying to fulfill our purpose in life. Our seeds were not created after our birth. Instead, we were born with a purpose and that purpose existed generations before we were ever born. The longer we wait to try and cultivate that purpose, the more difficult it becomes to fully complete what we were called to do and the less time we have to enjoy the fruits of our labor. Who we choose to partner with can have a grave effect on whether our seeds will ever amount to anything more than a dream.

This is why when you are dating, you must be able to recognize men who come bearing no fruit. No amount of love, sex, or devotion can change him. There is no way to guilt trip, manipulate, or force a man into being who you need him to be to get what you want out of life. He has to already possess within him the ability and commitment to create a life of abundance and the will to do so with you.

When you see that this is not the case, gather your things and walk away. Do not give your best years to someone who is not only incapable and unwilling to support you on your journey but who is also delaying your development. Shutting the door is a very critical component of the mastery phase of *The Market Mastery Model*™. You can set your intentions properly, seduce a man day and night, practice hypergamy, and sleep low all you want; but if you continue to grant access to men who mean you know good, your seeds will forever exist within a state of gestation, and you will die unable to give birth to your purpose. So shut the damn door, sis, and focus on yourself.

SHOOT YOUR SHOT

CHAPTER 31

IN OUR FINAL CHAPTER, WE DELVE into the final step of mastering the market: *Shoot Your Shot*. This principle is all about taking control of your dating life and going after exactly what you want. By now, you have learned to set your intentions, seduce the right man shamelessly, short-circuited your dating process, seize your setbacks, and shut the door on the things that do not serve you. The last skill you need to master is initiating the first move without letting the fear of rejection or awkwardness hold you back.

Making the first move is not about being aggressive or pushy, it is about being confident in your own worth and knowing that you deserve to have the things you desire. In this chapter, we will discuss the best ways to initiate contact with a potential partner, how to gauge their interest, and the best timing to take the next step. Knowing how and when to shoot your shot is a tell-tale sign that you have mastered the market and are dating on your own terms.

We will also cover common misconceptions and self-sabotaging behaviors that women often engage in when it comes to making the first move. From overthinking to fearing rejection, we will explore the reasons why women hold back and how to overcome these obstacles. By the end of this chapter, you will have the tools and confidence to make the first move with ease and grace and attract the right partner for you.

I know what you might be thinking: "But sis, what if he is not interested? What if I get rejected?" Let me tell you, rejection is not the end of the world. In fact, it is just a part of the dating process. If a man is not interested in you, it is not always because of something you did or did not do. Sometimes, he is just not interested. And, that is okay. While it is possible that a man may express his interest first, you do not have to wait for him to make the first move. This is where the art of 'shooting your shot' comes into play. By taking the initiative, you can actively participate in your dating life, express your interest, and potentially open the door to a new romantic opportunity.

Now, I am not talking about sliding into someone's DMs with a creepy pickup line. I am talking about being confident and assertive in expressing your interest. Shooting your shot is all about knowing when and how to make the first move. Before you do, it is important to make sure you are shooting at the right target. In chapter 24, we discussed the importance of knowing your market and identifying your ideal partner. Now it is time to put that knowledge to use. Think of it like you are playing darts. You can have the perfect aim and throw with precision, but if you are aiming at the wrong board, it does not matter. The same goes for dating. You can have all the confidence in the world to make the first move, but if you are not making it toward the right person, it is a wasted effort. So, before you shoot your shot, make sure you have got your sights set on the right target.

Knowing when to make the first move is just as important as knowing who to make it toward. Timing is everything, and it is crucial to read the signs and understand the situation before making your move. Are they single and available? Are they showing interest in you? Are they in a place in their life where they are open to a new relationship? These are all factors to consider before taking the plunge. Do not let fear hold you back. Remember, you are a market maker now, and that means you have the power to create opportunities for yourself. When the time is right, do not be afraid to shoot your shot. It might just be the bullseye you have been aiming for.

I know you might be thinking, "But what if I come across as desperate?" Sis, society has conditioned us to believe that suffering in silence is better than speaking up for our truth. Being assertive, confident, and showing genuine interest in someone is not desperate, it is attractive. Men appreciate a woman who knows what she wants and is not afraid to go after it. In fact, it would be more desperate to just wait around and accept any kind of man that shows interest.

Shooting your shot is about being deliberate in the choices you give yourself and the people you open up to. Your ideal partner is out there, and they will appreciate and respect you for being assertive and confident in your approach. Do not let society's narrow-minded views hold you back from getting what you truly want and deserve. Remember, mastery of the market means being in control of your own choices and taking the necessary steps to manifest the life and love that you desire. Shoot your shot, sis, and aim for the bullseye.

Now that you have mastered the art of shooting your shot, it is vital to remember that there are many different ways to make the first move. While seduction and flirting are certainly powerful tools in your arsenal, they are not the only options available to you. Now, let's explore some other strategies for making the first move in a subtle and confident manner.

One strategy to consider is using body language to signal your interest. This can include things like maintaining eye contact, smiling, and mirroring the other person's body language. By making small, subtle gestures that indicate you are interested, you can make it clear that you are open to a connection without being too forward or aggressive.

Another strategy to consider is initiating conversation. This can be as simple as striking up a conversation with someone you are interested in, or it can involve more subtle tactics like dropping a comment or question into an existing conversation. The key is to make it clear that you are interested in getting to know the other person without being overly pushy or aggressive.

Finally, consider becoming magnetically attractive. This means that you work on yourself, focus on positive thinking, develop good personal hygiene, and be good at your own life. By becoming the best version of yourself, you will naturally connect with like-minded people. It will almost feel like the work is done for you because you are so magnetically attractive.

There is no one right way to make the first move. Different people and situations will require different strategies. The key is to be confident, be yourself, and be open to new experiences. And remember, if you are struggling with any of these strategies, do not hesitate to revisit the chapter on seduction and flirting for more tips and advice.

On the next page, I have listed a few examples of what to do and what not to do when it comes to shooting your shot:

What to Do
Walking up to a guy at a bar and striking up a conversation with him. You're showing interest in a subtle and confident way, and you are leaving the ball in his court to take the conversation further or not.
Sending a flirty text to a guy you have been talking to. You're expressing your interest in a low-pressure way, and you are giving him the opportunity to respond or not.
Using body language to show a guy you are interested. This can include things like making eye contact, smiling, and touching your hair. These subtle cues can be a great way to show a guy you are interested without feeling too aggressive.

What NOT to Do
Stalking a guy on social media and sending him a message every day. This is not only creepy but also it will make you look desperate and might push him away.
Sending a guy a message that is too explicit or forward. Even if you are confident in your sexuality, it is important to remember that not everyone is comfortable with the same level of forwardness, and you do not want to make someone feel uncomfortable.
Waiting outside of a guy's work or home to talk to him. This is not only creepy but also it is not cool, and it might get you in trouble with the law.

As you can see, shooting your shot is not about being desperate, it is about being deliberate in the choices you give yourself and the people you open up to. So, take the time to practice these strategies, and do not be afraid to share your experiences and successes with other women. Remember, the goal is not just to land a date but to land the love of your life. So, go out there and shoot your shot, sis! It is time to land your bullseye.

A Moment to Reflect

As we conclude Part 6, let's take a moment to reflect on the key takeaways and engage in some introspective journaling. This will help consolidate your understanding and facilitate a deeper personal connection with the material.

Key Takeaways

1. Setting Your Intentions: Understanding the importance of setting clear intentions in your dating life can lead to more fulfilling relationships.

2. Mastering Seduction: Learning the art of seduction can empower you to attract the man of your choice.

3. Short-Circuiting the Dating Process: Gaining control over your dating process can lead to more efficient and successful dating experiences.

4. Seizing Setbacks: Learning to effectively handle setbacks can strengthen your resilience and improve your overall dating experience.

5. Shutting the Door on the Past: Closing the door on past relationships and negative thoughts can free you to fully engage in the present and future.

6. Shooting Your Shot: Taking the initiative to approach the men you desire can empower you to take control of your dating life.

Journaling/Reflection Prompts :

Remember, the purpose of this section is to empower you to take control of your dating life and to navigate the dating market with newfound assertiveness and self-assuredness. Use these reflections to explore your current approach, understand its impact on your dating experiences, and shape your future dating life.

1. Setting Intentions and Taking Initiative: Reflect on your intentions in your dating life. What are your desires and how can you set clear intentions to achieve them? How comfortable are you with taking the initiative in your dating life, and what steps can you take to become more assertive in approaching the men you desire?

2. Mastering Seduction and the Dating Process: How comfortable are you with the art of seduction? What steps can you take to improve your skills in this area? Additionally, consider how you can take more control over your dating process to make your experiences more efficient and successful.

3. Handling Setbacks: Reflect on a recent setback in your dating life. How did you handle it and what can you do differently next time? How can you use setbacks as opportunities for growth and resilience in your dating journey?

4. Closing the Door on the Past: Are there any past relationships or negative thoughts that you need to let go of? How can you start the process of closing the door on these to fully engage in the present and future?

CONCLUSION

MY FINAL
THOUGHTS

I remember filling out my online profile on a popular dating app over ten years ago. One of the sections required the users to state their ideal first date. At the time, I was a personal trainer in Los Angeles and hiked at least twice a week for pleasure. No matter how often I asked my previous partner if he would accompany me on my hikes or participate in my community-based fitness boot camps, he refused. So, to avoid finding myself in the same situation, I put on my dating profile that my ideal first date was to go hiking.

I matched with this amazing guy, a United States Army Veteran who currently worked in the Department of Veteran Affairs with a decent salary. He requested to take me to one of the most popular hiking trails in the city, and I could not have been more excited. Do not worry. It was in no way isolated or dangerous.

We met up in the parking lot, and he pulled out a host of new hiking equipment he believed could benefit the both of us. He had extra gloves, water bottles, light weights, and other things I cannot fully remember. I did not expect him to come with anything more than what he needed, so I was pleasantly surprised.

We put on our gear and enjoyed two hours in the blazing sun. We talked endlessly, laughed at ridiculous jokes until we cried, and stopped several times to see if we could still do proper pushups and sit-ups despite us both reaching muscle failure. And the best part of all? No matter where we were on the trail, my view was perfect because the man looked like he had come straight out of a magazine. I mean, we were in Los Angeles! I had a fantastic time.

After we returned to the parking lot, he looked at me and asked if I enjoyed myself enough to allow him to take me on a proper date—one that did not consist of us walking around half-naked and sweating profusely. I agreed, went home, got ready, and met at a nice restaurant for an even better time. I am not sure how we found more things to discuss, but it was by far one of my favorite first dates ever.

This story has always been an important one for me to tell because, on the surface, it goes against everything most people assume *Say No To Coffee Dates* is all about. But it is a prime example that every person is different. There is no universal "right" first date for every woman. It is also a reminder that whatever you desire, you can put into the universe and receive just that. I learned in a previous relationship that I did not want to be in another relationship with someone who did not value their health as much as I valued mine or who never took the time to exercise on their own or with me.

This did not mean that my potential partners needed to be gym heads or prep every meal they ate. It did not mean that I needed them to accompany me in all my crazy outdoor pursuits. But it did mean that we needed to share a similar interest in regular exercise—or at the very least, hiking!

Dating on your own terms will allow you to enjoy the experiences you value the most in your current season or stage. Hiking was free. It would have cost my date absolutely nothing but his time, which is the one thing he could not get back. He put forth an effort to show me that he was willing to invest more than just his time by purchasing new gear for both of us. Working out with a person who equally enjoyed it as much as I did was exactly what I wanted, and all that I needed to realize was that I could beg the wrong man for the simplest things for years, and I'd never receive it. Or I could make an odd request to the right guy, and he'd go beyond what was expected.

People have tried to say that he got over on me. But the truth is when you date on your own terms, you get to choose precisely what you want. After this date, I gained a newfound confidence that allowed me to state my desires to my potential suitors boldly. As a result, I have gone on dates that looked very different from the one described above, but they were all ideal at the time.

Subsequently, throughout my dating journey, I have encountered a diverse range of men, each with their own unique characteristics and experiences.

One man I dated was a successful sales executive, making substantial deals and earning large sums of money through his work with political party-affiliated companies. Though he was successful in his career, his personality was undesirable, and our relationship was short-lived.

Another man I encountered was a socially awkward yet brilliant individual who worked in artificial intelligence and helped prevent child exploitation. Our conversations were enlightening and opened my mind to new possibilities.

I also had the opportunity to date a man who had built a successful company through innovative financial strategies despite having the least technical skill set among the team he built, and he shared his valuable insights with me.

Additionally, I met a man who was a great communicator and provided valuable feedback on my goals and aspirations, despite coming from a wealthy background.

Lastly, I had a brief experience with a man who became financially successful at a young age. He taught me ways to get myself in rooms that would benefit me despite my inexperience or lack of expertise. However, he lacked moral integrity, and we parted ways.

These experiences provided valuable lessons and helped me grow as a person. The diversity of my dating experiences reflected the individuality of the men I encountered. Not all of them had a favorable outcome, yet I always approached each encounter proactively, allowing myself to extract value from each person and experience.

You see, the goal of The Market Maker MethodTM does not focus on obtaining a proposal from every man you date; instead, it emphasizes the significance of maintaining a positive attitude and resilience when courtships do not culminate in a fairy-tale ending.

You must have the belief, foresight, and mental fortitude to remain confident that your dating method is still leading you down your chosen path. You must also be willing to take the time to cultivate what you desire. It likely will not happen overnight, but it does not require years upon years once you have decided that you truly are ready to enter that long-term relationship. The only difference between the women who will become successful market makers and those who will not is their commitment to stay the course no matter what.

Before reading this book, you may have expected to learn about superficial aspects such as fashion, social venues, hairstyles, and tactics to appeal to men. However, it is now clear that these elements are not as significant as understanding one's own identity, embracing authenticity, and creating a path of the least resistance in your dating life.

Say No to Coffee Dates is not just a catchphrase; it is an expression representing the glory of your becoming, intended to illuminate the connectedness between your dating decisions and the life you intend to live. We understand that our future is partly dictated by the decisions we make from our choices. However, our egos are stroked with the idea that it takes nothing outside of ourselves to create the most amazing life possible.

Theorists have even debated for years whether we are products of nurture or nature. But as of recently, the findings have become clear. Your future is an amalgamation of who you are internally and the environment in which you exist. And contrary to popular belief, your environment is not a collection of places. Instead, it is an aggregation of people you hold space for. Thus, who you choose to spend most of your time with today, grossly impacts who you become tomorrow.

Your decision to invest time, energy, and effort into your romantic pursuits is a significant one and should not be trivialized or dismissed. Deeply ingrained in our humanity is the desire for connection and companionship, and the pursuit of a suitable partner is a fundamental aspect of human nature. To deny or belittle this desire is to ignore a fundamental aspect of our humanity. Choosing a partner is one of the most consequential choices we make in our lives, and it is vital to approach it with the same level of care and consideration as we would any other important decision. Consequently, embracing and prioritizing our romantic aspirations rather than feeling ashamed or dismissive of them is essential.

As a progressive woman, I almost hesitated to put pen to paper and write this book. I did not want others to perceive me as undermining women's progress in any way, and I fully acknowledge that there are many pressing issues that women are currently facing, many of which are of paramount importance. Say No to Coffee Dates is about more than simply selecting the person with whom a woman will share her time and body. It is about strategically preparing for the future and harnessing our innate desire for connection and reproduction to attain a life of abundance through the path of least resistance.

To truly reach the pinnacle of success in your romantic pursuits, it is essential to shed any limiting beliefs holding you back. One common misconception is that high-quality men are scarce, leading to competition and conflict among women vying for the same limited pool of potential partners. However, this is not the case. High-value men come in all shapes, sizes, and backgrounds, and it is crucial to have the self-awareness to recognize the type of man who aligns with your values and aspirations. By shedding these false beliefs and elevating your self-awareness, you can effortlessly attract and secure the type of partner who complements you, leading to a fulfilling and abundant life.

Becoming a market maker allows you to filter out men who are incompatible with you and fortifies your intolerance of those who offer low-effort dates. You now understand why men who are looking for quality over quantity would never ask you out for coffee. While it does not reflect their inherent value as a human, it does call into question their perceived value as a partner.

Let's face it. Men care about how women perceive them, who they believe are out of their league. They want to put their best foot forward if they are highly interested in a woman because they see the value in getting to know her. They do not want to appear broke or broken. If he truly is looking for substance, he is not going to waste his time offering a coffee date because he knows that the cheapest investments rarely yield the most favorable returns. And, just like you, he is not in the business of seeking out those unicorns which do. He'd prefer not to cheapen his experiences out of fear that they may not result in the outcome he sought. If the woman is not worth the risk, he does not invest any part of himself.

He knows what his offering is, trusts his discernment, and knows that a woman of a high caliber will find value in their time spent with one another, regardless of the outcome. Thus, he permits himself to respectfully walk away from any table where mutual respect is not on the menu, which is the sole reason he would believe that his time, money, and energy was wasted. He is a winner, a doer, and reserves no time for coffee dates to get to know a woman who could someday be his wife.

So, market maker, it is up to you. Making excuses for why coffee dates are acceptable, more accessible, or preferred is a thing of the past. Leave it there and elevate your thinking. Now is the time to harness whatever mental fortitude you need to walk away when the situation requires so you can stop making fear-based decisions to accept pre-dates from men over coffee.

You **do not need an excuse**
to leave the table, Sis.
Your self-respect is all that is required!

◆

GLOSSARY OF TERMS

Definitions from Shawdrism Languages

a woman's market - A dating market where women set the rules and the closing bell never rings.

a woman's place - The designated area for women to sit back, relax, and let men figure things out on their own or with the help of other men; a place where women thrive by letting the man 'MAN'.

affirmation - A positive statement or belief that compels the universe to grant your desires. Affirmations empower and inspire action toward achieving dreams.

anchoring - the process of establishing how you should be treated by associating your reputation with positive experiences from your past

authenticity - The ability to be who the hell you are while evolving into who the hell you want to be.

barriers of entry - The velvet ropes and bouncers of your dating sphere, keeping the undesirables at bay.

confluence - A harmonic convergence of internal and external metrics signaling when to enter or exit a relationship.

declaration - A powerful statement or principle that guides life, influencing decisions and shaping one's path. Disregarding declarations can lead to negative consequences and disrupt harmony.

decenter men - The liberating act of shifting the focus from pleasing men to prioritizing oneself; a radical reorientation towards self-love and empowerment.

dusty - a man who is broke and delusional with nothing to offer but audacity

edge - The unique blend of characteristics and qualities that set a woman apart, making her irresistibly attractive and intriguing in her own distinct way.

entry signal - The green light in your dating traffic system, indicating when it is safe to proceed into a romantic relationship.

exit strategy - Your pre-planned escape route from a relationship, designed to minimize collateral damage.

feminine energy - The nurturing force that births creation, honors intuition, and gracefully navigates life's winding paths.

glass ceiling - Invisible barriers in your relationship that only become apparent once you have bumped your head a few times.

habits - the defining factors of your future

high value traits - The golden threads woven into one's character that elevate their worth beyond the superficial, radiating an irresistible allure that is more than just skin deep.

hypergamy - The audacious action of leaving dusties right where they had you all the way f¥%ked up.

hypogamy - The bold act of choosing violence by settling for low-hanging fruit.

isogamy - The blissful luxury of basking in the afterglow of success.

intuition - That gut feeling that whispers the truth even when logic is still fumbling for the light switch.

invalidation point - The final straw that breaks the camel's back, prompting you to hit the eject button; your relationship's stop loss.

logic - The mental compass guiding decisions, built on the foundation of past knowledge and experience.

low-hanging fruit - a man who is for everybody; easy to get, harder to return and usually has very little to lose

manipulation - the art of lying to a man in order to enter a relationship you do not actually want; a short-sighted tactic for a long-term goal

market maker - A woman who sets her own dating rules, creating an exclusive market tailored to her needs.

masculine energy - The driving force that constructs, employs logic, and moves unswervingly along life's linear path.

peen - another word for "penis" used on social media to avoid being flagged for inappropriate language.

pick-me - a woman who is willing to sacrifice herself to win the approval of or receive validation from a man

pragmatist pick-me - a woman who, driven by a belief in practicality, tolerates men's undesirable behaviors, including infidelity, as a trade-off for preserving family cohesion and financial stability

pretty privilege - The golden ticket in the lottery of patriarchy, granting unearned perks to those who fit society's beauty standards.

representative pick-me - a woman who manipulates her own identity, either consciously or unconsciously, to align with her partner's desires, often sacrificing her authenticity for the sake of securing a relationship

rules of engagement - The relationship Geneva Conventions, outlining how conflicts will be handled in your romantic interactions.

seduction - The enchanting art of evoking strong emotional attraction in another person through slow, subtle actions that stimulate as many senses as possible

self-awareness - knowing who the hell you are, never will be, and ain't never been

self-selected woman - noun A woman who is a mastermind of her own life, opportunistic in her dating approach, and the heroin of her own story; the inverse of a pick- me woman

shadow - half of who you are and everything you do not want to be, the repressed side of the beautiful you!

The Poor Tax - the hidden costs women must pay when they are pursuing relationships while insolvent

The Rich Reward - the benefits and incentives that wealthy women receive when they are dating; a powerful advantage in the dating market

TROMP - An acronym for Top-tier Rotation of Marriageable Prospects; the crème de la crème of your dating options.

W2W convo - (Woman to Woman) A bad decision; the result of displaced fault from the culprit to a contender.

warrior pick-me - a woman who, driven by a sense of competition or submission, tolerates and endures unhealthy relationship dynamics, often sacrificing her own needs and self-respect, to maintain her status as "chosen"

wealth - passport to freedom

E N D N O T E S

Chapter 7:

1   Postmus, J. L., Plummer, S. B., McMahon, S., Murshid, N. S., & Kim, M. S. (2012). Understanding Economic Abuse in the Lives of Survivors. Journal of Interpersonal Violence, 27(3), 411–430. https://doi.org/10.1177/0886260511421669

2   Piquero, A. R., Riddell, J. R., Bishopp, S. A., Narvey, C., Reid, J. A., & Piquero, N. L. (2020). Staying Home, Staying Safe? A Short-Term Analysis of COVID-19 on Dallas Domestic Violence. American Journal of Criminal Justice, 45(4), 601-635. https://doi.org/10.1007/s12103-020-09531-7

Chapter 9: Busting the Myth of Virginity

3   Bellis MA, Hughes K, Hughes S, Ashton JR. Measuring paternal discrepancy and its public health consequences. J Epidemiol Community Health. 2005 Sep;59(9):749-54. doi: 10.1136/jech.2005.036517. PMID: 16100312; PMCID: PMC1733152.

4   Twenge, J.M., Sherman, R.A. & Wells, B.E. Changes in American Adults' Sexual Behavior and Attitudes, 1972–2012. Arch Sex Behav 44, 2273–2285 (2015). https://doi.org/10.1007/s10508-015-0540-2

Chapter 11: Design the Relationship

5   NFL Football Operations. (n.d.). NFL Instant Replay Process. Retrieved July 6, 2022, from https://operations.nfl.com/officiating/instant-replay/nfl-instant-replay-process/"

6   New York Post. (2022, September 6). Marilyn Loden, who coined the phrase 'glass ceiling,' dies at 76. Retrieved October 6, 2022, from https://nypost.com/2022/09/06/marilyn-loden-who-coined-the-phrase-glass-ceiling-dies-at-76/

Chapter 12: Establish Barriers of Entry

7   Financial Industry Regulatory Authority. (n.d.). Day trading margin requirements: Know the rules. Retrieved July 2, 2022, from https://www.finra.org/investors/learn-to-invest/advanced-investing/day-trading-margin-requirements-know-rules

Chapter 20: Wealth Accumulation

8   Baghai, P., Howard, O., Prakash, L., & Zucker, J. (2020). Women as the next wave of growth in US wealth management. McKinsey & Company. Retrieved from https://www.mckinsey.com/~/media/McKinsey/Industries/Financial%20Services/Our%20Insights/Women%20as%20the%20next%20wave%20of%20growth%20in%20US%20wealth%20management/Women-as-the-next-wave-of-growth-in-US-wealth-management.pdf

Part 6: Master The Market

9   Gladwell, M. (2008). Outliers: The story of success. Little, Brown and Company.

Chapter 29: Seize the Setback

10   Luks, A. M., Auerbach, P. S., Freer, L., Schoene, R. B., Zafren, K., & Hackett, P. H. (2019). Wilderness Medical Society Clinical Practice Guidelines for the Prevention and Treatment of Acute Altitude Illness: 2019 Update. Wilderness Medical Society. https://doi.org/10.1016/j.wem.2019.04.006

Chapter 30: Shut the Door

11   American Society for Reproductive Medicine. (2019, June). Infertility workup for the women's health specialist. American College of Obstetricians and Gynecologists, 133(6), E377-E384. https://www.acog.org/-/media/project/acog/acogorg/clinical/files/committee-opinion/articles/2019/06/infertility-workup-for-the-womens-health-specialist.pdf

12   Sansone A, Di Dato C, de Angelis C, Menafra D, Pozza C, Pivonello R, Isidori A, Gianfrilli D. Smoke, alcohol and drug addiction and male fertility. Reprod Biol Endocrinol. 2018 Jan 15;16(1):3. doi: 10.1186/s12958-018-0320-7. PMID: 29334961; PMCID: PMC5769315.

INDEX

M

N

O

P

T

The DECIDE Model™ xxviii, 93

Tolerant 243

tool 4, 10, 17, 43, 148, 156, 209, 212, 216, 218, 219

transformation xxvi, 4, 5, 7, 9, 38, 44, 94, 156, 218, 219, 224, 225, 270, 348, 351

TROMP xxix, 99, 101, 112, 113, 115, 134, 142, 188, 203, 207, 214, 245, 253, 275, 276, 293, 302, 311, 322, 323, 327

U

unicorn 113, 142, 195, 236

V

validation 3, 7, 44, 235, 247, 327

values 7, 9, 14, 19, 20, 27, 32, 37, 43, 44, 47, 52, 53, 56, 74, 79, 82, 85, 89, 94, 95, 104, 105, 118, 119, 129, 131, 144, 148, 150, 151, 157, 206, 207, 210, 211, 219, 225, 229, 243, 244, 259, 264, 265, 280, 281, 322

Values-Driven 243

vetting 34, 114, 119, 128, 130, 142, 146

Viginity xxix, 99, 101, 112, 113, 115, 134, 142, 188, 203, 207, 214, 245, 253, 275, 276, 293, 302, 311, 322, 323, 327

vocabulary 273, 274, 276

Vows 281, 282, 283

W

Wealth xxix, 99, 101, 112, 113, 115, 134, 142, 188, 203, 207, 214, 245, 253, 275, 276, 293, 302, 311, 322, 323, 327

The Rich Reward xxix, 99, 101, 112, 113, 115, 134, 142, 188, 203, 207, 214, 245, 253, 275, 276, 293, 302, 311, 322, 323, 327

Wilderness Medicine Society 299

X

Xenial 243

Y

Yearning for Growth 243

Z

Zealous 243

ACKNOWLEDGMENTS

As I sit down to pen the acknowledgments for my book, I am filled with gratitude for the unwavering support and guidance provided to me by the individuals who have played an instrumental role in bringing this project to fruition. This book is not only about learning how to date on your own terms, but also about understanding the significance of our closest relationships and how they shape us as we discover our true selves, embrace our unique paths, and strive to achieve our life's purpose. The journey of writing this book was not an easy one, but with the help and encouragement of the people listed below, I was able to overcome the obstacles and see my vision through to completion.

To my mother, KP: thank you for instilling in me at such an early age that I was capable of achieving anything I put my mind to. You have affirmed me throughout my entire life and used creative and fun ways to teach me how to affirm myself as well, whether it was through reciting short, yet empowering poems as a kid, memorizing scripture as a tween, or reminding me of who the hell I was as a young adult when I had forgotten my power. You were my first example of how a relationship can either deplete you or catapult you closer to the vision you have for yourself. At 4 years old, I wanted to marry you. Then, I tried to be just like you. And now, I have learned that just being your daughter was all that I ever had to be in order to receive your unwavering love and support. You will always be my hero!

To my father, Walter, Sr.: There was no man more capable than you who could have guided me into becoming the woman I am today. Through your wisdom I have learned the value of integrity and power of compassion. Through your unwavering love I have discovered the true meaning of family, loyalty, and commitment. And it is because of your grace that I gave myself permission to be courageous in my stages of becoming. You are everything a daughter could have asked for. You single-handedly taught me how a man should treat a woman and I am blessed to have you as my father. I know great men exist because I know you.

To my dad #2, Jerome: It is so funny because you have constantly told me that I was too smart for my own good. And now that I finally know what that means, it is completely shifted my perspective and how I make decisions in many areas of my life. You like to have your long talks, and that is just fine, because I love to listen. Thank you for always showing up, even when I did not know how to make space for you—And for being very vocal about your belief in me and my goals and showing your support in any way you can. I am forever grateful to have you in my life.

To Jonathan: I will forever be grateful for the support and encouragement you provided me throughout my writing process. More than anyone else, you listened to my countless rants about "Say No to Coffee Dates", and you did so with patience and attentiveness, always offering valuable insight and a unique perspective from a man's point of view. Your unwavering belief in my dreams and abilities, even when we didn't always see eye to eye, was invaluable to me throughout this journey. I am so grateful for the safe space you provided me, and for the impact you have made on my life. I appreciate you. I love you. I am a better woman because of you. Thank you from the bottom of my heart.

To my oldest, Anthony: You were hand selected, my greatest planned decision. There is not a day that goes by where I do not thank God for having you as my son, and the best example for your siblings to follow. It has been fairly easy parenting you and even more amazing watching you grow into a stellar young man right before my eyes. I am rooting for you in every way. And I am so proud to be your mom. I love you, always.

To my daughter, Halle: You became a #1 best selling author at the age of 8. So of course I think you are a pretty dope kid. But without that title, you are by far my greatest teacher and have served as an inspiration to me in so many ways. I have learned from you that success truly comes when preparation meets opportunity. And it has been an honor to share a love for writing with you, growing with you and guiding you as you blaze your own trail in this world. I love you Halle Amor.

To Jeremiah: Life's thrown us a curve ball, hasn't it? We've ended up on the same team without quite planning it, and what a story! You've become a part of my crazy, unique family and I wouldn't have it any other way. I hope you see this book as inspiration to complete your saga, soon! And thank you for teaching me about chess. I love you! Keep making me proud.

To my future NBA star, Andrew: You will probably never read this book. But if you surprise me, I just want to remind you that with your level of intelligence, athleticism, and work ethic, you can do anything you put your mind to, except beat me in a word game. You were born a winner and positioned for greatness. I'll bet on you any day. Thank you for being you. I love you, son.

And to my baby love, Zewdi: You came unexpectedly and changed my entire life. Mommy for sure would not have gone down this path had it not been for you. Mommy owes you big time!

To my siblings: First and foremost, I'd like to extend my heartfelt gratitude to my youngest brother, Robert. Our spirited debates, sometimes stretching for hours on end, have been instrumental in shaping and refining the topics in this book. I have no problem saying I lost some of those debates, especially because it meant I have become a better woman, partner, and teacher. Your insights, challenges, and unwavering engagement have been invaluable to this project.

To my sister, Destiny, with whom I've shared countless memories and a bond that time and distance can never erase, I hope this book serves as a testament to the complexities and nuances of relationships in all their forms. My dreams are manifesting in part due to you making all my dreams seem attainable, even the most outlandish ones.

To my other siblings, each of you holds a unique and special place in my heart and life. While not all of you were directly involved in the creation of this book, your influence on my life has indirectly shaped my perspectives and narratives. Our shared experiences, both the highs and the lows, have contributed to the person I am and the stories I tell. Thank you all.`

Now, to my friends, in alphabetical order- (whew) Throughout my writing process, I relied heavily on the support and guidance of my closest friends and family. So, in no particular order:

To Cecilia, my twin soul: thank you for being a consistent force of positivity in my life. Your wisdom, guidance and unwavering support have been invaluable to me as I navigate the ever-evolving journey of womanhood. Since we were teens, you have always been a sounding board for my thoughts and ideas, and your ability to speak life into me has been an inspiration. I am forever grateful for the friendship we share and the impact it has had on my life. You are a true friend. Thank you for all that you are and all that you do.

To Liza: Throughout the first year of my writing process, I relied heavily on your advice and feedback. You made me dig deep, really deep. You pushed my mind further than I even knew it could go. You reminded me how important it was for my voice to be heard, but even more for the readers to be led towards true transformation. I could not have done this without you. Your input and encouragement helped me to ensure that what I was writing was necessary and not just a collection of meaningless musings. I would be remiss if I did not acknowledge your integral role in this journey. Thank you, sis!

To my battle buddy turned bestie, Robyn: I never would have thought that my time in the military would have given me such a valuable and lifelong friend like you. From our days serving together, to the unforgettable memories we shared, and to even birthing our sons on the same day hours apart. No matter how distant we may be physically, I have always felt comforted in knowing that you are just a phone call away. You have always been there to lighten the mood and bring a sense of humor to even the toughest of situations, and I am forever grateful for that. Thank you for always remaining true to yourself and to our friendship, even when I struggled to do the same. I am so grateful to have you in my life.

To Sherry, my dear friend: You pushed this book harder than I did before it was even completed. Not only have you championed me and encouraged me to get it done, but you constantly reminded me that this message was bigger than me; that the ideas I had transcend race, religion, and creed, especially in these new millennial times. You came into my life in the season I needed you the most. I am never letting you go!

To my SWS ladies: You all are the Real MVPs. We laughed together, cried together, and learned together. Overnight, we became a community of like-minded women. And it is within our group that I was forced to evolve faster than I thought I was ready for. Yet, you all stood beside me while I was trying to figure everything out. Thank you for giving me a reason to keep going.

And to my readers, I hope this book provides you with the guidance and support you need to stop settling for less than you deserve, and to start demanding the relationships you desire. So, let's say no to coffee dates and start creating the relationships we truly want. Together, we can make it happen! Thank you for joining me on this journey, and I hope this book serves as a helpful guide as you navigate the dating world on your own terms.

ABOUT THE AUTHOR

Shaw Drake, a Dallas, TX, native and visionary dating expert, brings a fresh perspective to the world of relationships. With a background as a successful FOREX trader, Shaw has discovered powerful parallels between strategic navigation in the currency market and the dynamics of the dating world. She has harnessed these insights to create the groundbreaking 'Market Maker Method', which she shares in her acclaimed book.

In addition to her transformative teachings in her book, Shaw has developed an impactful dating course that has brought positive transformation to the lives of countless women. In 2021, she hosted her first international women's empowerment conference in Playa del Carmen, Mexico. Shaw is passionate about revolutionizing what it means to be a woman in a male-dominated world and empowering every woman to create the market in which her ideal partner exists.

Currently pursuing her Masters in Psychology at Harvard University, Shaw is deeply committed to increasing her knowledge on human behavior, evolutionary psychology, and interpersonal relationships. Through her captivating workshops and thought-provoking lectures, Shaw inspires women worldwide to take charge of their dating lives and say no to coffee dates once and for all.

Shaw is a mother to four and an inspiration to many. To learn more about her transformative work, book a one-on-one session, or join A Woman's Market community, visit her website at www.shawdrake.com.

Made in the USA
Columbia, SC
23 August 2023

21989193R00226